WILLING

As the fifth or sixth pretty girl appeared on the TV screen and smiled brightly, the man in the armchair sighed. They were all the same, these girls. Breezy, brainless and quite without character. Not like a real woman. Not like the woman sitting on the floor at his feet.

The woman, to whom men were open books, reached back and took hold of his hands. She guided them over her shoulders to her large breasts and placed them so he could gently mould and fondle the full firm flesh ...

Willing

Jennifer Cross

HEADLINE
DELTA

First published in 1995
by HEADLINE BOOK PUBLISHING

A HEADLINE DELTA paperback

10 9 8 7 6 5 4 3 2 1

ISBN 0 7472 4877 X

Phototypeset by Intype, London
Printed and bound in Great Britain by
Cox & Wyman Ltd, Reading, Berks.

HEADLINE BOOK PUBLISHING
A division of Hodder Headline PLC
338 Euston Road
London NW1 3BH

Willing

Prologue

As the fifth or sixth pretty girl in succession appeared on the TV screen, smiled brightly and started chatting about the weather, the man watching from his armchair sighed a sigh of mild irritation. So far they were all the damned same, these girls. Light, breezy, good-looking enough, rather brainless and without character. Not like a real woman. Not at all like the real woman who was watching with him.

She was sitting on the carpet, her back to the chair, between his knees. He looked at the top of her blonde head and remembered last night – and just the thought of it made his cock stir and forced him into an involuntary shift in his seat.

The woman, to whom men were open books, reached back and took hold of his hands. She guided them over her shoulders to her large breasts and placed them where they could gently mould and fondle the full, round flesh.

While his left hand stroked the nipple of her left

breast through the thin material of her V-neck wool and silk sweater, his right plunged down beneath the garment and grabbed as much as it could of the other naked globe. Idly he enjoyed the differences of playing with two generous tits, one clothed and one bare to his touch, while keeping an eye on the TV.

'When is she on?' he asked the woman, who removed his hands, stood up and turned with a challenging smile as she spoke.

'Katrina was eighteenth of the twenty to test. I make that another twelve minutes before she's on.'

The man also smiled. How was it that this woman, the one now standing on one leg while she took her first shoe off, could make a commonplace expression like 'twelve minutes' sound like the combined decadence of 200 years in the fall of the Roman Empire?

Both shoes were off now, and she was hitching up her skirt to unfasten her stockings from the suspenders. Each stocking was carefully draped around his neck, she knowing that when she leaned forward to do that he could see all of her marvellous bosom swinging free beneath the sweater.

She wriggled out of her skirt and panties and, last of all, pulled her sweater over her head. She was a beauty, a real beauty, still an absolute stunner even if she was the wrong side of thirty-five – or possibly even the wrong side of forty, thought the man, although she certainly didn't look it. After all, Katrina must be twenty at least, so unless she had her very young . . .

In fact, Katrina was nineteen and her mother,

Elspeth, was thirty-four. Elspeth had made one big mistake in her life, at the age of fifteen, and she was never, never going to make another.

She knelt before the man like a vision of lust, her left eyebrow raised quizzically and her mighty breasts squeezed between her arms as she carefully and slowly undid the clasp at the top of his trousers.

She pulled the zip down with deliberate patience and then fished inside for his cock. If it hadn't been quite as hard as it could be, through regular and recent exercise, it instantly became so. Her practised fingers curled round it and brought it out into the light. He leaned back in his chair, content to remain fully clothed while this naked goddess ran her hand up and down the fiercely curved and very large rod.

So strong was the curve and so big the member that she had to lean over a long way to get the end of it in her mouth, and this time the man's sigh showed no irritation whatever. This was a sigh of great delight, as he felt her tongue working on his glans and her lips grasped firmly the end of the hard body of his prick. Slowly at first she began to suck, and in time she moved her head up and down. She could feel his member bucking and twitching in her mouth, and each long suck and each slow slide of her lips brought another sigh and another spasm of movement from the eager organ, stiff and swollen in its heat.

She speeded up a little, but not much. Just enough to give him that extra impetus. She felt his cock positively vibrating in its anxiety and then she was swallowing,

swallowing like mad as she tried to cope with the sudden flood of come.

'Keep sucking, keep sucking, please!' urged the man, and she did, sucking and swallowing until the last drop was gone. Then she withdrew and knelt back on her heels, holding his cock in her hand and admiring its glistening redness with her head slightly to one side.

Her other hand wiped a little come from her bottom lip, a small ooze which had crept out in the rush, and then with both hands she carefully placed the still erect member back inside its underpants and trousers and zipped up.

She gave the bulge a pat.

'If that's still there after Katrina's been on, we'll have to do something about it, won't we?' Elspeth wondered to herself how she could sound so confident. Naturally she had been prepared for a full scale sexual encounter with this man, and anything would go, but she had not been prepared for such repetition, sometimes with deviation and always without any hesitation at all. This man was a sex engine. No sooner had he had some than he wanted some more. And he had one of the biggest cocks Elspeth had ever seen.

Now there were just two more of the boring, same-ish girls, then here was Katrina. Katrina was most definitely her mother's daughter. Tallish, blonde, plentiful – a proper bit of stuff to make a chap stir, thought the armchair critic as he noticed the full line of Katrina's breast as she turned to the weather chart.

This idea of his would knock the other breakfast

programmes sideways. They all had proper weather forecasters, men from the Met who talked like half-baked professors or bookish-looking girls with nothing whatever moving underneath their strait-laced bodices. He had taken a decision that with a proper script, a weather presenter needn't be an expert. What she needed to be was a knock-out, and Katrina certainly was that. She wasn't the only one, mind you, in the twenty. There were two or three others as attractive as her.

Elspeth had his hands on her naked tits again while they watched Katrina swing through her two minutes, and then she pulled him further forward so his fingers could reach down and find her tuft.

He kissed the top of her blonde head and shuffled forward in the chair so she could feel the hardness of his bump against the back of her skull.

'My, my, my,' she said. 'Is it never going to go down? We've done everything it's possible to do over the last twelve hours and he's still rearing up.'

'Not quite everything,' said the man, pulling his shirt over his head.

'Ah,' said Elspeth, and crawled slowly across the carpet to the couch, turning the TV off on the way. She lay, stomach down, along the length of the couch, her trunk balanced on the arm and her legs sticking out into the air. These legs she waved slightly, as if to guide the man to the right spot.

He was naked by now and walked across to her. He placed his hands on her buttocks, kneading them with pleasure. He put one hand to his mouth and deposited a large blob of spittle on a finger which he then transferred to the end of his cock. Both hands were on the buttocks again, and moving ever more closely to a hidden point in their clefted centre.

His two thumbs found the place and pulled the buttock flesh apart, so that the end of his cock could present itself at the forbidden gate. He pushed, but made no progress. Elspeth's hand reached round and found the questing knob, and with a wriggle and thrust gained it access.

Slowly the man pushed home, until the whole of his length was tightly sheathed in her arse, and then he began to thrust hard and deep. Now he'd had her in every orifice, mouth, quim and arsehole, and if ever she wanted any more favours from him, he'd make sure that he and two of his mates could have her in those places all at the same time.

As for now, the restrictions placed around his cock were bringing him swiftly to a climax. Harder and harder he went, faster and faster, until he felt the surge and whacked his pubis against her luscious bottom for the final time.

'And after that,' he said, pulling out, 'I think I can safely decide that Katrina has confirmed her undoubted talents in the screen test and will be offered the job of Satellite Morning Television's, and the nation's, first ever Weather Dish.'

'Why, thank you, sir,' said Elspeth, sliding and turning to lie full length on the couch, luxuriously stretching her nude body and tapping her love-skilful hand over a little yawn. 'I know she will give satisfaction in her work – and if you ever need any *other* form of satisfaction . . .'

Chapter One

The true professional

'If there ever were any doubts about whether I could cope, I sure as hell am proving it now.'

These were the thoughts of the stunningly attractive, vivacious blonde who smiled so cheerfully into the television camera as she felt the man's hand creeping slowly up the inside of her thigh. His fingers caressed the smooth warm skin of her leg, bare under the billowy white summer skirt. What very beautiful skin, his finger tips told the man, and so virginal-feeling.

Certainly the chirpy face of the TV announcer bore out the touch of her thigh-skin. She looked like the girl next door ought to look, but never does, and she prattled away about this little boy's birthday and that little girl's pet hamster as if such matters were the most important thing in her glamorous world right now.

'And it's Emma Foreshaw's turn, she's twelve today, and here's the card her classmates have sent from Turnberry Street County Primary – thank you all and what a very nice elephant – and now Robert Stark of 32, Anthills Road . . .'

Her mouth kept moving, the words kept coming out, the eyes and the smile never faltered, and the man's index finger pushed gently under the elastic of her panties.

'Knocker, you'll have to stop this. I can't get the birthdays out.'

Knocker, a large furry glove puppet who was supposed to be an otter but looked more like an elderly weasel, nodded in agreement that perhaps sticking his whiskers under the nice lady announcer's nose was going too far.

At the same time, you could have said that Knocker's operator was also going too far. Under the desk the fingers of his other hand inched further towards their goal. He had his index and middle fingers inside her pants now, and he was plucking at her pubic hairs with them. He felt his own organ rise and bulge as his fingers slipped into the sweet dampness of her slit, while up above, the knockabout Knocker remained uncharacteristically quiet for the rest of that day's stint on Boundary Birthdays.

Boundary Television's most presentable presenter kept up her act. Cards were brandished with the usual aplomb, and kids' names and addresses were read out with all the charm that had made her a local TV hit so quickly. But from the waist down she was aquiver as Knocker the Otter's owner and trainer got three fingers in her quim and began frigging her in depth.

10

At last she heard the producer's PA in her earphone. Just fifteen more seconds to go. Time to wind up and announce the next programme, and cheerio for now. Byeee . . .

Knocker's invisible alter ego, under the desk, expected her to get up and walk away, or perhaps to lean down and rattle him round the ear. Instead she opened her legs and wriggled her bottom forward on the chair, inviting his fingers further in. They obliged, as she called to the floor manager to ask him to pass her the glass and jug of orange juice which stood on a table on the other side of the small studio.

'God I'm exhausted,' she groaned to him in explanation of her leaning-back sitting position as he poured her some juice. 'Can I just sit here for a few minutes, or am I in the way?' The floor manager managed a mumble which tried to tell her that she could never be in the way as far as he was concerned, and her grateful lips parted in a smile which left his brain wordless and his loins twitching with unalloyed lust.

She drained the orange juice, put her hands behind her head, sat back even further in the chair, opened her legs wide and then closed them again. Knocker's man got the message, shifted his position, took his other hand out of Knocker the Otter and placed it instead at the disposal of another little furry animal, that one hiding beneath the tight, thin nylon of the TV dreamgirl's knickers.

The pants were pulled down with the help of a lift off the chair by the blonde girl's anxious bottom, and

Knocker's handler pushed his face up between her thighs as the legs opened again. His tongue searched tentatively inside the soft, hot lips and found the little hooded stem near the top. As the texture of his taste-buds rasped across her most sensitive and private part, and the stiffly-seeking tongue flexed with skill and enthusiasm, Katrina Mulloy, the darling of every sex-ually active male from Carlisle to Berwick-on-Tweed, sighed in sweet pleasure and gripped the causer of it tightly between her knees.

The man fell to his work with even more vigour. His reason for trying what he did with Katrina, a bombshell of a girl who had had no interest in him before, was that Knocker the Otter was to be put down in favour of a new, more sophisticated animal. Boundary Birthdays today, Saturday, was Knocker's goodnight and there would be no more pay cheques for his owner. And so, for the hell of it, he thought he'd try and get inside the legendary Katrina's pussy.

Legendary she certainly was, and the stories about her appetites, although generally satisfied with those who could do her some good in other ways, were enough to give ideas to anyone whose cock could be hardened. Bill Cousins, children's party magician and otter manipulator on one of Britain's smallest TV stations, had often had a hard cock as he knelt beside Katrina's delightful lower parts. Sometimes in a mini-skirt, some-times in shorts, sometimes as now in a floaty, muslin number, her legs moved with her voice and brought well-defined thoughts into the mind of the poor man condemned to the life of Tantalus, who could see the water he was desperate for but could never get near enough to drink it.

Since Katrina arrived at Boundary Television, Bill had never got up from his work with a soft prick. But he had thought he could do no good for Katrina's career and therefore had no chance. Now he found that, as his tongue flickered in and out of her ever wetter quim, he was wrong.

Katrina was having trouble keeping still. Her fingers gripped the desk edge, her knuckles showing white. She wanted to bounce her bottom up into the man's face, she wanted to wrap her legs around the back of his head, she wanted to slide under the desk altogether and grab hold of his cock and suck it madly while he brought her to a climax.

By now there were no other people in the studio or control room. The station went over to the network after Boundary Birthdays. She wondered if a camera had been left on and she was being recorded. She wondered whether to stand up, rip all her clothes off and fuck with the otter man on the desk top.

Instead she sat tight as she felt the waves begin to come. The man was gripping her enlarged clit with his lips now, and his hands had slid beneath her bottom cheeks and were massaging her flesh as he sipped at the fountain of her wantonness.

With a shudder she came, her legs pressing his head in a grateful vice, and as the last flourish of her orgasm died away Bill Cousins, a handsome enough man of about thirty-five, talentless in almost everything except sex and children's parties, withdrew his face, dripping wet with her juices, and stared along the insides of the most beautiful legs he had ever examined, up to a damp and curly-haired apex where lay the scene of his most recent triumph.

What would she do now? She was too good for poor Bill Cousins, obviously. She only shagged people of board-director level and above. She would just walk away.

And so she did. As Bill emerged from under the desk, her swaying hips in the thin, long white dress were approaching the studio double doors. The only difference between this and her usual rear view was that she was trailing a large toy otter behind her.

Bill needed no written invitation. He followed her to her dressing room and went in without knocking. She sat on a chair in front of her mirror with Knocker the Otter perched on the table top looking back at her. Bill's cock, already stiff inside his trousers, gave an extra heave as the famous smile flashed at him, reflected in the mirror, and the fingers of her right hand, so recently holding home-made birthday cards, undid the top two buttons of her dress.

As Bill walked towards her she swiveled round in her chair. As he arrived her perfect fingers unfastened the top of his trousers, and as he closed his eyes in bliss she slid the cumbersome cloth down, likewise the shorts, and grasped his wickedly hard cock in tender determination with one hand, while she undid his shoelaces with the other.

14

'Golly gosh,' she said. 'I'm going to enjoy this. I haven't seen one as big as this for weeks.'

Having got rid of shoes and other irritations, her head bent forward and her long blonde hair brushed against the man's thighs. Her mouth, felt on their cocks in dreams by thousands and thousands of men and growing boys, opened wide and enveloped the end of Bill Cousins' prick in sweet sensation. However, Bill did not awake to find wet come on his pyjamas. This was for real and, as she proved as she slowly moved her head back and forth and gently sucked, this girl was good.

This girl was also anxious to feel Bill's big member inside her, and when she was satisfied that it could get no harder and no bigger, she stopped sucking, admired the shiny subject of her ministrations briefly, stood, turned, lifted her skirt and bent over, legs wide and hands firmly on the make-up counter.

Her knickers just at that precise moment were being picked up from beneath a studio desk by a puzzled cleaning lady, so they weren't in the way of Bill as he took the necessary step forward, bent a little at the knees, and slid home.

She positively gurgled with delight as she felt the whole of his length push up and his balls tap gently against her skin. He began moving, slowly and thoroughly, and he watched fascinated in the mirror as, eyes closed, she moved one hand to her chest and undid the remaining buttons on the front of her dress. He could see her delicious breasts inside her bra flexing as he thrust, her cleavage opening and closing as his giant cock slid up and down her slipway.

Still watching in the mirror, he untied the bows of the thin straps over her shoulders and the dress dropped away, leaving the clasp of her bra to be undone and allowing his hands to slither around and beneath her arms until they found a plump breast each. He cradled them, feeling the powerfully erect nipples in the centres of his palms, and began to accelerate.

Katrina opened her eyes now and they met his in the mirror. The smile came again, the smile that would melt iron and, equally well, make flesh as hard as metal. Bill smiled back and pumped the more vigorously. She left his gaze to concentrate on what was happening, with her left hand holding his and helping to palpate her left tit while her right wandered down to where strong meat was bounding and rebounding between her legs.

She could tell he wasn't far off coming. Her index finger tip caressed her clitty as the rod steamed back and forth, faster now, and faster still, and faster again as Bill went into his last moments.

With the most tremendous pumping the man sent a stream of spunk hurtling into the dreamgirl's innermost portions while she, rubbing quickly, just caught the end of his coming with her own. Ahhhh!

She waited for a minute or two while the glorious feelings subsided and then withdrew from him. She took a tissue from her table and wiped his length with a sympathetic hand, sorry to see that its stiffness was going.

'Take a seat on the couch,' she said. 'I'll get changed and pour us a drink.'

There wasn't a screen in her dressing room like you see in the movies, so she didn't go behind it and hang articles of clothing one by one over the top. She just stood in front of him, stripped naked, and then put a thin and very tight T-shirt on. The outline of her breasts was superbly defined by the material, and the words 'TV Presenters do it with Mikes' were given undulations which no Pennine fell, Cheviot hill or Lake District mountain could ever match.

Mr Bill Cousins, otter manipulator, grinned at the T-shirt. She told him it was the only one of its kind in the world, especially made for her by someone she knew, and Bill never doubted what she said for an instant. The whole of her gorgeous bottom was revealed as she bent to pour drinks from the tray, and the shirt came to just below her belly button as she walked towards him, a glass in each hand.

She stood there in front of him, he sitting on the couch, she with one hand on hip while the other lifted her G & T to her lips. Bill took a swig.

'Do I need to change my name to Mike?' he asked.

'With a cock like that,' she replied, 'you could change your name to Claud Cecil Cedric Butterscotch and I'd still want to sit on the fucker. What is your name, by the way?'

She shifted her position slightly so she had her legs wider apart, and her free hand explored underneath the T-shirt as she took another drink. She was also keeping an eye on Bill's cock, which seemed to be waking up.

'Thanks for the compliment. I'm Bill. And he,' he

said, as he emptied his glass and pulled at his cock, 'is also at your service. Or at least will be in a minute.'

Katrina took Bill's glass and put it with her own back on the tray. She made her little return trip as slow as possible, carefully placing one foot in front of the other so that maximum wiggle was visible to the seated man. When once more she was standing in front of him, she could look down into his crutch and see his massive prick at almost full attention and being given what extra orders it needed by Bill's own hand.

She put her hands to the hem of the T-shirt and lifted it over her head. Once more the film-star body was displayed in all its cock-hardening beauty to the children's party man. She leaned forward and undid his shirt buttons. Soon, he too was completely naked. She picked up his ankles and swung them over the couch end so he was lying along the full length. A very brief kiss for the end of his bulging and burgeoning member was sufficient to put it at red alert, and with a knee on either side of his hips she lowered herself slowly onto what she had already named as cock of the month.

Her hand held the big nut of it at her entrance, and slid it around in the warm dampness. She felt her own juices begin to flow and with an exclamation, half of surprise and half of joy, she pushed the whole of it up as far as it would go.

Bill lay there watching as, with eyes closed again and an expression of total concentration on her face, she writhed and pushed and slid and wriggled her body up and down his shaft. He felt in control of his own coming. This was his third erection in half an hour. It would take a lot of writhing and wriggling to get him to come again.

So, Katrina had all the time in the world and she intended to make the most of it. Slowly, quickly, steadily, jerkily, she moved in a spontaneous dance on his may-pole, squeezing every atom of sensation from the best fuck she'd had in weeks.

She never even noticed when, to Bill's dismay, her dressing room door opened and the Boundary Birthday's PA poked her head round. When she saw what was going on she stepped inside, closed the door, and walked over. Bill, now believing that nothing that happened that day could surprise him, saw the PA's neat little hands close over Katrina's breasts from behind.

'Darling,' whispered the girl in the plummiest of accents. Boundary TV was no exception to the general rule that only girls from the very top drawer ever got the jobs. 'If you are going to be unfaithful to me, at least let me in on it.'

'But sweetheart,' groaned Katrina, eyes still closed, movements up and down Bill's cock unabated, 'fucking PAs get in on too much as it is. Now, be a good girl and see if you can lend a hand where it matters most.'

The PA cast her eye around the room and saw what she wanted – a large cushion. With a hand under Bill's buttocks she got him to raise up while the cushion was slid underneath. Now there was just room for her to get her head under the backs of his thighs, where she could watch her friend's quim lips slipping and sliding up and down Bill's cock.

The PA, of course, knew Bill well enough but gave a

little whistle to herself as she saw his cock in close-up. That blasted otter would have worked a lot better with his prick inside it instead of his hand, she thought, as she leaned forward and gave his balls a lick. By turning her head upwards a little she could also flick her tongue at Katrina's bumhole, which made her bounce around a bit.

It seemed, though, that of the two of them the partner requiring the most additional stimulation was Bill. He was calm while Katrina was jumping about on his cock with increasing abandon. So, the PA snaked herself as near as she could and took both of Bill's balls in her mouth. Gently she sucked them as, above her head, Katrina's bottom threatened to bash her through the couch.

Bill was getting really interested in this new form of double sex. He could feel the PA girl's tongue lightly massaging his testicles, while the rhythm of Katrina's ever more frenetic thrusts was repeated by a small pull on his balls caused by the regular collision of bounding arse cheek with the recumbent personal assistant's head.

Katrina was very nearly there now. Her head was back, her long blonde hair was flying, her eyes were open wide but seeing nothing, her mouth was open in a silent scream as, thrusting as fast as she could, she brought herself off in a mighty explosion of gasps and cries and then fell sideways off the couch to lie senseless on the floor.

The PA, a neatly-made, slim girl with short dark hair in a bob, looked slyly up at Bill, her mouth full of his bollocks. He looked at Katrina, then at the PA, and shrugged a little smile.

She stood, pushed her trainers off with her toes, slipped her jeans and panties off and pulled her sweatshirt over her head. She had small, pertly pointed tits, a thin waist and hips like a boy's. Between them, however, was a quim like a woman's, which Bill saw clearly as she swung her slim leg over and sank onto his shaft.

'If I'd known you had such a big one – mmmmmm,' she said, 'I could have – mmmmmahh – introduced you to the – mmmnngggikkimmm – programme controller's wife, and she would have – bleeding bloody hell – made sure you didn't – ffffffffffuck me pink – lose your job.'

Bill, beyond caring about his job as the feelings generated by the new quim began to shake his self composure, reached up for the little dangling titties and gave them a good squeeze. Then he pulled the girl down and turned the two of them over. By reaching under her legs he could get them up and over his shoulders so that she, her arse on the cushion, was as open and as close as she could be.

He began some serious thrusting, his huge cock plunging in and out at a steady pace. She, unable to say any more, made guttural noises in her throat with each plunging ram of his rod.

Katrina regained consciousness just in time to see the two bodies wildly clashing into each other in complete abandonment, her friend making mad groans as she pushed her small body into Bill's in time with his pumpings which, at climax, must have been making 200 revs a minute.

The local TV star sat up to watch the ex-otter man and the ex-public school girl, daughter of a lord and so nicely mannered, come together with the most tremendous bang. When they had eventually subsided, she spoke.

'Look, sorry chaps, but I've got a train to catch.'

'Well, darlings,' said the PA, her eyes closed and her arms around Bill like she would never let go, 'I've got some steak in the fridge back at my sweet little bijou residence in desirable downtown Carlisle. Would you like some, Bill?'

Before Bill could reply, Katrina was on her feet having just glanced at the clock.

'Shit. Look at the time. If you want to take any meat out of anywhere, start right now with his fucking dick and your fanny. Come on, please! I've got some serious getting ready to do.'

And so it was that an hour later, in an expensively furnished and extremely comfortable flat, a man replete with fillet steak and salad was watching his very large cock being daubed with sauce béarnaise by a petite, dark-haired twenty-one-year-old member of the aristocracy, while a nineteen-year-old TV presenter, of more humble origins but far greater ambitions, was eating soup in the restaurant of the London train. Of the half a dozen other diners, the only ones of interest were the two big red-haired Scotsmen, brothers obviously or possibly even twins, who were making no secret of their own very devout interest in Katrina.

Katrina, however, didn't want any more that night. She had a big day tomorrow. She would just concentrate on her soup and fish. The red-haired boys would have to miss out. Would there be freckles, she wondered, on their cocks?

Chapter Two

A vacancy has arisen . . .

. . . and so, Katrina was interested to note, had two Scotsmen. As their kilts swung past her on their way from the restaurant car to the bar, she noticed that their sporrans seemed to be forced out of alignment by something behind them. Here were two cabers that needed tossing, she thought. What a pity she was too tired – and too concerned about tomorrow – to see to it herself.

Even so, once the coffee was finished and there was nothing to do but retire to her bunk, Katrina found herself heading the wrong way and ending up in the buffet bar rather than the first class sleeping car. While getting a hot chocolate, supposedly for a nightcap, she was hardly surprised when the two ginger Mac-some-things appeared and tried to persuade her to have a brandy or a malt whisky with them instead.

Well, she might as well just stay up a few more minutes, but no more. Half an hour later, with nobody else in the buffet car and the barman out of sight,

Katrina was being asked to find out at first hand if it were true that the right-thinking Scot never wore anything under his kilt.

Katrina's searching fingers beneath the pleated plaid found a sturdy and stiff pillar of Scottish society beside her. Reaching across under the table, she found something very similar opposite. When the boys pointed out that a public railway carriage was not the best place for socio-demographic research, Katrina agreed that her sleeping car would be better. These were two burly lads, sixteen stones each of Highland muscle, and one at a time would definitely be enough on a railway bunk.

Katrina, with all the foreplay in the buffet car, had forgotten her tiredness and her responsibilities for the morrow and was eager now for some hot cock. As soon as the door was closed she stripped her clothes off without any attempt to disguise her hunger.

Colin and Calum McHarg tossed a coin, and Colin won. Katrina lay face down on the top bunk, her bottom raised and her legs apart. Colin clambered up and, watched at eye level by his jealous brother, thrust his red-fringed pole into Katrina's moistened slot. He tried to fuck her slowly at first but the rhythms of the train were too catchy, and the sight of Katrina's white arse and the feel of her great tits as he burrowed beneath her writhing body and wrapped his hands around them, were too compelling for Colin.

Soon he was shagging in time to the carriage wheels and at that speed he couldn't last long. With a gurgle of Gaelic triumph he spent, his last few thrusts going deeper and deeper, and he would have lain on top of the partly-satisfied Katrina had his brother not hauled him off and rolled her over onto her back.

He knelt astride her, fondled her beautiful breasts, pulled her head up and pushed his cock between her willing lips. Her eyes opened wide at the effort of getting so much of his mighty cannon into her mouth and then, as he settled into a gentle in-out, with her tongue providing special stimulation, Katrina placed one hand around his balls, cradling them as they swung and vibrated, and the other hand between her own legs. She caressed her little joy-stick while the ginger-and-white meat pudding, more rigid than anything in a butcher's window but not so different in size from a fat polony, caused her to slurp and swallow.

She almost choked when she felt another finger, not her own but much bigger, playfully tickle her other, more private entrance. While Calum's cock filled her mouth and her own fingers stroked her quim, a new sensation was caused by the tip of an index finger of Colin's, lubricated with spit, trying to wriggle its way into her bottom.

As Calum began to move faster, Katrina felt her own fingers follow his pace and her fulfilment came just as the Scottish spunk flooded her throat. Somehow she managed to swallow it and make her instinctive coming noises without anything going down the wrong way, but when she returned to normality she felt something else most definitely going the wrong way, not down it, but up it.

She quite liked the feeling and raised her hips so that Colin could get better access. Standing with his feet on the bunk below he could now get his tongue onto her quim while giving her arse the fiddler's elbow, and soon she was writhing again as she approached the throes of a second coming.

In a twinkling, she didn't quite know how, the boys lifted her off the bunk and stood her between them. Calum bent her head down to his cock, stiff and raring to go once more. As she bent, Colin withdrew his finger from her bum and replaced it with his prick.

Katrina almost bit Calum's cock off as she felt this great thick thing forcing its way into her vitals, and then she was being lifted, Colin's arms about her bosom from behind. Calum stepped forward, took her legs in his own arms and tucked them under his armpits. Now he could stick his cock in her cunt, while brother rammed his further and further up her arsehole.

Never had Katrina had so much cock in her at once before. She could say or do nothing as she hung, transfixed by two huge ones, and felt their iron hardness sliding up and down inside her, separated only by a thin membrane which, she was quite sure, would soon burst.

Then the two cocks would join together into one hellish, heavenly monster which would drive ever upwards until it emerged, triumphant, out of the top of her head. She was near unconscious as the relentless red pricks thrust and counter-thrust, two surging engines of pleasure giving her more cubic capacity then she'd ever known.

Her arms were around Calum's neck, her head on his shoulder. He held her buttocks in his paws while brother Colin banged from behind and grappled her tits.

They had no mercy, these two, and the speed and depth of their closing thrusts were too much for the girl. She made some strange noises and fainted while two dicks pumped their last drop into two different holes at once.

She awoke an hour later, tucked up between the sheets of the top bunk. It had been a dream, hadn't it? She couldn't have done what she just did, surely?

Then, as she stretched and felt her aching muscles, she knew. Two cocks at once. Wow. Well, she sighed as she dropped back off to sleep, there were still further possibilities. If the opportunity arose she could, she thought, manage three . . .

The TV company seemed empty of people. It was Sunday morning, but Sunday was a TV day like any other day – surely somebody should be about?

As Katrina stepped from the lift on the top floor there was more emptiness. She saw a reception area like a small football pitch of carpet with several deep and heavy Chesterfields, leather-covered, seemingly abandoned at various points near smoked-glass coffee tables and copies of celebrity magazines. Apart from the lift door that Katrina had come in by, there were only two more doors. One was obviously the way to the back stairs. The other looked like it must be the door to her future, next to the receptionist's desk and clearly made of some rare wood or other about a foot thick.

Katrina flumped onto a leather cushion and idly spun the pages of a magazine. It was full of photographs of drunk-looking women with their tits hanging out of their dresses, arriving or departing from some function or other on the arms of famous and even more drunk-looking men. Eyes were red, smiles were off centre, and cleavages were fully exposed. Well, thought Katrina, if that's what being famous does for you . . .

The heavy wood door swung open with the tiniest swish and a very glamorous young woman came out. Not noticing Katrina yet, she sat at her desk and took a moment looking in her pocket mirror to straighten a few strands of hair and check her make-up.

That, thought Katrina, is a secretary who has just been sitting on her boss's knee.

A little cough brought the secretary back to business. She rose with a bright smile, her gestures showing she was just ever so slightly uncertain about whether her skirt was on straight, and showed Katrina in to see the man, the same man who had watched the screen tests with Elspeth, Katrina's mother.

He had no trouble recognising the daughter. The same ravishing features, but younger. The same gorgeous blonde hair, but longer. And the same wonderful hourglass figure, except perhaps with a touch more on the tits and a touch less on the waist and on the hips. He got up, shook her hand and offered her the seat in front of the desk. He returned to sit in his swing chair and half-turned to the picture window. London's rooftops were spread for Katrina. Not a sheep to be seen anywhere. Here was the new world she had to conquer.

'Down there,' said the man, 'among those chimney pots, are millions of people who haven't got satellite dishes. Millions of them. We've tried everything. Sport. Italian housewives in their underwear. Old films back to back for a hundred years. Old costume drama and old comedies. And still the bastards won't buy our fucking satellite TV. What do you think of that?'

'Well, er . . .' This was not the course Katrina had expected the conversation to take.

'I'll tell you what it is,' said the man. 'The terrestrials have all got better front people. Their newsreaders are better. Their commentators are better. Their pundits, their station announcers, their everybody. All better. But that is going to change, and the change starts with you, Miss Mulloy. You are the first better presenter that satellite has had. Not the last. The first. Welcome to Satellite Morning Television. SMT is glad to have you.'

'Oh. You mean, I've got the job? I thought this . . .'

'You thought it was an interview? I've seen your screentest. I've asked around. I phoned all my friends who live up in sheep country and told them to watch you on Boundary Television. You are it. Def-in-itely. Now, there just remains one final little formality.'

The most powerful man in British satellite TV stood and walked around the desk. As he approached the seated Katrina he unzipped his fly and took out one of the biggest cocks she had ever seen. It was as hard as iron and curving to the sky. Obviously, whatever the secretary had been doing it hadn't gone very far. It was just a warm-up. The actual game was going to be played by Mulloy, Miss K.

Katrina rose instinctively, her eyes glued on the gigantic and menacing cock. Like lightning she whipped her panties off, sat herself on the edge of the man's desk, pulled her skirt up and opened her legs. He walked straight in as if he was calling at the newsagent's for a packet of cigarettes on the way to work. With some very rapid adjustments from Katrina the mighty prick went home without a pause.

The man stood still for a moment. His hands were on Katrina's shoulders, then they went down to her arse, pulling her towards him. Finally, he was satisfied that he was in position and began thrusting.

Katrina could only marvel at the size of the thing going in and out. The strangeness and unexpectedness of her situation took away the sexual sensations for a while, but gradually the friction of the biggest cock in television – bigger, even, than Bill Cousins the otter-operator's, thought Katrina, and I wonder what that little PA tart would make of this! – began to tell on her. She leaned back on her hands and pushed her pelvis forward. She leaned right back on her elbows, and drew her knees up so that her heels were just on the desk edge. She could not be more open, she thought, as the boss's bull-like pizzle measured its full length inside her, fifty times a minute.

The man had his hands flat on the desk and his eyes were closed. Faster and faster he began to move, and

Katrina began to grunt and cry. With amazing precision he withdrew his whole cock to the very entrance of her love tunnel, and then thrust the entire thing right up to her womb neck, again and again, more quickly still, and by now with such energy that the climax could not be far away.

For Katrina it was already here. With a yowl and a whoop she announced the arrival of the orgasm express, but still the man steamed on, pumping and thrusting. Katrina began to think she was tripping. Surely he had LSD on the end of his knob or something. This was not possible. How could he ... ? Suddenly he went into hyperdrive and after thirty or so uniquely fast jerks he was there. She felt the come gush and was glad. She couldn't have managed much more of it.

With no ceremony the man replaced his cock in his trousers and pressed the bell on his desk. Horrified, Katrina leaped onto the floor and just managed to get her skirt down from around her waist when the receptionist walked in.

With a glitteringly false attempt at a confident smile, SMT's newest star picked up her bag and swung from the room. The secretary, cooler than Katrina in the circumstances, did not forget to pick up also the tiny scrap of black lace from the arm of the office chair where Katrina had been for her interview.

Outside the office, the secretary gave her an understanding smile.

'Here. Put your knickers back on, dear, and I'll take you for a coffee and show you around. No, don't worry about a girls' room. Slip them on here and we'll be off.'

On the way to the canteen Katrina discovered a new word. She asked the secretary what she'd been doing to get her boss in that state, ready for the interview, and had been told that, far from a warm-up, the boss had been giving her the entire benefit of his length and girth and had come only those few seconds before Katrina arrived.

'There's a word for it,' said the secretary, a svelte redhead with the body of a swimsuit model. 'Priapism. He absolutely has to have six times more fucks than anybody normal. And he's the boss, so when his cock jumps, so do we.'

'We? You mean all the girls in the company?' Katrina wondered how often she would have to be split in half in the cause of her career.

'Good lord, no. You saw the size of his dick. I mean, a lot of the girls here would need an ambulance after that. No, what happens is that there is a small and exclusive pool of girls who can cope. There's a password each day. When he gets his first hard on, which is usually as soon as he gets to work in the morning, he calls in whoever is on the front desk – where I was today. After he's given her one and got his coffee and agenda for the day, he rings her and tells her the password. She rings the other girls on the network. Then, when he gets his next stiffy, he presses his fuck button—'

'Fuck button?' asked Katrina.

'Yes. It flashes a small green light on the receptionist's console. She calls whichever of the gang she thinks might be available and says "Swiss cheese" or whatever. If she's not free just to come at that moment, the selected girl has to phone another one of them up and get "Swiss cheese" into the conversation. We work as fast as we can to get someone there, because the longer he has to go without sticking his cock into something, the bigger his erection seems to get.'

'How many times a day does this happen?'

'Sometimes five, sometimes ten. The record is thirteen.'

'Thirteen? In one day?'

'Yes. And we had two of the pool off sick so that meant six of us had to take two fucks each and his own personal secretary took three. She, needless to say, was off sick the rest of the week.'

'Will he want me to be in the pool?' Katrina didn't know if she hoped for a yes or a no to the question.

'Don't know. I'd doubt it, personally, because he doesn't usually have any involvement with the on-screen performers – apart from the interview, of course. What he calls the little formality.'

'Bloody enormous formality, more like. So every female on screen, newsreaders, presenters, interviewers, they've all had his cock up them?'

'Every one. Even that fat old bird who does the agony aunting. She thought all her birthdays and Christmasses had come at once. You could hear her two floors down, never mind through the door, and it's supposed to be soundproof.'

'What about that intellectual female who does the

serious politics bit? Her as well? I mean, I'm sure she's frightfully brainy, but she looks a cold kind of fish.'

'Don't you believe it. She was the first job-interviewee in the history of employment to ask if she could have a second interview. The problem with her is keeping her away. She's always finding some excuse to request a meeting with the boss, and if she doesn't get the company's top fuck at least once a week she gets very tetchy. You watch her. If she's interviewing some poor member of parliament and giving him a really hard time, it's because she hasn't had it with bossy boy lately.'

'Well, I can see how you could get like that. It's the biggest one I've seen, and I've seen quite a few.'

'I've only ever seen one as big, and that was on an American footballer. Black, he was. Can't remember his name ... oh yes, Cliff. He does modelling work. Came here to film a commercial and I just happened to barge into his dressing room at an opportune moment to find him standing there in just his pants. Talk about a bulge! I almost turned around and walked out, but he was too quick. He reached inside his pants and flopped this thing out. I was mesmerised. I simply had to go and stroke it. And when I stroked it, it leaped up. Absolutely huge. So I could do nothing else but strip off and lie on the carpet. Wow. So, if ever you happen to meet a big black ex-footballer called Cliff, don't ask to see his credentials unless you really mean it. Now, enjoyed our chat. Must get back to work. Perhaps we'll have a night out together sometime. Could be a lot of fun. Bye.'

As she watched the elegantly swaying behind of the

secretary, Katrina smiled to herself. She was in. She had her big break. London, the TV scene, fame and fortune – it was all there for her. And all she had to do was be herself.

And if, on the way, she could jump on a few cocks and give herself some thrills, so much the better. But now, after her morning's work, she would get the first train back north and this time she would sleep all the way.

Chapter Three

It's not my fault . . .

. . . it's bred into me, thought Katrina Mulloy, Weather Dish of one week's experience and already being pursued by the tabloids and freelance paparazzi, but at this moment looking at some earlier and much different press coverage.

Unpacking a few things to put around her new London flat to make it more homely, she'd come across a scrapbook and a cutting from the local paper years ago about the school play. *Twelfth Night*! How she'd so desperately wanted the part of Viola – and how, but how, had she got it . . .

As a schoolgirl, Katrina had appeared to be her mother's pride and joy. Ever since she was old enough to understand, Elspeth had told about how she, Elspeth, had been bound for fame and fortune, built on her beauty and sparkling personality, only to fall pregnant at the age of fifteen.

The fortunate result had been Katrina. The unfortunate result had been a single-minded determination in

Elspeth to ensure that Katrina had the fame that mother missed, and was not exposed to the dangers of sexual relationships, even though she was clearly born to be very active in this particular field.

As Katrina grew up and became more womanly, Elspeth increased the frequency and power of her warnings. But, of course, the more she warned, the more Katrina wanted to try. And the more she expressed conscious and unconscious interest in men, the more pressure the men put on – and the more Katrina learned about the power a sexually attractive female has over the male of the species.

By the time she was finishing her first year in the sixth form, despite her mother's hawk-like watching, Katrina had done everything except 'it'. She had felt, and been felt. She had allowed boys to undo her bra beneath her sweater and then to fondle her wonderful tits. Eventually she had allowed one boy, who had a car, to take her sweater off in the back seat. She would not, however, let him go any further, nor would she touch his cock, but she watched with great interest as he wanked himself off in front of her, catching the spunk in his handkerchief.

Another boy with another car was able to strip her completely naked, and to put his inexperienced fingers in between her thighs, but not his bulging, eager cock. She was happy to watch him wriggle his pants down, and let him stroke her tits with his prick, and although she was a bit shocked by the come surging over her nipples the first time, she got to like it the second time, and the third time actually reached up and skinned the hard knob for herself.

Gradually she was ripening, and yet another boy, or rather a young man, a lad with a job and a car of his own, not his father's, was a main beneficiary of the work of all those explorers who had gone before.

Katrina liked the boys to feel her tits. She liked the fingers probing inside her, and she liked the feeling of skin on skin as they rubbed their rocky rods on her stomach and breasts.

She liked the strange feel of a cock, how it was hard and warm and yet had this velvet smoothness. And now, for the first time, she found she liked the feel of it inside her – but not yet in her quim. In her mouth.

Not many young men could claim to have been often sucked off, much less by a girl like Katrina, and she found that no sooner had she put her new boyfriend's cock in her mouth but the spunk ran. At first she used to spit it out, then she got to swallow it and preferred it that way.

Most of the boys who had participated in the education of Katrina were totally besotted with her, but realised that she was so special that no one boy of their age could hope to tie her down. Also, she began to realise, as once again her boyfriend groaned in pleasurable wonder and his cock sent a stream of instant come down her throat, that if she was to be properly introduced to full sex, it had better not be with one of these wham-bam boys. She would have to find a man who would take care with the introductions. So far she had only had hints of the great sensations which she had read and heard about. Boys' fingers, and her own, had given her clues about what might be in store, but it would need an experienced and sensitive older man to make her deflowering any more than a quick thrust.

There were some quite desirable teachers at the school. Should she set her cap at one of them? There were her mother's boyfriends – plenty of those, and willing, but with her mother being so careful and sensitive to the slightest hint, what chance would she have of succeeding there?

After some thought she took a route many had taken before her – the father of the child to be babysat. Not that Katrina was the babysitting type, but some of her school friends were, and they talked, and one of them admitted to being shown the way by a rather dishy dad who took his time and who had the most creative tongue, and quite a big dick, although it was what he did with it that mattered.

Katrina wanted to know how her friend had made it plain that she was available. After all, most older men (this man was in fact a mere twenty-nine) would be hesitant about making advances to young girls, wouldn't they?

Well, yes, they would, a bit. But it was incredible what a soft glance and a trembling hand on a knee could do. He'd nearly gone in the ditch the first night she'd stroked the inside of his thigh as they were driving home.

It was agreed that next time she was wanted for

babysitting, she would be indisposed but would send her friend Katrina – and my, how that man's eyebrows shot up when he saw what was on the doorstep.

'I got a lift here,' Katrina said, looking into his eyes, 'but I hope you'll be able to take me home.'

Clearly, nothing would please the man more, and his cock was twitching all evening as he sat with his wife at a business dinner. He kept his wine drinking to strict moderation, but he made sure his wife had the four glasses he'd found were enough to make bed and sleep an immediate necessity when they got home.

As predicted, she went straight upstairs, calling in to see the offspring but then disappearing for the night, leaving her husband to pay and convey the babysitter.

Katrina was carefully posed when he came into the sitting room. She was sitting on the couch, her legs under her, with her skirt placed so that a large expanse of white thigh was visible. As she got up, held onto the chair arm and bent down to pick up her shoes, she knew her miraculous bosoms were well in sight as the man stared, fascinated, down the neckline of her loose T-shirt top. She was wearing no bra, naturally, and had even thought of dispensing with knickers – but no, that was probably going too far.

'Would you, er, like a coffee before we go?' said the man, trying his damnedest to be casual but failing completely.

'Oh, thank you,' said Katrina. 'That would be nice.'

She was sitting on the hearth rug when the man returned, her skirt once again riding up her long, long legs and her tits swinging beneath the thin shirt as she turned the pages of a magazine.

The man's cock jumped and began an unstoppable rise. As Katrina's eyes lifted from the magazine they caught sight of the desired swelling and paused there, before continuing up to the coffee mugs and the man's face.

'I think you'll spill that coffee in a minute,' she smiled. 'Why don't you put it down over there and come and sit next to me? I think there's something you and I need to talk about. Or, perhaps, not talk about.'

Within twenty seconds his mouth was on hers and his hands were her breasts. She lay back on the rug. He lay beside her, propped up on one elbow, and idly ran his hand under her shirt.

'What brilliant, brilliant tits,' he sighed.

'Yes, aren't they?' said Katrina, lifting up her arms to make easier the passage of the shirt over her head.

Next she lifted up her bum so the man could pull her skirt down, and then her knickers. The shoes were kicked off long ago.

'Now, look here,' she said. 'I've got no clothes on, and you've got all yours. So you stand up again and take off that jacket – so – and the tie. Shoes and socks. Good boy. Shirt and trousers. No – leave that bit to me.'

She knelt in front of him, naked, and stroked the iron curve of his cock through the flimsy cotton of his briefs, which were all he now had on. Slowly her hands went round behind and pulled, inch by inch, until the pants were well down at the back over his buttocks but held up at the front only by his cock. Her hands came to the front again and dived inside the straining material and pulled out his stiff dong.

While she skinned it with one hand, she pulled the briefs down with the other so he could step out of them. She knelt a little closer and took the end of his cock in her mouth.

He pulled her head towards him, forcing the cock further in than she was used to. She spluttered and pulled back.

'Sorry,' he said, sliding down on to the rug once more. 'Here. You lie back. Let me do the work.'

She'd never felt the skilful ministrations of a man's tongue before and it was simply sensational. She forgot all her concerns about being a virgin and just let herself go. Her knees were soon up and wide apart and her pelvis was thrusting spasmodically into the man's face as he licked her and speared her and caressed her to the point of orgasm.

As her moans became more insistent and her hands began to scrabble at the back of his head, he pulled back and slid up her body so that her nipples now were the object of his questing tongue, and at the same moment pushed the end of his cock into the wet and welcoming warmth below.

There was some pain for her, but she had been well manipulated and she was able to contain it easily enough as she felt the hot sword slide into her scabbard. The man began pumping slowly. She instinctively wrapped her legs around his back and her arms around his neck. With his face buried in her chest he increased his speed. She was going to come first, he thought, and soon.

He was right. Within two minutes of being deflowered, Katrina Mulloy was biting her lip in an effort to stop herself shouting loud enough to wake the sleeping wife above as wave after wave of delicious sensation swept through her young body.

And still the man kept going! Faster and faster he thrust until he too, with a low and sighing grunt, spilled his semen in her ex-maiden passage.

Katrina lay with the still man in her arms. This certainly was something, this sex business. She liked it. She liked it very much.

'Can we do that again?' she asked the man . . .

Now a TV personality – as yet on a fairly small scale, admittedly – and veteran of many successful romps, the older and wiser Katrina Mulloy, Weather Dish Extraordinaire, smiled at the memory. He had become a bit of a problem, that chap. Wouldn't leave her alone after that. Wanted to leave his wife for her. Stupid man! Didn't realise that a fuck was just a fuck – not, she thought, as she re-read the local paper's review of Katrina Mulloy as Viola, like Mr Simpson, the English teacher . . .

When it came to casting *Twelfth Night*, Katrina was clearly in the running for a leading role, but so were half a dozen other girls, some of them more established in the school's actress clique. After the first reading Katrina felt she was up against it. After the second reading she knew it was slipping away.

Next day, English was her last lesson. She claimed to be having trouble understanding a certain passage in *The Canterbury Tales*, and could Sir please explain it to her after class?

Sir didn't seem all that keen on the thought of doing overtime, but perked up during the lesson when he noticed that Katrina had very nice legs, as currently being revealed by the blue gingham school dress, already quite short, seemingly accidentally slipping up almost to knicker level.

He could also see, as she bent forward to write notes for the next homework and absentmindedly undid the top two buttons of the dress, that there was a remarkably fine cleavage under there.

One or two knowing looks were exchanged among Katrina's friends as they filed out of the classroom, leaving the best-looking girl in the school alone with one of the few sexy teachers.

'Well, Katrina, what can I do for you?' said Mr Simpson.

'It's this passage from *The Nun's Priest's Tale*,' she said. 'Here.'

Mr Simpson followed her pointing finger and found himself reading aloud.

'This gentil cok had in his governaunce
Sevene hennes for to doon al his pleasaunce,
Whiche were his sustres and his paramours . . .'

Katrina sat with one leg on the edge of his desk

and thoughtfully scratched at the soft white skin thus revealed.

'Olivia,' she said. 'Maria. Viola. Three leading ladies in *Twelfth Night*, and rather more than sevene hennes wanting to be those ladies.'

'Well, yes, it is a bit of a problem,' said Mr Simpson. 'In fact, I think the part of Maria is settled. I've always thought of her as a shortish, plumpish sort of woman and most of the top actress girls here are too tall. So that leaves Olivia and Viola and, as you say, rather more hennes than parts.'

'And how will the gentil cok be able to make his selection, I wonder?' said Katrina. 'If there's nothing in it for acting, the choice will have to be made some other way.'

'The gentil cok,' said Mr Simpson, seemingly assured but as disturbed as any man would be by the thoughts which were going through his mind, 'is having a hard time of it, if you will pardon the expression.'

'Look, Mr Simpson,' said Katrina in her most sultry voice. 'I want to be Viola. And I don't care who I have to fuck to get it.'

'I see,' said Sir, now more than slightly flustered by her directness. He had always seen himself as a smooth seducer, one so subtle and devastating that no woman or school girl selected for the process could ever resist him – nor, indeed, such a good lover would he be, ever split on him afterwards.

'Good. I'm glad you see,' said Katrina, sliding off the desk top and standing with one hand on hip while the other fingered the third button of her blouse. 'Well, I can get under the desk and suck you off now, or we could try and sneak into the art-room cupboard, or I could come round to your place later. Which do you fancy?'

'I think a suck now, under the desk, definitely gets you a part in the play. An hour or two later in my bed would surely be enough to make necessary the learning of Viola's lines.'

'You drive a hard bargain, Mr Simpson.'

'One day, I want to be able to say – you talk about that Katrina Mulloy, the famous and beautiful celebrity? I had her. Twice. Once under the desk and once in bed . . .'

'Famous? You really think so?'

'Katrina. I don't see how you can fail. Mmmm. That's nice.'

The thing which stuck out in Katrina's memory now was the time in his flat later. Sex so far had been enough of itself at every stage. No artificial aids had been required, but Mr Simpson had asked her which she preferred, mayonnaise or condensed milk. Katrina, with more of a savoury taste than a sweet, had said she liked mayonnaise, and in particular she liked the curry-flavoured one.

In front of a full-length mirror Mr Simpson had carefully spooned curry mayonnaise onto his dick as he stood there, naked, while she, also naked, knelt before him and licked it off. She must have had about six teaspoons full of it. Then she had to lie on his bed while he squeezed condensed milk from a tube onto her nipples and up into her quim. It had been nice when he sucked it off, but the whole procedure had been too prolonged for the hot, passionate novice Katrina who, after her experiences as a babysitter, just wanted a big cock inside her as soon and as long as possible.

But he came good in the end, that Mr Simpson. Once the picnic was over, he'd got her to sit on his face, then on his cock, and she'd been able to ride herself to two separate orgasms before he came. What a difference between a man and a boy, thought Katrina.

The rehearsals for *Twelfth Night* and the performance were a bit of a blur now in Katrina's mind, but the after-show party wasn't. That had got out of hand, most definitely.

Full of herself and the applause she'd received for her admittedly excellent portrayal, Viola had had one or two glasses of wine too many at Orsino's house, where the party was held, starting at midnight, after the official do at the school was over.

Orsino had played the romantic lead mostly because he was large and aristocratic-looking rather than through any great thespian talents. The party was at his place not because he was the best-liked life and soul, but mostly because he was the son of wealthy parents, with a large detached house currently his to do what he liked with as said parents were away on their fourth holiday of the year.

Orsino was a bit of a prat, actually, thought Katrina looking back.

There are not many female players in *Twelfth Night*, even including the ladies-in-waiting, and so the larger number of males at this party were keen to make their passes as soon as possible. The lad who was Malvolio was highly intelligent and streetwise, and it was he who made sure the girls, particularly Katrina, had plenty to drink and that the conversation soon came round to sex.

Of the eight girls there, six were silent on the subject. Of the fourteen boys, only three or four had nothing to say. A democratic majority, then, was interested in sex and had had, or wanted, some experience of it. A vote was proposed. They would have a game of strip quiz.

A quiz book was found and the rules explained. Each person in turn nominated a page number and a question number. If they could answer that question correctly, they could keep everything they had on and could ask for another question. If they got that right, they could put back on an item of clothing they had lost, or one anybody else had lost.

If they got a question wrong, they took off two items.

This was quite clever of Malvolio. The girls who were shy and innocent tended to be the more studious anyway and so more likely to know the answers, while the extroverts – like Katrina – could always answer a question wrong on purpose, as indeed could the prattish show-offs like Orsino . . .

Within twenty minutes, Katrina was wearing only her bra and knickers and Orsino only his underpants, with Katrina's blouse tied around his neck.

The others were in various stages. One of the girls,

one of the shy ones in fact, was down to bra and pants but not caring too much after her fifth glass of Moroccan red. Another, the not-so-shy buxom one who had played Maria, was topless but had everything else on – skirt, shoes, the lot. She was just slightly pissed and proud of her tits.

All of the boys had lost shoes and socks, some had lost shirts, but all were decent.

Katrina it was to answer the next question. Page forty-seven, number six. Who wrote *Hiawatha*? Well, she knew it was Longfellow, but what the hell.

'Something to do with length,' she said with a giggle. 'By the big sea shining water, Stands the whatsit with a hard-on, Big Chief Dick-head with a hard-on, Wanks his willy in the moonlight.'

She stood up slowly in the middle of a silent circle of gaping boys and wondering girls and, without saying a word, unhooked her bra, held it by finger and thumb at arm's length, and dropped it in Orsino's lap. She did a twirl, arms in the air, and then took down her panties, dropping them on Malvolio's head.

'Fuck knows,' she said, and sat back in her place, arms around knees, as if nothing had happened.

It was Orsino's turn. Page sixty-nine, number one. Who said 'Roll up that map of Europe. It will not be wanted these ten years?'

'Miss Smedley,' said Orsino, which was quite witty for him, since Miss S was the geography teacher. He stood and walked over to Katrina, his underpants bulging with confidence. He took the blouse from round his neck, and waited. Katrina shrugged, knelt, and pulled down his pants.

Most of the girls in the room had never seen an erect penis before. Some blushed. Some looked closer. Some – plus most of the boys – giggled nervously.

Orsino thrust his hips at Katrina, making his quite large and very stiff cock wobble and sway.

'Have you ever done it, my lord Duke Orsino?' said Malvolio.

'Course I have.'

'Who with?' said the topless, not-so-shy girl who had played Maria.

'Loads of girls. Loads of 'em.'

'Well,' said Katrina, 'you had better give us the benefit of your experience with a demonstration. I'm sure we all have something to learn.'

This raised a laugh. They all knew who was the most experienced person there.

'Now,' continued Katrina, 'how many of you girls are virgins? All of you? Well, I know that isn't true' (Mr Simpson had chosen Olivia in rather the same way as he had Viola, and Maria had a certain reputation in the school) 'but we'll leave that for now. I suppose even if you weren't you wouldn't admit it, and thus run the awful risk of having to do the demo with Orsino. All right. I'll do it.'

She drained her glass and held it out for Malvolio to fill up. Orsino was made to lie on the carpet and Katrina knelt beside him, gently running her hand up and down his cock.

'Now girls, pay attention please. Today's sex education lesson takes the form of a practical, and please watch closely as you may be asked to show us all later just how much you have learned.'

With the wine and the dramatic atmosphere, few of the girls seemed to mind the implications of this and none of them left the room. Katrina continued.

'This item here is the penis, also known as the cock, prick, dick, dong and the pork sword. It is in its erect state, ready for insertion into the vagina, quim or cunt.'

There was a groan from Orsino, and a couple of the boys not quite at the front to watch were allowing their hands to stroke their own cocks through their trousers. Topless Maria allowed her hand to be placed on the trousered bump of the boy who had played Antonio. One of the ladies-in-waiting snatched her hand away as Sir Toby tried to get her to do the same thing.

'Girls, I must tell you, it is very important to have the penis as stiff and enlarged as possible, so that the female will enjoy the sex act to the utmost, and to this end it is often useful to give the penis a little oral stimulation, like this.'

The naked Katrina bent towards Orsino's cock and gave the end a little lick. Then, slowly, she lowered her lips over it and took in the first three inches. Orsino moaned again. Katrina straightened up and continued her slow skinning of the hot and anxious rod.

'Mmm. Now, when we are quite sure that the penis is as hard as possible, it is time to . . . oh.'

Five spurts of come shot into the air, the first landing

on her shoulder, the second on her right tit, the rest on Orsino.

'Olivia, I know you've seen this sort of thing before. Be a darling and get me some kitchen towel, will you? Poor my lord Duke couldn't last the pace. We shall have to continue the demonstration with somebody else.'

The girl who played Olivia, who was in bra and jeans, dashed to the kitchen and back and took not a little special care to wipe the come from Katrina's luscious form. Meanwhile a quick election was held among the girls and they voted Malvolio to be the next subject for Katrina's lesson.

The boldest two or three of the girls stripped him naked. Maria gave his cock a stroke. One of the shy girls, who had managed to lose only her shoes in the quiz, permitted her go-for-it friend Maria to place her shy little hand around the unfamiliar silky warmth of a hardened man. She blushed, but clearly liked it.

Malvolio lay down and Katrina began slowly wanking him.

'Where was I, before I was so rudely ejaculated? Ah yes. Give the penis a bit of a lick and a suck, like this . . . and, when you are sure he's ready, throw your leg over his recumbent form, thus . . . and lower yourself onto the penis, holding it the while to make sure it goes in the right place. There. Mmm-hmmm.'

Katrina lifted and lowered herself a few times, pulling her wonderful bottom up to the very tip of Malvolio's cock, so they could all see, and then sliding gently down. She also leaned forward so that her magnificent breasts dangled in front of Malvolio's face.

'Now, girls, with most boys, their only objective is to stick their cocks in and fuck you as fast as possible. This does not do a lot for the feminine orgasm. In order to make the most of the potential of any given fuck, you should take control. You want the man to play with your breasts, like Malvolio is doing, and you want the cock to move inside you in the way you like it best. You can, if you wish, give yourself a little extra stimulation by tickling your clitty with your finger while you are sliding up and down his shaft. Mmmmmmm.'

Only one girl in the room was now empty-handed. She watched, riveted, but was too inhibited to take any part. Maria stood between two boys and had a cock in each hand and was wanking them both with a will. Olivia stood behind Sir Andrew Aguecheek and reached around his waist and dug both hands inside his trousers. All the other girls had a cock to wank, and the boys left out were wanking their own.

Katrina stopped talking now and looked into Malvolio's eyes. They smiled, and went at it. Katrina speeded up and began making noises. One of Maria's boys shot his load onto the carpet. The boys who were wanking themselves were going as fast as they could, and they all came more or less at once.

Katrina, with one last yelp, sat down hard on Malvolio's cock and felt her own violent sensations wash over her as the boy pumped his flood up into her. She collapsed on top of him, half-drunk and very happy.

Maria's second cock was still strong. She looked up

at the boy, who winked. She took off all her remaining clothes, walked him across the room by the balls, and placed him on the carpet beside the exhausted Malvolio and Katrina.

'Now, what was it again? Kiss it ... suck it ... and mount it. There. That slipped in all right. Funny. I must have done this before, it went in so easily. Oh yes, I remember. It was with Mr Simpson.'

'You too?' said Katrina and Olivia simultaneously.

'The bastard,' said Katrina, now awake and watching Maria wriggle and thrust her plump little body up and down the boy's long pole.

When that was over, and people had got partly dressed again, and had another drink and the remains of the bought-in food, there still seemed no way that everybody could get paired off with whom they wanted, or at all, and so Katrina stepped in once more with another dramatic idea.

'What we need is a sacrificial maiden,' she said. 'Come on, you boys. Pick one out. And don't pick me or Olivia or Maria.'

The boys muttered among themselves and announced their selection. It was Maureen, a very bright type whose excellent good looks were somewhat disguised by bookish spectacles and hair done up in a bun. Her clothes, always long and roomy, hid they knew not what, although during the strip quiz they had noticed a couple of good points when she pulled off her jumper.

Maureen, not used to drink, was feeling very relaxed.

She allowed Katrina and the others to take her into the next room.

'While we're gone, you boys draw lots. I want two volunteers.'

The girls stripped Maureen naked and one or two, including Maria and Katrina, could not resist stroking her breasts in admiration. This Maureen was what they used to call statuesque. Her tits jutted out in plentiful firmness, her tummy was flat, her buttocks round and muscular, her legs long and strong. Quite a girl.

Two girls were sent to search Orsino's mother's bedroom and quickly came back with a floaty, see-through negligee. They put that on Maureen, tied her hands together in front of her with a silk scarf and blindfolded her with another.

Naked except for the negligee, bound and blindfolded, she was led into the main room. The boys stopped talking as they saw the light from the doorway outline Maureen's blissful form through the diaphanous material.

Katrina and the other girls, themselves mostly dressed in T-shirt, and jeans, or jumper and knickers, displayed their captive to the gawping boys. Then they undid the wrist binding and slowly, ever so slowly, removed the negligee.

Maureen stood, nervous but willing, while they retied her hands, this time behind her back.

'Who are the two volunteers? Let them step forth!' Katrina commanded.

The rest of the girls had the boys stark naked in a

few moments, and they were made to lie on their backs on the floor, arms widely stretched, legs a little apart, with the soles of their feet touching.

Four of the girls took off their jeans and knickers and sat, one on each of the four outstretched hands. Maureen, still blindfolded and bound, was made to step across the boys so that her cleft was over their feet. She was helped to a kneeling position, and then encouraged to lean forward so she could take the cock in front of her in her mouth.

As she relaxed her kneeling she could feel toes questing around her wet pussy. She sucked with a will, and wriggled herself on the boys' toes. Katrina turned to the two remaining girls who were so far not involved in the tableau and looked at them questioningly. One shook her head. The other got up from her seat and found a little space on the carpet where she could catch hold of the cock of the boy not being sucked and wank it, with enthusiasm if not with much skill.

Katrina went and sat beside the girl left out.

'What's the matter? Why won't you join in?' she asked, gently.

'I'd join in if it was all girls,' replied the head-shaker. 'I just like girls. I don't like boys. I've tried it and I don't like it.'

'What do you do together, then, with another girl?'

There was much moaning and groaning from the tableau. The two cocks were spouting come all over and five females were wriggling their young and tender arses on all kinds of combinations of fingers and toes.

'I'll show you if you like,' said the young disciple of Sappho, who was called Marilyn. 'Let's sneak upstairs now, while all this is going on.'

And so they did, Katrina remembered, and for the first time she had found out what a girl's tongue can do, and a girl's fingers. It was nice, she smiled in fond memory, and she'd done it quite a few times since, but overall she preferred cock.

Later that night, with young boys still able to get hard-ons and young girls still willing to give them what they wanted, Katrina had had a chance fuck with Feste the Jester. Very nice too. A nice long one, wasn't it?

Katrina, Weather Dish, smiled to herself again at her memories. She'd got quite serious with Feste for a while. He was a very good fucker. His cock reached right into your vitals. But, they lost touch when he went to university and she began her first job. Ah well. Such is life. But a walking shadow, a poor player that struts and frets his hour upon the stage and then is heard no more. So. Better make the most of it.

Chapter Four

Some mothers do have them . . .

. . . brilliant ideas, that is. Elspeth felt very pleased with herself, a) that she'd had the impulse to ask this very classy young man out to lunch, and b) had managed to get from him some information, which, despite the horny and disreputable thoughts currently occupying the animal section of her brain, had triggered a notion labelled 'commercially cunning' in the more sober, intellectual portion of her grey matter.

The young man – well, younger than Elspeth, about twenty-seven, twenty-eight – was an account executive with AQPR, the hottest of creative hot shops in London's advertising world. She'd invited him to lunch after meeting him at a cocktail party the previous week. Five minutes' standing with a glass of New Zealand white and looking up into his James Bond features had decided her that she would simply have to get inside his trousers. However, the conversation at the much anticipated lunch, over the roast beef and Yorkshire, had turned out to be about the poor boy's business problems, not about his cock.

The agency was developing the launch advertising for a new range of upmarket bath products with exotic perfumes called Luxor Egyptian. The basic idea was to have a luscious female in the bath, foam up to her chin, who would be astonished when a man came walking into the bathroom wanting to borrow a towel, wanting to mend the tap, wanting to ask the way to the M4, whatever.

She would use a different bath oil in each ad, and a different man would come into the bathroom. Most of the thirty seconds would be spent watching her soak luxuriously, then suddenly in would come the man to say, 'Excuse me, can I borrow a cup of sugar?' Cut to astonished girl's face. Zoom in to very misty close-up of soapy skin as she appears to rise from the bath to answer the request. Close on copy line – 'Luxor Egyptian. For girls who can cope.'

Elspeth's lunch companion had been given the job of finding the girl in the bath. She would become a national figure, that was for sure, but she could not be an established famous person to start with. They wanted a minor celebrity, very minor, or an unknown, but someone who was so stunning that she would have had to live in a cave not to have become famous. It was an impossible job. Where was he going to start looking for the world's most beautiful unknown bath girl – who also, incidentally, had to have no past. AQPR couldn't have her being exposed in the papers as having slept with six government ministers.

'What does "unknown" actually mean in your terms?'

'Not on national telly – at least, not on any of the four main channels.'

'How about someone who was about to begin broadcasting on Satellite Uptime?'

'Uptime? Well, that would be all right. They've only got 2.3 viewers a week.'

'At the moment they have. But the word is that things are changing. And there's a girl coming on there who's having her job-finalising meeting even now as we speak, who has the looks and the ability to add six noughts to that 2.3.'

'And if our advertising campaign could coincide with her rise and rise . . .'

'Exactly. I'll declare an interest. I'm her agent, sort of. Kind of manager. Informally, you know. I'll get some pictures to your office this afternoon. I presume you want nude studies? To see what she'll look like in the bath?'

The young man coughed. As she said the phrase 'nude studies', Elspeth's hand had gone to her left nipple, sticking prominently through the skinny ribbed sweater she was wearing. Idly and seemingly unconsciously, she scratched the nipple with her index fingernail.

'Nude, yes, that will be fine,' said the man, stirring in his seat as he felt a tremor in his underpants. What happened next took him a while to work out.

Something was stroking his cock through his trousers. Elspeth, busy with cream and sugar for her coffee, had both hands visible. She looked up at him and winked. The man put his hands to where his napkin should have been and found instead a stocking. She'd kicked her shoe off and was wanking him with the sole of her foot.

'Look,' said the man. 'We have a flat near here. For visitors from out of town. I've got the key. Shall we . . .?'

'Of course,' said Elspeth. 'Just a quickie, though. We've got work to do.'

Elspeth's work was very thorough. She found out that the director who did all AQPR's commercials was a homosexual and therefore not open to her usual form of persuasion but – and here was the chink of opportunity she wanted – his favourite cameraman, or camera person, was a girl with money troubles. She was also a lapsed lesbian, in that she liked girls mostly but had a weakness for very big and very black men.

Once it was confirmed that Katrina Mulloy, Britain's first Weather Dish, was also to be the Luxor Egyptian Bath Girl – a formality as soon as the agency saw those pictures – Elspeth got on the phone to Carole the Camera and invited her for a little chat.

When she arrived at Elspeth's terraced town-house in Islington, Carole was dressed – as always – in jeans and sloppy sweater. Elspeth was in a smart business suit but Carole's sexual instincts were immediately aroused by the impression that there was nothing underneath it. She couldn't see, there was no real evidence, but Carole just had this feeling that if the tailored jacket was unbuttoned then out would fall a large pair of naked tits, and if the skirt was lifted up the sun-tanned legs, no panties would be there to hinder progress.

Elspeth showed Carole a miniature camera and a pile of twenty-pound notes.

'These are closely linked,' she said. They were sitting at a low coffee table in the long lounge made, Carole assumed, from two rooms knocked into one. 'You get this,' continued Elspeth, pointing to the money, 'if you use this.'

'Obviously the where and the when are a bit ticklish, or you wouldn't be offering me all this cash for a happy snap.'

'Quite so. You will shortly be camera operator on the commercial for Luxor Egyptian Bath Oils?'

'Yes, how did you . . .'

'And the star of the show will be naked but will have her important little places covered all the time with lovely foamy bubbles?'

'Well, yes, I mean they wouldn't want anything actually showing, I suppose.'

Elspeth leaned over the low table towards Carole. The girl could see down the front of Elspeth's suit. Her instincts had been right. There was nothing there except for a large and luscious pair of breasts. Carole felt a slight dampness and was glad that she at least was wearing knickers.

'There will come a point,' continued Elspeth, 'when the model will stand up to get out of the bath. She will reveal all then, with a certain amount of disguise through foam clinging to her. If you were to use this camera, you would be able to get a picture of her which would be of enormous interest at a future date to the readers of one of our famous newspapers. Luxor Bath Girl Starkers! Read all about it! Weather Dish shows warm front!'

'Weather Dish?'

'Yes, didn't you know? The Luxor Bath Girl is to be Katrina Mulloy, TV weather's newest and most dishiest. And, already, after one week, putting tens of thousands on Satellite Uptime's viewing figures.'

'Katrina Mulloy? But your name's Mulloy. And I've seen her. I heard it when somebody in the office said ... and you look quite a bit like her.'

'Elder sister. Looking after her interests. Stardom beckons. I'm just helping it to come that bit sooner. And talking of coming ...'

Elspeth stood, and lifted the girl Carole to her feet also. Elspeth was taller than her young friend, and found it easy to bend a willing head back so that she could plant a fierce kiss on the girl's lips. At first the lips stayed firm and closed, and then they softened, and opened, and two tongues coiled and searched in a passionate embrace.

Carole moaned as she felt Elspeth's hand searching beneath her sweater for her bra catch, finding that there was no bra and switching the search to the front. Carole's breasts were small, hard cones which demanded strong handling. Elspeth moulded and massaged them without gentle preliminaries. Carole, she felt, was a girl who liked to go for it.

Indeed, while Elspeth was busy on her tits Carole was keeping her lips and tongue busy and at the same time hurrying off her own jeans and pants, and no sooner were they clear than Elspeth's jacket was opened and her skirt unzipped. The two women collapsed to the floor, hands everywhere, clothes being shrugged and kicked away, locked in each other's enthusiastic explorations.

Carole was on her back. Elspeth straddled her face, looking down the young, firm body, and lowered her fleshy parts onto Carole's stiff tongue. While the younger girl gasped and reached into every crevice, Elspeth slowly kissed and licked her way down past the hard little cones and across the flat tummy to Carole's own most sensitive region. Now they were in the perfect sixty-nine, tongues working furiously.

In two minutes, Carole was crying out. Elspeth, the mistress of sexual technique, had sucked Carole's clitty with such skill that the flood of sensation swept over her sooner than ever before. This was in Elspeth's interests. She would have all-girl sex, if it was necessary, but she didn't really like it. She much, much preferred men, especially men like Cliff who, listening at the door, decided that now was the time to make his entrance.

Cliff was on Elspeth's employer's books as a model. He was an American ex-footballer, a linebacker who had come over to help promote the game in Britain, got injured and stayed.

Cliff was indeed built like the geological features after which he was named. He stood over the two women's entangled bodies and felt his cock jump as Elspeth, a frequent companion, dismounted from the smaller, slimmer, younger girl.

Carole seemed out for the count. In fact she had

opened one eye and seen Cliff towering above her, his enormous private parts captured in a black leather posing pouch, the only thing he had on. In terror of what might happen to her, she closed her eyes and played dead.

Elspeth pulled Cliff onto the carpet beside her and gently stroked the mountain ridge covered in posing leather.

'I think the string is going to break,' she said. 'I'd better undo it.'

Carole could not resist a glimpse through half-open eyes and needed all her self-control not to squeak in fright at what she saw. Never, never, never had she dreamed that a man's cock could be so big. It was vast. It was a foot long and thick in proportion. Elspeth's white hand, sliding ever so slowly up and down its black enormity, looked like a butterfly on a tree trunk.

Carole closed her eyes, unable to deal with this situation at all. This was too, too real. Carole's weakness for big black men had not been gratified very often – in fact, until now it had been largely confined to fingering herself while looking at magazine pictures which her male homosexual friends got for her. To see the real thing this close was a terrible shock.

Carole, her mind racing, heard a slurp.

'Fucking hell, Cliff,' said Elspeth's dreamy voice. 'I'll swear it gets bigger every time. I can't get my mouth over it at all these days.'

The reply was a deep laugh. Cliff was a man of few words.

'Cliff. Stay there while I get the jelly.'

Elspeth continued talking while she got up, walked a short distance, and returned.

'Sex with girls is all right, but there ain't nothin' like having a fucking great prick stuffed right up your pussy. There. There we are. Just a little blob right on the end, and smooth it around, we'll just have a bit more, there, just right . . . and now, let me get comfortable, that's it. Right. I'm ready. Give me that cock. All of it.'

Carole heard shuffling as Elspeth laid back on the carpet and Cliff positioned himself above her. There was that deep laugh again, and then a sound from Elspeth like people usually make when they're thumped in the solar plexus.

Carole had a look. As if asleep she turned her body and opened an eye. A few feet from her along the carpet was Elspeth's bottom. It was jumping about like a dribbling basketball. And being thrust into it, as fast as it bounced, was the foot-long black pile driver.

Elspeth's legs began to wave in the air. Carole had seen people make similar movements with their arms when they'd scored a goal or holed a winning putt. Here it was a lovely, tanned, shapely pair of female legs which were jerking and pushing in total emotional release.

Cliff speeded up. Elspeth was a frantic, palpitating, out-of-control automaton which flailed and wailed as the gigantic ramrod went in and out at unbelievable speed.

'Aaaaaagh!' she shouted. 'Aaaaaagh! Cliffeeeeeeee!'

Cliff's last thrust went home and Elspeth collapsed,

exhausted. Carole, wide-eyed by this time, watched in awe as Cliff slowly withdrew his grotesquely oversized dong, inch by gleaming inch.

Out and out it came. It kept coming, like those joke films when twenty people get out of one side of a tiny motor car. When eventually it was all out, still stiff, Carole thought she had never seen anything so magnificent. If only she was at home lying on her bed. Her fingers itched to creep towards her pussy. Her eyes closed as she tried to imagine bringing herself off with a picture of Cliff in front of her, his cock in his hand and his eyes looking straight to camera.

There was more shuffling. Carole kept her eyes closed. She heard a door open and close. Who had gone out? Was she alone with Cliff? Oh my god. Aaagh!

She gave a squeal as she felt a hand on her naked buttock. She didn't dare look to see who it was, but from the size of the hand she didn't have much doubt. The hand stroked her firm, tight buttocks with a surprising gentleness, and she made no resistance when another hand arrived and helped to turn her over. Fingers now searched between her thighs. She had to open them. Had to. Couldn't stop herself.

She looked, and saw Cliff's smiling face. Cliff, looking down, saw a frightened little rabbit. His smile broadened.

'Hey, baby. It's all right.'

Carole raised herself on her elbows and gazed in wonderment at the biggest cock in history. To her, everything was far from all right. She imagined she was about to be put to death by battering ram. This was nothing like a girl's tongue, nothing like a vibrator, nothing like the dildos she'd used.

'What . . . what . . . what about some jelly?' she gulped.

'I don't need no jelly. I just been done fucked Elspeth. I'm lubricated just fine.'

He presented the head of his cock at her entrance. She raised her knees and opened her legs as wide as she could, still watching from her elbow-propped position. Cliff raised himself up from her as far as he could, understanding that she would want to witness the next few minutes as fully as possible.

He pushed. It wouldn't go. He held his super-cannon in his hand and pushed again. No progress.

She lay back flat, reached down, and took his cock in both hands. No matter how she guided and adjusted, and no matter how or where he thrust, it would not go in.

'You lie back and I'll try sitting on it,' said Carole, now treating this as a challenge. They got the same result. Nothing.

Elspeth, in her bedroom, reading a book while reclining on the duvet, was surprised to hear an anxious little tap on the door.

'Elspeth!' the voice said. 'It's Carole. I can't get it in. Can you help?'

The resulting sight of two naked women walking towards him made Cliff's cock stand even stiffer. Elspeth knelt down and anointed him with jelly and then lay alongside him, at a slight angle, with her head in his lap. At her signal, Carole got into a straddle and lowered herself, not onto Cliff's cock but onto Elspeth's tongue. The cock slid up her tummy, the end of it reaching as far as her waist.

Elspeth's hands were working her buttocks as her tongue wriggled and licked inside her quim. A thumb made a questing feel around her puckered back passage. Another rubbed her clit while the tongue thrust in deeper. Carole began to feel the first waves of an orgasm approaching and moaned out loud.

Elspeth pushed up with her hands. As Carole's buttocks rose in answer, Elspeth grabbed Cliff's cock and placed it in position. As Carole came down, in it went, right before Elspeth's eyes.

The sounds which now came from Carole were hardly human. She was utterly transported. Pure animal instinct made her move up and down on Cliff's gigantic prick, and with each movement her eyes opened wide in a mad stare and her mouth, also hanging wide open, emitted wild gargles.

Elspeth watched, fascinated, as Carole's wet fanny lips slid over and back, a few inches from her face. Her hand strayed to Cliff's balls and gently massaged them. She smiled. This camera operator would do anything, anything at all, now she'd had a taste of Cliff.

Carole was moving faster now, and emitting high-pitched wails like a train in a tunnel. Cliff was lying back with his head resting on his hands. He was happy. He had one slim young female jumping on his cock while another, more ample and luxurious specimen, stroked his balls and breathed on his thigh.

Carole came to a fantastic climax, her movements a mad judder and her head thrown back in a last primeval cry. A moment later, unconscious, she fell off Cliff's cock and lay still on the carpet. Cliff smiled at Elspeth.

'Hey, baby. I ain't creamed. Just open your mouth and say after me, come, baby, come.'

Elspeth knelt beside her favourite footballer and lowered her wide-open lips. She could just get the first couple of inches of the massive head into her mouth. Her fingers scratched his cock root and stroked his balls as she did her best to suck him. After a minute or two of this, an idea occurred to her.

Lifting her mouth off his cock she took it in both hands, and, bending her head a little to one side, began to lick it. She concentrated on the rim of the glans and in particular on the point where the foreskin is joined to it. She rubbed her tastebuds against his most sensitive point and was rewarded immediately with a sighing moan. She rubbed harder. Another moan.

She sat back for a moment on her heels to admire her work, and then, with both hands, one above the other as if she was holding a ceremonial banner, she slowly moved the skin up and down his shaft. What an absolutely magnificent cock, she thought. If only all men possessed such a beast – but, on the other hand, maybe best not. She leant forward again and did her rough-tongue trick. This time there were two moans – one from Cliff and one from Carole who, coming round from her orgasm-induced coma, saw first the instrument of her downfall.

Carole roused herself and knelt on the other side of the recumbent footballer and watched the tastebud technique.

'Can I have a go at that?' she asked.

'Surely,' said Elspeth. 'I'd have thought there was enough room on this cock for both our tongues and more besides.'

And so the two girls bent to their work, rasping Cliff's rampant dong, working his shaft with their hands and softly fondling his balls.

Even Cliff could not take such attentions for long. His groans and thigh-writhings told the experienced Elspeth that the time was fast approaching. She showed Carole how to wank him with both hands and then leaned forward so that the end of his cock was buried between her two swaying tits. She pushed her magnificent pair together with her hands. Cliff shoved upwards so that he was poking her in the tits from underneath while the rest of his length was being skinned faster and faster by the panting Carole.

Suddenly his hips gave a great heave. Elspeth squeezed her tits in. Carole gave a few final and extra rapid flicks of the wrist, and the two girls watched, fascinated, as a steady stream of come oozed through Elspeth's cleavage.

Cliff sank back with a final, low, satisfied growl.

'Hey, man. That was some fuck. I ain't never been

licked by two tongues before and I'm here to tell you, babes, I like it.'

'All right, lovey, now just ease yourself up a bit. I want to be able to see the pink, dear, see the pink. No, I don't want you breaking the surface like a couple of bloody porpoises, lovey. I just want to see the pink, lurking, under the bubbles. Yes. That's it. Perfect, lovey.'

The director of the TV commercial was trying to get Katrina in the most revealing position without actually revealing anything. She lay in the bath, foam potentially up to her chin, with one knee raised and her two arms lying flat along the tops of the bath's sides. As the camera came in close, the dim shapes of her superb breasts could be seen, and beneath the whiteness of the bubbles there had to be a strong hint of pinky-brown-ness where her two large nipples searched for air.

Carole on the camera-trolley was a true professional but even she could not help feeling a slight dampness in her crutch at the gorgeous sight of Katrina Mulloy, Weather Dish, with no clothes on. The tiny stills camera had already clicked her marvellous rear view as she climbed into the bath. Now she had to make sure she filmed her commercial to her usual high standards, and somehow during it took a snap of the full frontal of Katrina with soapy bubbles flowing down her curves.

'OK, lovies, we've got enough of that but Katrina, stay in the position. Do not move. Keep your porpoises below the surface. Goodness knows how you get near enough to that weather chart with all that warm front moving down the country. And I bet nobody's ever said that before, have they? Now, Brian sweetheart, this is your moment. We'll get the shot of you coming through the door later. What I want now is where we cut to your back view, and zoom in over your shoulder to see the lovely Katrina looking up at you in pleased surprise.'

Katrina was thinking that the water was getting a bit cool, but they'd better not disturb it for the sake of continuity in the commercial. She gave her pleased and surprised look on request and held it while Brian said his line – 'Oh, hello, I'm the carpet layer. Where would you like me to . . . ?'

'Right, lovies, last shot for Katrina in the bath. Now, when he says 'like me to', dot dot dot, Katrina's got to stand up. We'll only use the first half second of it, just enough to get the tiniest teeny-weeny sighting of a couple of pink porpoises, but the movement's got to be right so, Katrina my pet, do the whole stand up as if you mean it. OK, Carole? You ready? Rolling? Sound rolling? Right, action!'

Katrina, allowing her pleased and surprised look to develop into an amused, quizzical and rather knowing frankness which would devastate every man who was the recipient of it, stood. Brian, an actor from an Australian soap, decided at that moment that he could not go back down under before he'd wiped the froth off this one with his chest hairs. What a piece! Those tits! That look!

'OK, lovies, that's a wrap. Breakies time. Brian, we'll do your door-opening bit after coffee and bickies. Come along, Katrina. You don't have to stand in the bath posing like Botticelli's fucking Venus coming out of the waves. Go and get your knickers on.'

Katrina had in fact posed a little longer than necessary after the camera stopped running. She was looking at the bulge in Brian's trousers and was making a resolution not dissimilar to his own. Meanwhile, Carole had had plenty of time to click her little camera.

The bathrobe was thrown casually over a chair. Katrina, already acquiring the professional model's total disregard for her nakedness while in working company, hung it by a finger over her shoulder and made for the door.

'Excuse me,' she said, demurely, smiling up at Brian as she passed him and making sure that some foam from her breasts got onto his shirt. 'I've got to go and get my knickers on, lovey. Bye.'

Brian sighed a deep, deep sigh of resignation. How he would have loved to follow that perfect set of rotating buttocks, but alas there was work to do. Later, Brian swore to himself, those buttocks would writhe in his palms.

Chapter Five

The best party you've ever been to . . .

. . . or anyone had ever been to, Elspeth resolved as she read the memo from her boss at the agency.

A small but very high powered delegation of American TV producers was coming over in three weeks' time, with the objective of casting a new blockbuster mini-series. It was to be about the Pilgrim Fathers and the first settlements in the New World, based on a phenomenally successful, five-inch-thick novel and, contrary to standard American practice, the actors were to be authentic British with authentic British regional accents.

There were several more unusual features about this project. The producers were seeing three theatrical agents rather like a manufacturer might ask advertising agencies to pitch for his account. The producers wanted to work with a team, that is one agent who would supply the whole cast, so that this very difficult aspect could be delegated completely. There were to be no big names – just good British professionals plus a leavening of young hopefuls and stars of tomorrow, the memo said.

The other remarkable thing about the Americans was that they were all female. Eight of them, what ages Elspeth didn't know, were called Paula, Tammy, Sue-Ellen and so on. Her boss, the memo instructed Elspeth, would be especially delighted if these Americans were to be given a memorable and entertaining party, the night before the presentation. He, the boss, would be speaking to an audience which, he hoped, had already been made receptive and susceptible by whatever pleasures Elspeth could cook up.

He guessed that such experienced campaigners would not fall for the usual cocktails and let's-get-them-pissed stratagem. Something special would have to be planned. Could Elspeth please have three ideas ready for discussion by the morning?

Three ideas my arse, thought Elspeth. There is one idea, and one idea only. She picked up the phone and dialled Cliff's number.

'Darling Cliffy,' she breathed as the massive footballer's economical tones came down the line. 'How's your cock?'

'Hey, Elspeth baby. How you doin'?'

'Cliffy, my pet, you will remember our conversation of last week, when we were discussing a certain theatrical venture for you and some of your more architectural friends?'

'You mean the Brick Shithouse Boys? Yeah, man, wowsville.'

'That was our private name for the act, Cliff dear.

You will remember we settled on something rather more tasteful for the actual name.'

'Oh, yeah. The Steelyards. Still don't get it, but you know best, baby.'

'Precisely. Well, I want you to get on the phone to all your biggest, blackest and best-endowed friends in the sporting world and get them together for rehearsals. We are making our debut in three weeks' time, at a private party for eight American TV producers, all women.'

'We? Are you coming on with us? Hey, man, there'll be ructions and fucktions.'

'Don't be silly, dear boy. Now, do as I say. I'll hire a rehearsal room, a choreographer and a pianist. You get the boys all ready to start, and swear them to secrecy. Soon as you've got their agreement, ring me, and we'll begin.'

Rehearsals over the following weeks proved a lot of fun, to say the least. The pianist, a repetiteur from the musicals circuit, was a wonderfully funny old queen who confessed that, raddled and debilitated as he was by half a century of ceaseless indulgence, he could still feel a tremor while these boys were strutting their stuff. When the boys in question were not falling about laughing at the pianist's interjections, they were laughing at each other as they tried bravely and, eventually, successfully to master the dance movements which the choreographer had designed for them.

She, the choreographer, was an ex-ballerina, a very good one in her day, who had left the ballet company when the tabloid newspapers exposed her sideline, which was sleeping, occasionally and very selectively, with very rich men for very large sums of money.

The boys, eight of them, were all sports stars, and all retired early for various reasons. Cliff and two others were American footballers. Drugs and extra, unofficial match fees had ended their careers. Two were rugby players – one had played for England, one for Wales – who had left the Union code, joined League clubs and just not made it. Three were field and track athletes, past their best, and the last one was, of all things, a Cambridge rowing Blue who had become a doctor and then got struck off for misbehaving with a socialite patient.

These eight had a number of things in common. They were all black, all big – from 6′ 2″ to 6′ 6″ – and they were all glisteningly fit. They had very fine bodies, muscular and magnificent without being grossly overdeveloped and, as Elspeth and the choreographer had found out at the first rehearsal/audition, they all had big cocks.

Cliff had turned up with his seven dwarves, as he called them, since they were indeed all slightly smaller than him. Sue, their new dance teacher, had played some rock and roll, and some smoochie, and some disco-beat, and just watched. Some were very good movers, some adequate and none, thank goodness, were total lemons.

Sue agreed with Elspeth that they need look no further for their troupe – providing, that is, they all came up to scratch in the intimate physique department.

They were asked to strip to their pants. Sue and

Elspeth held hands to steady each other. Never had they seen such a collection of masculine perfection.

'And now,' Elspeth squeaked, 'sorry, errhum, and now, we need to see you with nothing on at all.'

'How much we gettin' paid for this, Cliff?' said one of the rugby players.

'Five grand,' Cliff replied, and eight pairs of skimpy briefs were pushed to the floor.

'Hands above your heads,' commanded Sue. 'And turn around. Thank you, gentlemen.'

While the boys dressed and chatted, Elspeth and Sue tried to stop gulping and hiccupping. Eight huge members had dangled from eight perfect torsos, and they were running wet with their excitement.

This, Elspeth now knew for certain, would absolutely be the best party ever. She could book The Covington with no qualms.

The Covington was a small country-house hotel which had secured its place at the very top end of the market by acquiring one of the finest chefs in France, providing accommodation and conference facilities of the very highest standard, and ensuring that all their guests' requirements were met.

Discretion also was a very strong point, and this Elspeth felt the need to emphasise while negotiating her booking with the owner.

'No one must hear about this party,' she said. 'Things may happen which our guests may wish to forget afterwards.'

The owner assured her that no problems would occur.

The menus were agreed, plus the refitting of the main conference room as a small theatre, plus a price which would ensure there was no temptation to accept any more residents that weekend. The six already booked in would be given free weekends at the nearest comparable establishment.

Came the day, and Elspeth waited at Heathrow for her party of American women. She was taking a chance, she had increasingly realised lately. Supposing these were born-again types, or battle-hymn Republicans? Even worse, suppose they were Los Angeles lesbians?

Elspeth, told to organise a fun evening, had gone steaming ahead with the kind of fun which she herself would enjoy. Now the doubts were setting in, and now the girls were arriving!

Through the green gate swept a group of females which was unmistakably Elspeth's. These were business types, and how. All in the thirty to forty age group, all with hair like a president's wife, suits from the thousand-dollar rack, eyes like tigresses and smiles like mother's milk.

Elspeth breathed a sigh of relief. No dykes here, no religious maniacs, nothing odd at all. These were orthodox with a capital O, and as such would be warm putty in Elspeth's skilful fingers.

Two big limos swished them away the thirty or so miles to The Covington. For most it was their first visit to England. Those who had been before had only ever seen hotels and offices in central London, so the oak beams and huge stone fireplaces of The Covington, once manor house of a family favourite of Queen Elizabeth I, were 'just awesome, Mary-Jo.'

One or two of the more observant ladies in the party couldn't help noticing that the porters didn't seem especially used to the job, but their size and gleaming black beauty made up for any shortcomings. Curiously, thought one lady, the hunk who carried her bags up to the bedroom didn't seem to get the hint when she put one leg up on a chair to rub her tired thigh. Maybe, she thought, they're under instruction not to fraternise with the guests. Pity, in that case.

Another lady, taking tea in the library and looking out of the French windows, thought she recognised the guy sweeping the gravel. She said to her companion that surely that couldn't be Billy Whosit who used to play for her husband's college football team? Billy Whosit, said her friend? I tell you, Whosit Schmoosit, I'd like to know what a man like that is doing sweeping gravel when he could be pushing my brush! How's about some of that wine they have in England? What do they call it? Sherry?

Two more of the ladies, out for a stroll around the grounds, noticed the extraordinary physiques of the men who were painting the tennis pavilion. Another black Apollo was spotted fiddling under the bonnet of one of the hotel cars.

Not knowing Elspeth well enough yet, none of them felt able to ask her later at the cocktail reception why it was that a little ol' English country hotel seemed to have all its most menial jobs done by 250–pound bodybuilders from the ethnic minorities who might be better suited as models in a calendar than picking leaves off a lawn.

Anyway, none of these menials appeared during dinner, which was served by highly professional waitresses, also – the Americans couldn't help noticing – all very good-looking. This was because most of the trade at The Covington was with businessmen, and businessmen liked to be served by pretty waitresses and, even better, like to take pretty waitresses to bed, and pretty waitresses would often rather earn two hundred pounds a night for a fuck than rely on restaurant tips. Staff at The Covington were therefore selected with this in mind.

After dinner, Elspeth stood and announced that if the ladies would kindly repair to the conference room, a little light entertainment had been arranged for their delectation and delight.

It didn't look much like a conference room, the Americans thought. Conference rooms didn't usually have a group of small tables and chairs in the centre, with couches and chaises longues around the walls, and soft red lighting, and bottles of champagne in buckets on every table, and a little stage at the end. This was more like a night club than a conference room. Oh well, who were they to complain? Let's get with the champagne, girls.

Elspeth watched until they'd settled down and got their glasses full, then cued the boys backstage. A drum rolled. A single spotlight shone on centre stage. And a big black guy in top hat and tails walked on, bowed, and smiled.

'Ladies,' he growled in an impossibly deep voice. 'It is my pride and privilege to introduce to you, for the very first time on this planet, The Steeeeeeelyaaards.'

The spotlight clicked off, and was instantly replaced by a flashing, circling, multi-coloured lighting display and a sudden and very loud and very recognisable guitar chord. As The Beatles sang *Hard Day's Night*, in processed the seven other dancers to join Cliff in a bouncing, strutting, spinning, flexing routine that had every eyeball in the place riveted.

Champagne stood, forgotten, as the women watched. Champagne was remembered, grabbed, gulped and refilled as the dancers incorporated some new moves into their slick and sparky set, moves which resulted in hats and coats being sent flying through the air, and trousers likewise, until all that remained between an open-mouthed, absolutely silent audience and eight sets of male organs were eight black leather pouches.

The song finished, the lights went out, and there was no sound but the rapid intake of champagne. Then, the bravest one began applauding. Within half a second they were all on their feet, clapping, whooping, stamping and demanding more.

Elspeth's voice came over the microphone from her tiny vantage point in the wings, stage left.

'Champagne bottles will be brought to your tables while the boys change for their next act. We do hope you will forgive them if their performance is less than perfect but, as Cliff pointed out, this is their first time, and their debut here today is especially for you and for this private party.'

She hoped that would make the message clear, took a long swig at her own drink, a treble whisky, and settled back for the next number.

There was a pause of a minute or two, during which the waitresses delivered champagne and the American TV producers spoke in hushed and reverential tones about the bodies they had just seen. Most of the speculation surrounded the contents of the pouches. Could there really be no kidding? Was what was in there all natural, or was there padding? Did you see the way that really big guy's pouch bulged, the guy who came on first? Did you see? If that's a cock I'll eat my hat. If that's a cock, said another, you'd have to eat your hat because you sure as hell wouldn't be able to eat that cock, not in one sitting, anyway.

The lights came on again and the boys entered from stage right in twos, dressed in British police uniforms. This time they were more direct in their approach. Within a short time, mostly spent marching about to the tune of *The Bold Gendarmes*, they were down to helmets and pouches only, with handcuffs in one hand and truncheons in the other.

Carefully they made a pile of the handcuffs at the front of the stage, then took off their helmets and hung them on the ends of their truncheons. There were a few calls from the audience now, and inhibitions were beginning to be cast away.

The boys stood in lines of four, swaying to the music and holding their truncheons out in front of their groins with the big coppers' helmets on the ends. With his free hand the dancer on the end of the back row undid his string and let his pouch fall to the floor. This action was repeated all the way along both rows, and now the near hysterical audience was confronted by eight naked men whose manhoods were hidden from view by helmets swinging on ten-inch mahogany rods.

Still, none of the girls made a definite move. It had to be Elspeth to show them the way.

Keeping her back to the audience she slipped onto the stage and went right up to the nearest naked man. The top of her head reached halfway up his chest while her hands reached behind the helmet. The truncheon was placed on the ground, as was the helmet, with Elspeth's back as the screen between screaming women and bare meat.

After a moment's fumbling she stepped aside and disappeared offstage. After another moment's silence the audience erupted as they recognised what Elspeth had done. There, before them, was a totally naked, godlike man with a cardboard fancy-dress policeman's helmet hanging by its elastic chinstrap off the end of his enormously erect dick.

And there, suddenly, beside their champagne bottles, were further supplies of cardboard helmets.

The women hesitated, then one got up. Sue-Ellen waved a toy helmet gaily to her colleagues, put the elastic between her teeth, made the three steps up onto the stage, picked her man, and put both her hands behind the big hard blue hat. This time the man passed his truncheon to his left-hand colleague and his helmet to his right, leaving the woman to work his half-erect cock into rapid and full tumescence. She knelt in front of him and, with a little judicious nodding of the head and prodding with the tongue, got the little toy hat to move from her clenched teeth to the end of his cock. That done she stood and led him to the very front of the stage. She bent and picked up one of the pairs of handcuffs and locked the man's wrists together behind his back.

He was still swaying to the music, his gigantic member sticking out in a great curve with its light burden just managing to stay put.

The woman stood in front of him again and addressed herself once more to a two-handed massage of the magnificent dong, preceded by a careless flick of the toy hat over her shoulder. When she was satisfied it couldn't get any bigger, she stepped aside to let the other girls see. There were gasps. It was massive.

The sight on stage was mindboggling: six huge and exemplary male specimens holding truncheons and police helmets, another, the largest, with a cardboard hat on his dick, and one with nothing on at all being slowly wanked by a small white hand.

Perhaps in other theatres and with other audiences the men would have been mobbed and even injured. Here the eight women out front were red-blooded, sure, and hetero, very much so, and emotionally stimulated, not half, but they were experienced and level-headed business people too – and they could count. Eight men, eight women, no undignified scramble necessary.

Four girls on the first table spun a cigarette lighter. The flame end finished up pointing at Paula. She was first to select a mighty black cock.

The three girls on the other table did paper-stone-knife until just Mary-Jo was left. She too could go and place her order for Cumberland sausage for supper.

Meanwhile Sue-Ellen had led her chap down from the stage to lay him out, still with his hands locked behind his back, on one of the couches. She stared at his incredibly manly frame, and his incredibly big dick, and licked her lips. Kneeling, she began licking his cock too, and slowly covered its entire surface with her warm and slippery spit. Then, standing, she began taking off her own clothes.

Like all the girls at the party she had come casual-jeans, a blouse, trainers, fun socks. Soon she had nothing on but the socks, which were white with a red and blue stripe.

First she sat astride his chest, rubbing her wet quim up and down on the rock-hard muscle. As she got herself wetter and hotter, she moved up a little and rubbed herself on his face. He tried to reach her with his tongue but she wasn't interested. She just wanted to rub herself all over him, ready for the slippery slide down his torso to the hard pole standing ready.

She reached behind her and pointed it skywards as she reared above him and then sank slowly onto the shaft. With no trouble at all the entire length slipped inside, and Sue-Ellen began bucking and jagging, with a slow, majestic rhythm at first but soon speeding up as she felt the helpless waves of sensation begin to take her over.

Her hands gripped his shoulders tightly as she thrust herself madly, piercing her deepest innards with a throbbing violence that could end only one way. With a great gasp of abandoned passion she came, and collapsed.

She could stay there. For the moment. Paula, the cigarette lighter spin winner, had been watching and her knickers were soaked, so she stripped at the table, carefully folding her clothes over the back of the chair, and then walked across to the men on stage with a refreshing glass of champers. While her chosen guy swigged the champers, she massaged his prick. As the last of the wine went down, Paula reached up in a vain attempt to put her arms around his neck. He passed the champagne glass to the nearest colleague, grabbed little Paula by the waist and lifted her three feet off the floor. Slowly, he lowered her and she, perfectly safe in his strong grip, guided his cock home. Now, seated on his cock, she could get her arms around his neck and so for the first time in her life she was (a) fucked while completely off the ground, (b) fucked by an ex-Welsh international rugby player and (c) fucked live on stage in front of an audience.

The experience was more than novel. It was wild and wonderful. And while she was groaning in ecstasy, Mary-Jo was also making progress. She liked the one on the end of the front row – a squarer build than the others and with a dick not so long but massive in thickness. She rubbed herself up against him and danced a few steps to the music, which had now changed to a raunchy rock beat, and then began a classic striptease. Anyone would have thought she'd done it before. She even took her jeans off as if they were the seven veils. Elspeth, watching with a great sense of self-sacrifice, made a mental note to check on the early career of Mary-Jo.

Naked, Mary-Jo stood with her back to her man. She brought his hands around to cover her breasts, and for a comical moment tried to get his cock to appear between her legs. Since his cock root was about level with the small of her back, this was not a feasible idea. Oh well, never mind the showbiz, let's get with the real biz. She led him to one of the couches, lay on it with her knees drawn up to her chin, and closed her eyes in bliss as the fattest cock she had ever experienced began grinding its irresistible motions in her quivering love-pocket.

All over the room similar scenes were being enacted. Elspeth, peeking from behind the curtain, could see slim, muscular black bottoms heaving and rounder, plumper white bottoms writhing and wriggling. There were little screams, whoops, giggles, moans, and lots and lots of grunts and squelching.

If one girl was temporarily out of commission, another would be recovering and making an approach to whichever of the massive men was available. The men had all taken an orgasm-impeding drug and were behaving simply as shagging machines, thrusting until the woman came and then standing at the ready for whichever one wanted a fuck next.

Gradually the pace slowed. Women, gorged and totally fucked out, lounged around in careless nakedness, drawing on cigarettes and drinking champagne, making the occasional comments to colleagues about the remaining ones still at it.

The last girl, and it had to be Sue-Ellen, was sitting astride Cliff for the third time and riding him to oblivion. Her eyes were tight shut and her face was grimly determined as she bounced up and down until, with a last gasp, she fell exhausted across his prone body.

One of the others went over, helped her up and brought her back to the group. Here was some champagne, which would revive her. Here was a cigarette. Congratulations. The first and the last fucker.

The men took one last bow from the stage, wondering when this no–come drug would wear off. The girls applauded, wondering if they might get enough energy later for a more private session in their bedrooms.

Elspeth congratulated the guys in their dressing room. 'Terrific. Here is five in cash for each of you. Now, you must all hang around in the cocktail bar in case they want any more. I'd just like to say that I'm in room six, and if any of you don't get the call, make sure you come up and see me. As many of you as there might be. Because I have to tell you that after that performance any normal female would be desperate for cock, and I am a lot more normal than most. Duty calls. I must phone my boss. But don't forget. Room six.'

Chapter Six

'We can expect things to get hot . . .

. . . wet and sticky by the evening, but as this high builds up over the south-east there should be a breeze later, perhaps a nice stiff one.'

Katrina Mulloy, Satellite Morning Television's stunningly successful Weather Dish, gave a tiny, hardly-perceptible wink to camera, plus her intimate little secret smile she had developed over the isobars, and said, 'Well, let's hope so anyway.'

The way Katrina did the weather forecast had breakfast-time viewers totally enthralled. The men enjoyed her double-entendres hugely, her seemingly accidental fluffs and her mass flirting. Female viewers, unless they were the miserable old bag type of woman, mostly wished they could be like Katrina.

A few acidic remarks were passed from wife to husband over the cornflakes as the sight and sound of Katrina Mulloy rendered everything else invisible and inaudible to men who were otherwise models of domesticity. Nevertheless, the wife would often be thankful to

Katrina for demonstrating that the boring old fart who could only get excited once every other blue moon had in fact got life in him yet.

Many a wife, after sarcastically wondering why the weather forecast had suddenly got so riveting, decided that a spicier kind of home video, a stronger kind of canned beer and a little more effort with the feminine charms might, after all, revive a sex life long ago presumed defunct.

If the weather slots on SMT did not provide enough of Katrina for British breakfasters, they would soon be able to look inside a certain Sunday newspaper with which Elspeth had been having clandestine negotiations over pictures taken during the shooting of a particular beauty-product commercial. Katrina had been a Weather Dish for three months now. Ratings were high, sales of satellite equipment were soaring, and at the peak of the wave Elspeth judged it was the time to leap on the surfboard of sensation which would, she was sure, carry Katrina to a brilliant next career move. But that was a week or two away. Meanwhile Katrina, her audience, her boss and her new found friends at SMT carried on as usual.

This morning, the breakfast show over, Katrina was changing into her jeans and T-shirt for a shopping trip before returning to her flat for a light lunch and an afternoon nap. The dressing room phone went. It was the boss, summoning her. She'd be there in just two shakes.

The two shakes in question were the ones she brought

about from her ample breasts as she whipped her shirt off, unfastened her bra, dropped it on the chair and put her shirt back on again. No point in making life for the boss more difficult than it need be.

Nicole, the redheaded secretary who had been on duty at Katrina's interview, was there again today as Katrina arrived at top-floor reception. They were good pals by now, and Nicole was quick to notice the increased movement beneath Katrina's T-shirt.

'Katrina darling,' she said. 'I think we've forgotten to put on our corset. If you go in with those things swinging about you'll knock the poor bugger over.'

'Nicole, you are a jealous old tart. Just because you could get both your tits in a teacup.'

'Some might say that was more refined than having a big display in a window box. Or in your case, two hanging baskets. Tits aren't everything, anyway. Why, only the other day when I was shagging [and here she named a famous BBC interviewer], he said how much he preferred my little saucers with the cherry in the middle to those great lolloping overstuffed pillows which Katrina Mulloy had nearly suffocated him with.'

'Bollocks. He's never been near my tits.'

'Ah. So that's one rumour that isn't true. Anyway, sweetheart, I think you'd better go in. The satyr of SMT is waiting.'

She pressed a button and the red light came on over the boss's door as Katrina walked through. He was on the phone. He waved her towards him and then beckoned her around to his side of the desk. He was talking numbers – percentages of this, increased points in that – and with total concentration, seemingly, except that as Katrina arrived beside him he pointed to his crutch. There, beneath the pinstripe worsted, Katrina could see a major swelling.

She knelt beside him and got busy with the buttons. She had no trouble finding her way into the boxer shorts – presumably, she thought, they didn't make briefs big or strong enough to contain the boss's tackle – and straight away brought his enormous dick out into the open.

She admired it, and stroked it with both hands. It really was quite something. Not quite knowing what to do next she looked up, her cheek resting against the rock-hard column. He looked down at her, winked, and carried on talking.

Katrina decided that for the moment she had the background job. She kissed the end of his cock, sucked it a little, licked it, skinned it gently up and down with right hand, left hand and both at once, sucked it a little more, and was feeling decidedly randy by the time the phone conversation eventually came to an end.

'Katrina!' said the boss. 'Kindly get your knickers off for the boss man while I tell you how wonderful you are.'

Katrina stood and began stripping.

'You are the best thing to happen to Satellite Morning Television since I gave birth to it. That was the MD of Footprint Europe I was talking to. We're going to merge our two companies and you, my dear, will be forecasting the weather in every European country as soon as we can get the business through. Let me look at you.'

Katrina, naked, stood before her boss, one hand on hip, the other playing with a nipple. With a subtle sway of the hips she turned to show him her back view and then walked as suggestively as she could over to a couch. By the time she got there and draped herself over it, the boss had all his clothes off and was striding rapidly towards her, huge cock waving in front of him.

Katrina was kneeling on the seat, thighs as apart as she could comfortably get them, facing the couch back. Her head rested on her arms and she watched over her shoulder as the gigantic prick waggled its way towards her. The boss man stood as close as he could, leaned forward so his weight was on her back, and thrust upwards.

Anxious not to find this mighty weapon suddenly surging into the wrong orifice, Katrina reached behind and guided him to his orthodox home – and so he took her, from behind, with no further ceremony or romantic ritual. He was just a plain old shagger, this priapic man of power and influence, but this was enough for almost all women (and too much for many!) simply because of the enormity of his tool.

The Weather Dish luxuriated in the gorgeous fullness of her love tunnel and, like an exhausted person sinking into a hot bath, let it all wash over her. He began to increase his speed. She groaned. He moved even faster. She cried out. He went into his last frantic sequence of great bangs, his torso whacking with tremendous loud slaps against her buttock cheeks. She could only wail her helplessness as she came in a rush, moments before she felt his own come flowing into her.

His last thrust, the deepest and hardest of all, brought about a second, smaller orgasm for Katrina who cried out once more, this time in surprise as well as delight.

'Thank you, Weather Dish,' said the boss man. 'Now, get your clothes back on. I have an important guest arriving. A male, unfortunately.'

He was wiping his cock on some tissues as Katrina, bemused and slightly dizzy, got dressed and walked unsteadily from the room. Outside, Nicole was all smiles.

'Sounds like you had a very productive meeting,' she said, offhandedly.

'Yes, temperatures did rise a little above the seasonal average. But – I mean – well, he's just a machine, isn't he? There's no sensuality, no . . .'

'No wantonness? No sexiness? No, there isn't. He's just a plain fucker. But what a fucker.'

'Oh yes, I'm not complaining, really, I just think I'd prefer, well, er . . .'

'A smaller cock and more intimacy.'

'Exactly. Anyway, I'm off. I've had my pep talk. Now I'm going to buy some new clothes.'

'What are you doing tonight, Katrina?' asked the slim, redhaired Nicole.

'Not a lot. Why?'

'Be at my flat at six. I've got a few friends coming round. All girls together.'

'It won't be a late do, will it? I'm due to be performing in half a million television sets at six o'clock tomorrow morning.'

'Mine at six. Pissed by eight. Taxis at ten. OK?'

'OK. Bring a bottle?'

'Two. See you.'

'Honestly! Is that true? He couldn't get it up? Him? The great macho guy of all time? What was the matter, brewer's droop?'

'Pharmacologist's droop, more like. He can't get through anything more stressful than his morning shite without shooting something, snorting something or swallowing something. He's not a poof or anything. He likes girls. He likes to watch girls. He liked watching me, taking my clothes off, playing with myself. Eventually I got to playing with the chauffeur sort of valet chap he had.'

'What, in front of him? You and the valet in front of . . .'

'Robbin' with batman, you might say.'

It was after eight. The girls had started with G&T, eaten the Chinese takeaway which had been delivered and were now on the crisp, dry and white. Talk, as always, was of men and one of the group, Lucy, a big-breasted blonde who at one time was headed for Hollywood but didn't quite make it, was relating the story of her affair with a famous American actor who, a few years before, had been a raging success in a series of films about a comic-book superhero.

'Weren't you terribly disappointed? I mean, to get him into your bed and then find out he's like, just come out of the sea at Scarborough . . .'

'With a willy like a winkle . . .'

'Not a winkle but a crinkle . . .'

The girls were a mass of giggles. Everything was a scream and another couple of bottles of wine were opened.

'Never mind,' said Lucy. 'The valet made up for it. Italian, he was. What a lover. Only trouble was . . .'

'His cock tasted of garlic!'

'No, Nicole, that was not the trouble. What I was about to say was . . . what was I about to say? Can't remember.'

'You were about to tell us the story of the biggest boy in your street,' said Nicole. 'The one with the wonker donker.'

'Not that one again. You've all heard it.'

'Katrina hasn't. Have you, Katrina? One about the wonker donker?'

Katrina, unable to say anything coherent although otherwise in control of her faculties, shook her head vigorously. She really must not have any more wine, she thought. Oh, thanks, she nodded, as Nicole filled her glass.

'Well,' began Lucy, 'this all happened when I was about seventeen years old. And my step-brother was sixteen. You see, we were rather protected, my brother and me, and not allowed to stray. So I didn't know any boys except him, and he didn't know any girls except me. I had developed the very fine and very wonderful body which you and many others have seen in all its glory in the paper and on the silver screen, and I was interested to know what to do with this set of attributes in order to gain the best advantage. So, I used to do naughty little things, like leave my bedroom door open, or not fasten my dressing gown, when I knew my little brother was about. I wanted to see what turned him on, in my innocent way. You know. Did boys like tits, or thighs, or all of it, or some of it? Was it best to hide a lot and show a little, or the other way around? I must have thought that all men were the same and my brother would answer for all of them. How sweet I was.'

Lucy drained her glass, held it out for a refill, and lapsed into silence.

'Go on!' said Nicole. 'You've hardly started.'

'Oh yes. Sorry. So, yes, I was showing the little bit the boys admire, wasn't I? And it so happened that one day our parents were out and I was taking a bath and I left the door open and in little brother walked, pretending not to know I was there. He said sorry and went to his room. I got out, dried, and tiptoed to his room also. And there he was, on the bed, having a wank. Now, I hadn't seen this before, so I just went right in and asked him what he was doing. He said "Nothing!" So I said, well let me have a try at nothing. So I did. But the point was, you see, he couldn't. No matter how fast I did it, or how slow, or how hard, or how gentle, and no matter how much I let him look at my tits, he couldn't. Not pubic enough. My step-brother was a slow developer.

'I'd never seen a boy come, of course, and I promised that I would wank him every week until we managed it. And I told my friend about it, and she came along too, and every week on a Saturday afternoon, when my dad was at football and my mum was out shopping, we would meet in my brother's bedroom and wank him until our arms were tired. Nothing. No success. And then something new happened.

'One Saturday my friend and me walked into my brother's room and there was somebody else there as well. A boy. A big dark-haired boy with a grin on his face. My brother said he was Joe, who he knew from school and who had just moved from further away into our street. Joe, apparently, could do it.

'My friend and me were a bit reluctant, particularly about the topless part. We always used to take our jumpers and bras off to wank my brother, because we thought we were more likely to get results that way. So, we compromised. We would wank Joe, but not take anything off ourselves.

'Joe lay back on the bed, hands behind his head, and smiled. We were obviously supposed to do all the work. My friend undid his fly zip and then whispered something to me about donkeys. I didn't know what she was on about. So, I undid the belt and the top button and pulled the trousers down. Now I could see what she was on about! Under his underpants, and very nearly escaping on its own, was a prick about twice the size of my little brother's!

'It was my friend's turn to make a move, but she

wouldn't. So I did. I pulled his pants down and, well, we both just gasped. It was huge. A great curving red and white thing. My little brother was watching with rapt attention. "Go on, then!" he said. "Get hold of it."

'So I did. I gave it a few strokes. Then my friend did. And then I did. And then it happened. Instead of us wanking and wanking until our arms were about to fall off, Joe with his giant jerker shot his load in about two minutes. All over the place it went. But Joe just smiled. And then he said, "Come on. You've seen mine. Now I want to see yours." It seemed fair enough, and by the time we'd shown him our tits and let him touch them – after great discussion – and refused point blank to show him any more, his cock was up again. My friend and I put a hand on it each. And this time we caught the stuff in a hanky.

'Saturdays were never the same after that. Joe and my brother would be there. Me and my friend would go in and talk in mock German. Vot ist meinen herren zat do for you ze frauleins kannst? And Joe would say, Ein vanke, danke. And what with Whopper Chopper and Vanke Danke, we eventually got to call his cock the Wonker Donker, and gradually we got more and more advanced in what we were doing. After about three months all four of us were naked, and my brother was helping to wank Joe, or maybe stroking my friend's tits while she wanked Joe, or Joe was fingering my hot spots while I wanked my brother and my friend rubbed her tits on Joe's cock.

'Well, three things had to happen. The first one

happened in about the fourth month. I just got carried away, swung my leg over Joe and sat on his cock. I shouted and I howled, but in it went and after two or three quick thrusts he came.

'I thought, shit, is that it, but my friend had been reading a book and she showed Joe and my brother how to use their fingers better, and how to use their tongues, and we found that if we wanked Joe twice and then had a fuck, he would last longer.

'And then the second thing happened. My brother actually managed it. I was wanking him at the time, and there it was, not a lot, but some. After that we got totally carefree. We would fuck and wank and finger, all of us in any combination, and then the third thing happened. The football was postponed because of a waterlogged pitch, my dad came home, heard the noise and found us. Well, he went bananas. Joe and my friend were banned for ever, my brother and I were both whipped with a dog lead and I don't think my dad ever recovered. Which was why I left home at seventeen, put my tits on Page Three and the rest is history.'

'Except for your friend,' said Nicole.

'Oh yes, my friend. Very clever she was. Went to Oxford, got a First, stood for parliament in a hopeless constituency, lost, joined the Barnsley Chronicle and then, after two years, got on The Times. And now she writes the comment column at the age of twenty-six.'

'What, you mean . . .?' Katrina had found her voice.

'Exactly. The most feared interviewer in journalism. Remember if you ever get cornered by her, and the way you're going you will be, just smile sweetly and say the dreaded words.'

'Wonker Donker?'

'You have it in one. More wine?'

After another glass or two Katrina told her after-play party story, and then Janine, a dark-haired girl from America, also with a very full figure, said she had another story about keeping it in the family.

'The part of the States where I'm from is very strait-laced. No sex before marriage, all that kind of thing. So I was at college, one year above my little cousin, except he wasn't so little, and there's him and all his friends who play football and work out in the gym and never ever get to see a pair of tits, much less get laid. All the girls in college, well, almost all, put their hair in a pony tail, wear glasses and a tartan skirt and study every hour of the day. As far as they know, a cock is just a rude word for a rooster.

'So my cousin started to plead with me. The guys just want a look. They'll pay. Just a look. Well, in fact, I didn't mind at all, but I said I did just to get the price up. No way was I going to show even my ankle for that money. So eventually I got them up to ten dollars each, and said there had to be ten of them. No more, or it could get out of hand. But no less. One hundred dollars a show.

'The first time was outdoors. A summer evening. A quiet part of the lakeside near the college which had woodland coming down to the shore. The boys all sat as good as gold, my cousin played guitar and I took my clothes off. I started with a pony tail, a pair of glasses, a frumpy sweater and a tartan skirt, and I finished stark naked. I showed them everything I had, picked up my clothes, and walked off.

'Cousin came by next day and suggested a new twist. They'd each put five more dollars in, and I'd pick one of their names from a bag, and I'd give him a wank in front of the others. OK. It was funny. I was wanking this guy, and he was lying on his back with his eyes staring madly in disbelief at his good fortune, and I just looked up from my work and there were nine other guys all with their cocks out, all wanking like crazy. Next time it was the same, and the next. Then they decided to take turns with me rather than risk the lottery, and after I'd been through them all, including my cousin, they got more pushy. Twenty dollars each. And after my strip I had to wank one and suck one.

'I said no. Cousin said they had pictures. Cousin showed me some of the pictures. I said yes. The first time it didn't work. They all got so excited watching me suck this guy off that they all came in their pants. There was nobody to wank. I mean, there would have been, but we had our time limits. My strip took ten minutes. The suck took five. Leaving another five minutes only, and nobody was going to get a hard-on in that time. So next time I stripped and did the wank first, then the suck. I got to like the suck. At first I used to spit the come out, but then I started to swallow and, boy, did that make the other guys wank harder. They were going at it like fiddlers playing a jig. And then the inevitable happened. They started to bring beer. The party began to last longer. I'd let one of them finger me while I sucked the other guy. And then one day I was on my knees sucking, and a guy was fingering me from behind, when my arms were held and a cock went up my cunt!

'I wriggled, I struggled, but it was no good. The cock went right in, stayed in, and came. When he pulled out, I ran off with my clothes, all tears and threats, but to tell you the truth I was glad. I'd done it at last. I'd always wanted to, but never dared. I didn't want it to happen like that, of course, but it had happened, and now I felt free to do it again. And so I did. A lot.

'The parties stopped after that. Finals were coming up anyway, for me, and I was tired of the public show. I just selected certain individuals, took them to my room in secret, and showed them what to do. Ah. There's the taxi.'

The doorbell was ringing and this party was over too. Back at the flat Katrina was in bed in record time, her alarm clock set and she was away into a deep sleep.

And then the dreams came. She was doing the weather forecast in the nude and all the cameramen and floor managers were wanking. Then they were all on her, before a surprised nation. 'This is live TV, folks' she managed to say before a huge cock filled her mouth. Another was in her quim, another up her bumhole, and she had one in each hand. She had to get them all to come at exactly the right moment, five seconds before they cut to the news. She'd never do it. She'd lose her job. The boss would . . .

Katrina woke, sweating. Never, but never again,

would she drink so much wine. In future she would stick to safer things, like fucking men, instead of going to an all-girls' night in.

Chapter Seven

Only girls . . .

. . . and horses work, she thought to herself. Phew! Day off. After ten consecutive days of early rising and TV weather forecasts with smiles and sexiness, whatever she felt like, Katrina was ready for a couple of days of doing nothing.

After the (late) morning soak in the bathtub, and the slow drying with the new fluffy towels, and the lazy anointing of her luscious person with various perfumed creams, and the half-hour brushing the hair and placing the outfit of the moment upon the torso and limbs, Katrina was ready to do something she had never yet done in London. She was ready to go to the supermarket.

Life had been far too hectic and crammed with urgent matters for such a commonplace thing as going to the food shop. Her meals had consisted entirely of SMT canteen breakfasts, dinner at other peoples' houses, takeaways and tins of baked beans with sausages on toast, the tins and the sliced white bread got on flying visits to the open-all-hours corner store.

Now, Katrina decided, she would stock up her larder and her fridge with proper fresh food and start looking after herself. Her face and body were at least three-quarters of her fortune and so she had better start giving the system what it needed for maximum beneficial effect.

These thoughts turned over idly in her mind as she drove the two miles to the nearest supermarket, parked, and began her tour of the aisles. She bought fruit, fresh vegetables, eggs, butter, yoghurt, milk, granary bread, steak, chops, a big bag of frozen prawns, more fruit, more meat, some pantry-cupboard basics like spices, flour, brown sugar, coffee, tea, hot chocolate, now, what about fruit juice?

She was standing in front of the massed boxes of fruit juice, wavering between the English apple and the freshly squeezed orange, when her trolley was the innocent party in a traffic accident.

'I'm terribly sorry,' said the other driver, a very smart-looking female with a Sloane Square accent, Pringle sweater and tweed skirt. 'I was trying to remember what I'd forgotten, and looking back to see if I could see it . . . oh dear, how stupid. Anyway, look, I'm Lavinia, Lavinia Hampson, well, it's Drax-Hampson actually, bit of a bore so I don't bother with the Drax part much . . . I say, don't I know you from somewhere?'

'I don't think so,' said Katrina, smiling and holding out her hand. 'Katrina Mulloy. I must have parked my trolley in an awkward place. I've never been here before.'

'Oh, that's it! Katrina Mulloy. Seen you on the box. Oh I say, fancy crashing trolleys with a telly person. Look, have you got much more to get? Come back for a coffee. Or lunch. It's nearly lunchtime. I've got some super pizzas here, or a couple of microwave curries. And there's low-calorie chicken à la king boil-in-the-bag.'

Katrina's smile grew even wider as she looked at her new acquaintance's shopping trolley and saw nothing but boxes of factory-made meals.

'OK,' she said. 'You make the coffee. I'll make the lunch.'

Lavinia Drax-Hampson's flat showed all the signs of family money. The rooms were huge, the furniture antique, the pictures original, the carpets impossibly thick and deep. Katrina looked and admired while Lavinia got the coffee.

'You have a lovely flat,' said Katrina when they'd settled with their cups and their filtered Blue Mountain. 'Looks like it's full of heirlooms.'

'Some of them are. I mean, nobody could afford to buy a Monet these days. That's one my great-grand-father bought in a pawn shop in Paris. But otherwise I've done it myself. I do so like a little luxury, don't you? Makes life worthwhile, I think.'

'I think I'll have to put that in the future tense,' replied Katrina. 'Eighteen months on Boundary Television doesn't make you rich, nor does a couple of weeks on SMT. But we're getting there. What do you do, actually?'

At the reply, Katrina choked on her coffee and very

nearly dropped the cup onto the Chinese mother-of-pearl inlay table, from which it would have bounced onto a Persian silk rug whose value she could only guess at.

'I'm a tart,' said Lavinia. 'Frightfully high class, of course, darling, but a tart nevertheless.' She watched Katrina's reaction with some amusement. 'Surely you don't disapprove. No girl does it for nothing. I just happen to do it for cash only.'

'No, no, I don't disapprove,' said Katrina, recovering. 'It's just not what I expected to hear. I mean, you're so . . .'

'Upper? Oh yes, I'm upper all right. At least, I appear to be. That wasn't true about the Monet. My great-grandfather didn't buy it in a pawn shop in Paris. My father nicked it from a gallery in Manchester. One of the many unsolved crimes he perpetrated. And with parents like that – my mother was what they used to call an exotic dancer – a girl's got to do what a girl's got to do, and I thought if I'm going to fuck for a living, I might as well fuck the richest men in England. Or anywhere else. And so I dropped my Burnley accent and my Burnley name – don't laugh, I'm really called Gracie Copthorne – hey, you said you wouldn't laugh – and became frightfully super. And with a little practice I became frightfully good at my work, and so now I only have to turn three tricks a week to keep myself in the style to which I have become accustomed. See?'

'Yes, I see.' Katrina was amazed – at the frankness of her latest friend, and at the amounts of money she obviously made, and at the amazing contrast between Lavinia's appearance – very County, respectable, all pearls and Labradors – and her profession. Is this the look that turns on the rich guys, she wondered?

'I know what you're thinking,' said Lavinia. 'What's a tart doing dressed like a country-house weekend? Disguise, my dear, disguise. Wouldn't do for the neighbours to know that my gentlemen visitors are here for certain special services. If I always appear like this, and they see a Tory MP knocking at my door, they think he's here on party business. As opposed to just business. Now, I've got my shopping to put away and some ironing to do. Will lunch be ready by then? There's most of a bottle of Chablis in the fridge.'

About an hour later, as they opened the next bottle of Chablis to accompany the lunch – crudités with a garlic and mustard dressing, Cajun pork fillet with mange touts and courgettes, fruit salad – Katrina was fully briefed on the life of a high-class call girl, and Lavinia was confirmed in her belief that no girl does it for nothing.

'So your mother fucks your way to the top as well as you?' she asked, as Katrina told her about the Weather Dish screen tests.

'Yes, but she doesn't know I know. Nor does she know that I do it as well. I suppose she'll find out one day. But all I get for my fucks is promotion. What's it like to get a pile of ten pound notes for it?'

'Fifties, darling, fifties. It's brilliant. No better feeling. I tell you, once the chap has passed over the sponduliks, and you pop them in your purse, you are willing to do anything. Well, almost anything. What's the matter? You've gone all pensive.'

'No, nothing's the matter. I was just . . .'

'Thinking that you'd like to try?'

'Good lord, no, I couldn't possibly. I wouldn't have the nerve.'

'Of course you would. I should say you were very well equipped for the job. Very well equipped indeed.'

'I must admit it's a tempting thought. I'm a sucker for anything new. I mean, new to me. And exciting. And a bit risky. Have you got any customers today? No, but anyway, I've just thought, what happens if they're SMT viewers? Suppose they recognise me and realise they're paying for a quick one with the Weather Dish?'

'Tell you what we'll do. You pop back home and sort yourself out, have a nap, and turn up here at about eight. I'll fix you with a dark wig and some coloured lenses – you wear lenses, don't you? Thought so. And some different make-up. And we'll do the hotels. The two of us. That's how I started. They won't recognise me now. Or you. And we'll pick up a couple of punters. How's that? Be like old times.'

At ten o'clock that evening two of the most beautiful girls anyone could wish to see walked smoothly into the cocktail bar of the Winchester Royal Park Hotel in Mayfair, sat at a table not entirely out of sight but not centre stage either, and ordered two dry white wines.

One had shining blue-black hair parted at the centre and falling wonderfully to a curve under her perfect chin. She had deep brown eyes, bright red lips, and the little black dress she was wearing showed a mind-blowing expanse of creamy white cleavage as well as endlessly long legs.

Her friend was equally stunning – also dark but with longer hair and more lightly built, wearing an oatmeal business suit which clearly cost a fortune, was couturier designed, and was never meant for any office. Under the jacket the waiter saw virtually all of a perfect and delicate pair of breasts as he bent over with the drinks.

The two girls lit Balkan Sobranies, sipped their wine, and were patient. They didn't have to be patient for long.

A distinguished-looking gentleman detached himself from the shadows and beckoned the waiter with a raising of the eyebrow. Would the waiter kindly take the two young ladies further examples of whatever it is they are drinking?

A smile of thanks from Lavinia was enough to bring the gentleman over, and he sat with them, and ordered a large single malt, and they chatted. It turned out that he was staying in the hotel on business, to do with aeroplanes, and couldn't bear talking about his job.

'I know a lot of men do that. Bore other people silly with the daily grind. But what about you ladies? What do you do for your daily grind?'

'We're solicitors, darling,' said Lavinia.

'I see,' said the man, trying hard to disguise his delight. It had been a dull week so far. Not an attractive female in sight. 'And what kind of clients do you specialise in? Commercial?'

'Oh yes,' said Lavinia, uncrossing and crossing her

legs and watching the man twitch in desire as the silken flesh slithered and slid before his greedy eyes. 'We are business people.'

The man seemed unable to make the next move. Surely he couldn't need more confirmation that the girls were professionals? Lavinia looked at Katrina. Katrina looked puzzled. Lavinia decided she would need to take the lead.

'Tell me – er – '

'David.'

'Tell me, David. Are you looking for business tonight? Business of the personal kind?'

'Well, yes, I could be.'

'Five hundred pounds for the two of us.'

'That seems rather a lot,' said the man while Katrina gazed at Lavinia with her mouth open. The two of us? Nothing had been mentioned about a double act.

'Perhaps. But you get us for it. Us. Not two slags off the street. And we do anything. Don't we, Caroline?'

'Caroline', remembering that she was a professional for the evening, nodded and narrowed her eyes promisingly.

'All right,' said the man. 'Shall we go? I think now would be a good time. I can see there's nobody on the desk.'

The barman and the waiter watched in mixed scorn and envy as the man, in his mid-fifties, walked through the cocktail lounge door followed by two absolutely cracking birds.

'Never had to pay for it myself,' said the barman. 'And never would either.'

'But what it must be like to have the money to pay for it, eh, Dicky boy? What about having the money to pay for it? And I'll tell you what. You'd never get no fucking birds like them two unless you did pay for it, would you?'

The man was right. There was nobody on the desk and so they crossed the lobby to the lifts unobserved. Once in the lift, and safely on their way, the girls relaxed a bit. Lavinia made small talk. Katrina played with the silver filigree pendant which nestled so temptingly between the swell of her breasts. The man tried to reply politely to Lavinia while his eyes were glued to Katrina's knockers.

Once in the room the man also relaxed. He bustled about getting them a drink from the minibar while Lavinia and Katrina put down their handbags and disposed themselves on chairs.

'Five hundred pounds, you said? Will you take a cheque?'

'Don't you have the cash?'

'Not that much.'

'We'll take whatever cash you have and the balance by cheque. Leave the payee space blank.'

'Three hundred and fifty pounds cash, one hundred and fifty pounds cheque. Unless you take Deutschmarks. I've got some of those.'

'The cheque will be fine. Thank you. Now, why don't you sit in that chair and watch Caroline and me take our clothes off?'

119

The man sat as directed, chain-smoking and swallowing hard on a big whisky, while Lavinia unzipped the back of Katrina's dress, then turned to allow Katrina to unzip the suit skirt. Katrina stood in bra, pants, suspender belt, stockings – all black – and red high-heeled shoes. Lavinia wore white underwear and still had the suit jacket on.

She bent forward to allow the man to undo the buttons. His fingers shook as he struggled with them, but when the three were free she stood, shrugged off the jacket, and stood bare-breasted. She had perfect little plums of breasts, not too small but certainly just a nice handful each. Katrina, on the other handful . . .

Lavinia undid Katrina's bra and let her large bosoms swing in liberation. The man gasped when he saw them, big and bouncy but firm enough to stand proud. The two girls stood in front of the man and, without rehearsal but with instinctive timing, removed the rest of their clothes in unison – left shoe, right shoe, left stocking, right stocking, suspender belt and, finally, they wriggled their panties down and together walked naked towards the man.

They helped him onto the double bed and knelt one on either side. They soon had him stripped to his pants and then hesitated. Katrina looked at Lavinia. There didn't seem to be a very big bump inside the pants. Lavinia winked, thrust her hand down the waistband and began fondling.

'Soon have him up and ready for action. Been on the

beer, have we? Naughty boy. Here, Kat-Caroline, give that a kiss while I find the oil.'

Katrina bent and took the now almost erect penis in her mouth. The man groaned as her tongue worked around its rim while her hand gently slid up and down the shaft. He put up his own hands, reaching for Katrina's mighty tits. She put a leg across him so her pussy hovered over his face and he could reach both tits easily as she continued her sucking on his cock.

Lavinia came in, saw Katrina's arse waving in the air and gave it a slap.

'Ow! What was that for, Lavinia?'

'Too much too soon. I've told you before about that. Now get off and we'll do the massage.'

She laid a towel on the bed, got the man to lie face down on it, and knelt across his body. From an elegant bottle she dribbled a few drops of oil, smelling strongly of almonds and something else that Katrina couldn't identify, onto the small of his back. With both hands she rubbed the oil into the man's shoulders, back and buttocks, at the same time caressing his skin lightly with her tush. The man groaned again. Lavinia poured some oil into Katrina's hands, dismounted, and rolled the man over. His cock was standing well now, a good strong curve of hard, hot meat.

Katrina wondered where to put the oil. On his chest, said Lavinia's eyes.

Gently at first, and with increasing vigour and confidence, Katrina rubbed the man's chest with oil, gradually moving down his body until the tips of her fingers were brushing against the head of his cock as it lay like a solid red-and-white rainbow against his stomach.

While Katrina continued her tantalising touchings, Lavinia took the man's cock firmly in her hand.

'Who would you like first? Me or Caroline?'

'I don't really mind, honestly,' croaked the man. 'Either. Any. I don't mind.'

At Lavinia's signal, Katrina sat on the man's chest and rubbed her pussy on his nipples. Lavinia mounted behind her, taking the man's cock into her quim and then putting her hands on Katrina's breasts. The man, looking up from his prone position, could see one beautiful girl sliding her quim lips up and down his skin while having her tits felt from behind by another beautiful girl who was riding slowly on his cock.

He put his hands behind his head. This was a sight and a sensation to be relished. This was going to be worth five hundred pounds.

Lavinia got off and held the cock for Katrina to slip onto. While Katrina wriggled and writhed, Lavinia lay down beside the man and offered her tits to his mouth. He gratefully ate the fruit while running his hands up and down Katrina's thighs.

Time for the big one, thought Lavinia. She pulled Katrina down beside her onto the bed and kissed her on the lips. Their bodies entwined in passionate embrace, their hands grabbed and gripped and their legs were everywhere. The man's dilemma was soon resolved, however, when Lavinia hoisted Katrina on top of her and held her there, pushing her legs apart with her own.

Offered to the man's steaming and jumping cock were two quims, one on top of the other. Lavinia lay on her back, thrusting her pelvis upwards, while Katrina lay face to face with her and pressed herself as open as possible, hoping the man wouldn't decide to go for the other orifice which was no doubt visible to him.

The man gazed in delight for a moment, then knelt between the women's legs. With his right hand he directed his cock downwards and with his left he opened Lavinia's entrance. He gave her six thrusts, then pulled out and gave Katrina six.

He did it again, six each, and again.

'Caroline,' said the man. 'I wonder if you'd mind turning over? If that's all right, I mean, you lying with your back on Lavinia like that.'

Katrina turned and lay back, trying not to crush Lavinia beneath her. The man could now see two quims, the same way up as it were, but just as important to him at that moment he could also see two tits, two fantastic tits, which he could bury his head in while his cock plunged in and out of whichever quim it chose.

His hands folded and groped and stroked while he kissed and licked and his arse bounced faster and faster. He had no idea which quim he was in, or if he was alternating or not, he just went for it.

In fact he was fucking Katrina as well as feeling her tits, so she felt obliged to respond although actually she was more concerned about squashing poor Lavinia.

'Oh, oh, oh, yes, yes, yes,' she cried, while the man drove into her in a frenzy. 'Aaaaah,' she sighed as she felt the come spurt up her, and thank goodness she said to herself as the man slid off, and she could get up from the somewhat flattened Lavinia.

'What do we do now?' Katrina mouthed silently. Lavinia nodded towards the heaps of clothes, which they took up in their arms and marched with to the bathroom.

The man lay on his bed, shaking his head in wonder at the experience he had just been through. He, at the age of fifty-four, had just fucked two of the best-looking and most sophisticated women he had ever met, and all for the price of a couple of days in this hotel. Wow. And wow again.

They emerged, dressed and immaculate, and picked up their handbags.

'Before you go,' said the man. 'I wonder, I mean, whether, tomorrow perhaps?'

'We could do it again? Well, what about it, Caroline?'

'I'm sorry. I'm booked up for the rest of the week.'

'Here's my card,' said Lavinia. 'Call me. You can come round to my place. Same price. Just one of me, of course, but we can do it twice. Bye now.'

They didn't speak in the lift, gave a little giggle at the young assistant manager who stood gawping at them from behind the reception desk, and then burst into laughter outside. They were still laughing when they were in the taxi. Lavinia gave the driver Katrina's address and then her own.

'There you are, colleague Caroline. Two hundred and fifty quid. Cash. Not bad for an evening's work.'

'Oh, I know, but I don't think I could do it all the

time. I mean, you never know who you're going to get or what they're going to do.'

'And is that so different from TV executives?'

'No, I suppose not. It's just . . . I don't know. I suppose I'm . . .'

'An amateur? Dabbling in dicks to help your living rather than to make it.'

'Yes, I suppose that's it. You're the true professional. Anyway, thank you for the experience. I'm going to bed now and I'm not getting up for two days. Goodnight. We'll keep in touch. You never know, if you come across a really, really good thing, you could always lend me another wig.'

Chapter Eight

Time to put the wind up . . .

. . . the weather forecast, thought Elspeth, studying the
TV industry figures over her morning coffee in her office
at the agency. Katrina had been weather-dishing for six
months now and the rate of increase in her audience
was levelling off. Her popularity was still rising steadily,
but not fast enough for Elspeth. The installation rate of
new satellite TV aerials was also slowing.

Was it time to release the pictures of Katrina, nude
in the advertising bath? Elspeth had almost done a deal
once already then pulled out, deciding the time wasn't
right. Certainly the advertising campaign was widely
and loudly acclaimed and had become part of British
pub folk lore. Carpet layers throughout the country had
acquired an elevated status as those tradesmen privi-
leged to walk in on a naked Weather Dish. 'To be
carpeted' no longer meant getting a bollocking from the
boss, and men on a promise would refuse that extra pint
on the grounds that they had to lay a carpet when they
got home.

Common chat-up lines in every disco followed the same theme. Girls were forever looking for a good carpet layer to see to their underfelt, and boys made confident assertions of their sexual prowess in carpet code. 'Let's get together on the Axminster and I'll show you my stretcher.' 'Feel the quality of my Wilton. I'm the man who can fit your rug.'

The only problem had been that while the ads had become part of everybody's consciousness, the products had not, and there was much to-ing and fro-ing just now about another series. Elspeth guessed that the company might pull out of television, in which case the pictures of Katrina might be worth a lot less. Perhaps now was the time to release them.

An article in the trade magazine caught her eye. 'Sponsor looks for outlet for his spare cash,' the headline said, and went on to describe how Richard Fleming, the reclusive, introverted computer-software millionaire, had been persuaded by his company directors that the Fleming name needed to be put about a bit more. Sponsorship was the answer and currently the snooker world championships, starting tomorrow, were being looked at with a view to Fleming Software taking over from the tobacco company. Would the Crucible Theatre in Sheffield next year be hosting the Fleming Software World Snooker Championships? It would if the telly and the cigarette manufacturer had anything to do with it. Snooker was losing a great deal of ground as a spectator sport and it wasn't clear who was more desperate – the telly fellows to find a new sponsor, or the tobacco company to get out of its two-more-years contract.

'Fuck snooker,' said Elspeth aloud. 'If Mr Fleming's got that kind of money, I can think of a lot better place for it.'

She reached for the phone and booked herself a room at the best hotel in Sheffield for the first three days of the tournament. The price was frightening – there was only the second of the two penthouse suites left free – but as Elspeth read out her credit card number through gritted teeth she only hoped that it was Richard Fleming who had the other suite.

With that arrangement made she called the editor of a certain Sunday newspaper. She was ready to do a deal. The previous price was OK, and the pictures would be handed over. The editor must agree, however, not to publish until he received one more phone call to say that systems were go. That was fine.

Elspeth worked frantically for the rest of the day and most of the next to clear her desk and then was on her way to Sheffield. She checked in, found out that the other penthouse was being occupied by one of the more flamboyant snooker players, not Fleming, and so bathed, dressed and went to the ball game.

Richard Fleming was there, surrounded by TV executives. He looked unhappy. He liked snooker and wanted to watch, and these Flash Harrys wouldn't let him, with all their talk about ratings and returns on investment and awareness profiles and market segment penetration. Elspeth waited until he got up to go to the loo and then put herself in his way as he came out of the gents. She strolled back to the playing area with him, kind of next to him below his shoulder, and naturally started a conversation.

'I thought that young boy made a mistake with shot selection in that last frame, didn't you? I mean, if he'd laid a snooker behind the pink instead of going for that long pot on the yellow, he might have won it.'

Elspeth had been reading up about snooker on the train and had brought a miniature TV in her handbag. Through the headphone she had been listening to the commentary and was thus as knowledgeable as anybody at home on the frame they had just been watching.

Richard Fleming fell for it, of course. This was the sort of talk he preferred, and the person talking, although female – and therefore a little frightening – and older than him – even more frightening – did seem a pleasant, smiling sort of a woman and also rather attractive.

'Yes,' said Fleming. 'I think you're right. I, er, I mean . . .'

'Where are you sitting?' asked Elspeth. 'Have you a good view? I've got a free seat next to me and you can see really excellently.'

'Oh, well, yes, that would be . . .'

As Elspeth led the way she had her strategy only vaguely planned. Never mind. This Fleming guy, brilliant software genius though he was, would melt before whatever fire she decided to light. He had no chance. Putty in her hot little hands.

They introduced themselves – Elspeth Mulloy,

theatrical agent, Richard Fleming, 'in computers' – and watched the next couple of frames more or less in silence. Elspeth couldn't stay long or those hungry TV executives, furious at this woman who had pinched their fat fish right out of their gaping jaws, would be asking a lot of awkward questions. Best to keep it looking like a chance encounter.

There was an interval, during which the chairman of the tobacco company made a presentation for lifetime services to an elderly TV commentator who was retiring after this championship. As usual at such moments, there was a line of a dozen identically-beautiful suntanned girls, smiling and applauding at the right moments and allowing themselves to be chastely kissed by the award winner, the award presenter and anyone else important who happened to be near by.

To Elspeth they were just so many dolls, all out of the same box. Lovely long blonde hair worn straight, pretty and symmetrical faces, flashing teeth, big tits, narrow waists, slender hips, long legs, but dolls. Judging by his reactions, however, Richard Fleming it would seem liked dolls and maybe, Elspeth thought, had a secret yearning to play with them.

Fleming was gazing open-mouthed at the line of talent. Elspeth formed her plan, then took a chance and whispered in his ear.

'Isn't it amazing how they find so many who look so alike?'

'Oh. I wasn't . . . I mean . . . was it that obvious? It's just that I've never seen so many nice-looking girls all at once, just, you know, being nice and not sort of competing like they do at Miss Great Britain and so on.'

Elspeth gave him her eyeball contact handshake and said she had to go. Fleming was clearly disappointed. Elspeth would meet him again tomorrow. Fine. And so Elspeth left the poor millionaire to the TV sharks for that night at least. She hoped they wouldn't eat him up just yet. She wanted that pleasure for herself. And in order to ensure that such a momentous meal would be available when she wanted it, a few little arrangements had to be made.

Richard Fleming returned to his hotel room feeling that TV sponsorship was not for him. Those chaps with the sharp suits and sharp brains were very tiring company. How had his fellow directors persuaded him to be here, alone in this hotel with a shoal of snapping barracudas waiting for him outside? He could have been at home now, working on his new suite of business programs, and he couldn't do it here because they hadn't let him bring his laptop in case he spent the whole time working instead of going to the snooker. Oh well. Bed, and what a big one. It must be seven feet in both directions. Anyway. Perhaps I'll see Elspeth tomorrow. At least she isn't pushing for something like those man-eating underwater snakes.

He awoke half an hour later in the sure and certain knowledge that there was somebody in his room. He could hear breathing. He could sense the presence of

people. There was more than one. The door was closing.
They were inside. Who were they? A girl's voice whispered something about light switches.

Richard Fleming, in self-defence, reached out and
pressed the nearest switch. It was the one for the bed-
side lamp. He was in light but they were in shadow –
and they were a source of total astonishment. Three
girls, all with long blonde hair, standing demurely with
hands clasped in front of them at the foot of his bed,
smiled and in unison softly said, 'Hello, Mr Fleming.'

They were cigarette girls! They were three of the line
that he'd seen at the snooker award ceremony!

Fleming managed to say hello back but his surprise
was still the master of him. One of the girls came and
sat on the edge of his bed and stroked his arm. Then
she leaned over and kissed him, a long, warm, luscious
kiss with soft lips and sweet breath, the kind of kiss that
sends vibrations through every organ in your body.

Another girl got onto the other side of his bed, rolled
across beside him and stroked his other arm, and then
his chest. Somehow, these lookalike dolls presented no
threat to Fleming. They weren't going to try and form
a relationship, they weren't going to try and persuade
him out of short-sleeved Fair Isle sweaters into Armani
suits, they weren't going to fuss over him like mother
hens. For the first time in his life, Fleming could be with
a woman and not feel that she was going to smother
him, change him or put two long sharp teeth into his
neck.

In fact, one of them was biting his neck – well, not

133

biting exactly, more sort of nuzzling. She rubbed his neck with her nose and kissed him in the hollow of his collar bone, and then her lips brushed across his chest as her hand went under the sheet and began a slow advance towards his private parts.

Fleming had had very little experience with girls. He'd had girlfriends, of course, at university and since, but they'd either been intellectuals like himself, anxious to discuss obscure ideas, or of late he'd had more the gold-digger type. In neither case had there been much in the way of bed sport. The intellectuals were usually feminists, rattling on about non-penetrative sex and only giving him a wank if he spent half an hour drowning in their bony quims. The gold-diggers were too obvious, hurrying him into bed with such speed that he usually found his cock went limp as soon as they got a hold of it in their greedy paws.

In all, he recalled, as the cigarette girl found his prick and began gently playing with it, he could remember only three distinct occasions when he had had what you might call proper sex with a woman. And here tonight were three . . . Good heavens above! Was he going to double his entire life of sex in one night?

He opened his eyes as the girl at his neck drew back. The third girl had taken some of her clothes off and was busy unfastening her bra. Fleming watched, enthralled, as the garment fell away and she turned towards him, a blonde and sun-browned goddess, her hair swinging to partly cover her breasts. She smiled, a sunbeam of a smile, as she bent towards him to take down her panties. The hair fell again, and the breasts swung in its framework, and then she straightened up and walked towards the bed.

The other two girls pulled the sheet aside and revealed Fleming naked. One of them took his cock in her hand and moved the skin up and down, slowly. The cock was very hard, and quite big, the girls noted. And the man didn't seem too shy about it. Perhaps this job wasn't going to be quite such a problem as Elspeth had led them to believe. The girl on the other side of the bed, also with her clothes still on, leant over and put the end of his cock in her mouth. She felt it judder. She pulled back.

The first girl held the cock upright as the third girl, the undressed one, swung herself over Richard Fleming. She placed a hand on either side of his head and let her gorgeous hair fall on his face, then moved herself forward so her pendulous breasts could be in easy reach of his hands – except that one of the other girls had to get his hands and put them on the right spots. Tentatively he squeezed the firm flesh and felt the smoothness of the skin as she made a small adjustment to the position of her hips and then, with the guiding help of her colleague, sank onto his prick.

She saw his eyes open wide and felt his hands go still on her tits, so she immediately began a gyrating kind of plunging which sucked his cock upwards into her and enveloped the whole of it in a warm, wet, pressing grip which moved, held and massaged all at the same time.

Fleming came within ten seconds of this expert

ministration. The girl felt him shoot, as she knew he would, and smiled her encouragement to him. Well done, my boy, her smile seemed to say, and she allowed herself to sink onto him as if grateful, and kissed him, and cuddled him, and wrapped herself around him, holding his cock inside her for as long as possible.

When it did slip out she said it was a pity. Such a nice one. It was lovely to have it so. Perhaps they would be able to do that again?

Fleming wasn't sure until he sat up and saw what the other two girls were up to. They had stripped naked during the brief encounter and were lying together beside him on this huge penthouse suite bed, kissing and fondling each other's tits. Fleming had never seen two girls together before and the effect was strangely stimulating. His prick stirred and began to rise as he saw one of the girls take her hand from her friend's left breast and move it down between her legs. The other opened her thighs slightly and Fleming could see the three fingers going up inside her slit and moving steadily in and out, in and out.

Then something even more remarkable happened. The other girl's hand moved too, and now both of them had three fingers inside the other, and both had a hand on the other's tits, and they were kissing with enormous passion. Fleming's cock was rearing now, a fact not unnoticed by his attendant girl who wrapped her hand around it and gave it the little extra stimulation it needed to become fully rampant.

'Mr Fleming,' she said. 'I'll lie on my back next to my friends, and you can watch them while you put John

Thomas here to a useful task, OK?'

She turned over slowly and luxuriantly, arranged her hair on the pillow, raised her knees up to her elbows and with one finger beckoned the willing Fleming into her receptive body. As she placed his cock in position and he thrust forward, the other two were getting more and more excited. Many oohs and aahs were issuing forth, and Fleming watched goggle-eyed as fingertips massaged clitorises made visible through wide opening of legs and careful manipulation.

His own body was banging automatically, thrusting his now much-enlarged cock up into his girl, and for the second time that night his sperm, unused to any call except from his own right hand, found the current situation much more urgent and rushed out into the inside world.

The two girls next to him reached their own climaxes at much the same time, and so two couples could roll apart on the vast expanse of bed and lie with comfort and satisfaction. Of course the girl who had been fucked twice by Fleming was not satisfied sexually although she was pleased enough at the way she'd done her duty.

After a while, she went to the bathroom. She had two lots of Fleming's spunk inside her and it was dribbling down her leg. When she came back, Fleming got up and went too. He came back with a washed and dried cock which was now much smaller than hitherto.

After another interval of silence, Fleming had to speak. Most men in his position might have asked the girls why they were there.

'How did you get in here?' said the software genius.

'This is Tamsin, this is Melissa,' said Fleming's recent partner of the two lying on the far side, 'and I'm Annabel. And we got in with a key, silly.'

'A key? Where did you get a key?'

'From the head porter. It's not difficult for girls like us to get keys from head porters.'

'Oh. I see. Well, it's very nice of you. That is, assuming you're nothing to do with those TV people. No, you couldn't be. You work for the current sponsor. You won't want me to take over. So what are you doing here?'

Fleming's mind, so adept at tracing the intricacies of the most complex computer programes, had at last hit on the sixty-four thousand dollar question about three naked blondes being in bed with him at the same time.

'Actually we don't work for the sponsor. We work for a PR company. And Elspeth sent us,' said Annabel.

'Elspeth? Who is Elspeth? What? That Elspeth? The one I met tonight?'

'That Elspeth,' cooed Melissa. 'She said you liked us when we were at the award ceremony. She came to tell us specially.'

'Oh, I see,' said Fleming, not seeing at all and deciding he'd better give up trying. 'Well, I'm sure, I . . .'

Tamsin got up off the bed and wiggled her delightful bottom in a most entrancing way as she walked over to the far side of the room. There was the cool box they had brought, with its bottles of Krug inside and its four flutes.

Fleming had never seen anything quite like a naked

Tamsin, blonde hair swinging, tits likewise, little blonde tush winking, opening a bottle of champagne, pouring it into four glasses, and bringing them over to the bed two at a time. As they drank, the girls each put a hand on his privates. One had his cock lying limply between finger and thumb. One idly scratched his pubic mound, and one cradled his balls.

Fleming gulped his champers and watched eagerly to see what might happen next. Tamsin and Annabel gave their empty glasses to Melissa, ran their hands up his body and lay down beside him. Tamsin began putting her tongue in his ear while she lightly touched the skin of his body. Annabel pushed herself up so that her tits were next to his mouth and he could lick and suck her nipples. Melissa meanwhile had bent her head over the still fairly limp cock, and Fleming could feel her hair brushing his thighs as her warm mouth encircled the end of his prick.

He took a census of his feelings. Down below was the sensation of the tip of Melissa's tongue sliding around the rim of his cock while her long blonde hair tickled his stomach and legs, and much nearer was another tongue working inside his ear, and a pair of tits squashed against his face, and then the tongue on his cock became a full surrounding feeling as she took it into her mouth and sucked with her cheeks.

He couldn't actually see very much even if he had been able to stop his eyes closing with the sheer indulgent bliss of it all, and so wasn't entirely certain what was happening as he felt his cock go deeper and deeper into what at first he thought was Melissa's mouth and then thought couldn't be because he was going in so far.

But Melissa was one of those able to conquer the urge to gag, and so could take the whole of any cock except the very largest ones right into her mouth and down her throat, and that was what she was doing.

Fleming could feel the abrasiveness of her teeth around the base of his cock, and the touch of her tongue, although that was fairly still, and the constriction of her throat around his glans made him want to come.

Melissa sensed this, and although she could take a cock as deep as she liked she could not take a flood of come, and so she withdrew, and wanked him hard, and watched in dismay as his erection collapsed.

Her little cry of disappointment brought the other two upright and they saw the shrinking organ in her hand. Fleming could only gaze in total lack of comprehension as Tamsin straddled him, bum to his face, and bent her head to the task. The sight of her full and firm buttocks with the secret little place in their midst, bouncing up and down as she put maximum effort into raising his cock, had the desired effect.

He could not stop his hands going to those globes of beauty, nor could he refrain from exploring the forbidden puckered entrance with the fingertips of one hand while the other fondled and gripped her twin hemispheres.

Annabel saw this, rolled off the bed and went to her handbag. She brought back a tube of jelly and squeezed a little on Tamsin's bumhole. Fleming rubbed it in and managed to get a finger inside the orifice. More jelly was applied. Tamsin rearranged her knees to give him more access, and soon he had half his index finger thrust up her. She sat back as she raised her head from his cock and pushed the whole finger in, while Annabel turned her attention and her jelly to the now stiff and glistening red prick.

Gently Melissa took Fleming's hand and held it while Tamsin lifted her bottom from it and shuffled forwards. Annabel held the shining, lubricated cock and Tamsin reached behind her to make sure the end was pointing precisely in the right direction.

With Annabel holding it firm she sank her buttocks onto it and gasped as she felt this thing, much larger than any finger, nose its way into her.

For Fleming the sensation was utterly wonderful. He could see his cock gradually disappearing between two gorgeous arse cheeks, and he could see the jelly oozing, and then he could watch as, very slowly at first and then with increasing momentum, the lovely Tamsin raised and lowered herself on his flagpole.

How tight was her passage! How exciting was the sight of his member being taken into it, and then being released, and then in again! Once more Fleming felt it coming, and he grabbed Tamsin's thighs and pushed his cock in as far as he could, and she cried out as his rod, now up to its fullest size, speared her to the depths and spurted hot sperm into her bowels!

Five, six, seven spurts he made, and then relaxed back

onto the bed. Tamsin bowed her head, exhausted and, she felt, split in two. As Fleming's eyes closed in sleep, the other two girls helped Tamsin off him and to the bathroom. There they ran a bath perfumed with oils and laid her in it. While she relaxed, Melissa got some more champagne and a packet of the sponsor's cigarettes. They made small whistling noises, and shook their heads and smiled, and discussed what to do next.

'I'm not sure if we need do anything,' said Melissa. 'I mean, what more does he want? He's been up Annabel twice, down my throat and up Tamsin's arsehole. I call that a fair old carry-on for a software millionaire.'

Annabel drew on her cigarette, took a swig of champers, and agreed.

'No question his hardware has gone soft, and I don't know if he could manage any more anyway, but we did say to Elspeth that we would stay all night if necessary.'

'But is it necessary?' said a quiet voice from the bathtub. 'I don't want anything as big as that up my bottom ever again.'

'Oh shut up, Tamsin. You know you like it that way. You set it up, sucking his cock like that and waving your bum in front of his face. It was the same that time with that wotsisname, that chap who lost in the final last year. You asked him if you could chalk his cue for him and ended up buggered as hell.'

'Yes, but he didn't have a big cock, did he? Just a little one. I don't mind little ones. Little ones are best for arse-fucking. Nothing bigger than a felt-tip pen.'

The three of them giggled and began to feel like

getting ever so slightly drunk, and so another bottle was opened, and more cigarettes were lit.

'Hey, remember that time at the car factory? What was the name of that MP who opened it? I can't remember now. Big fat cow with hair like steel wool. She kept looking at Melissa as if she would eat her for lunch.'

'Are you implying that I am attractive to lesbian politicians, Tamsin? Because if you are, I shall arrange for a certain cricketer to visit you and give you the benefit of his famous stump up your arse. That'll sort you out.'

'Oh my god, not him. He's the one the other players refuse to shower with. His cock hangs down to his knees, and they can't find a jockstrap big enough to curl it up in.'

'Let me tell you,' said Annabel, 'I happened to find myself not unadjacent to the member in question once, and when it's stiff it is terrifying. You can't believe it as it grows. You start off with this python in your hand, and it rears up, and suddenly it's a telegraph pole. But my oh my, once you've got it inside you – in the right place, of course – what a corker.'

'Corker?' spluttered Tamsin, now fully recovered. 'Corker? What kind of a word's that for the biggest cock in English cricket?'

'If not in all cricket,' said Annabel. 'I've been to bed with half the West Indies team and they haven't got anything like it. Not even that big fast bowler, you know him, the one who enjoyed me sucking his balls while you two licked his cock end.'

The girls fell about laughing at their memories of

adventures in the cause of cigarette promotion and soon the fourth bottle of champagne was finished.

'I'll go and get another,' gurgled Melissa, and she swayed out of the bathroom and across the bedroom, which was still brightly lit. Fleming stirred and opened his eyes in time to see Melissa's gorgeous bottom bent over the champagne store, a sight which brought an involuntary cough from a man who had already seen and done more in one night than he had in the rest of his life.

Melissa turned, her perfectly-proportioned naked body framed by her long blonde hair.

'Fancy a drop?' she said, as she removed the foil and carefully prised the cork from the bottle neck. It made a pop but, having been opened with experience, did not foam over. Melissa raised the bottle but, instead of placing it to her lips, poured a slow and steady rivulet of liquid bubbly onto the top of her left breast.

By pushing her tits together with her elbows she could make the champagne run from left to right, and then it found its way between them in a thin dark chasm, to emerge on the roundness of her belly and then to trickle into the forest of her Venus hairs. From there it chose to go both right and left, and Fleming watched in fascination as the stream, occasionally catching a sparkling reflection from the room lights, trickled down both her legs, across her feet, to disappear into the carpet between her toes.

Gulping, Fleming could only nod his approval of the drinking idea. Melissa walked slowly and deliberately towards him, for the moment stopping her pouring, and then she waited just short of the bed. She parted her legs more and stood with right hand on hip as she tipped another bubbly tide onto her breasts. This time it went round the outside of her mountains before arriving as two separate streams on the plain below, and these streams joined just below her tummy-button and entered the blonde pampas together.

Legs astride, Melissa gave a little stripper's bump and a small fountain of champers spurted out, making a glittering curve like a little boy's pee. Fleming found himself climbing out of bed and getting on his knees in front of the river goddess, ready to drink from her pure spring should she choose to allow another flow from her source.

Annabel and Tamsin, wondering what was taking Melissa so long, peeped around the bathroom door and saw their friend, hand on hip, bottle in other hand, standing like a cowboy on the booze, and they saw her tip another rivulet of champagne onto her jutting bosom, and they saw it run and trickle this way and that until it arrived in blonde-grass country and there, with a skilful flick of her hips, she transformed it into a curving jet, some of which Fleming managed to catch in his mouth but most of which splashed his face.

Fleming crawled forwards and placed his mouth directly to Melissa's tush. She poured again. After a few moments, he drank, his lips and tongue guzzling the bubbly spring water. She poured again, and opened her legs slightly wider. He drank again, and this time kept guzzling long after the stream had dried up. Now he was eating rather than drinking, and Melissa's pussy responded with a rising spring of her own fluids. Fleming put his arms around her bottom to bring her closer. She closed her eyes, moaned, and thrust her hips forward.

Her friend Annabel, practical as ever, tiptoed over to get the champagne bottle, went back, and shared a drink with Tamsin.

Melissa could now put her hands on the back of Fleming's head as he grunted and snorted inside her thighs, and she was bumping and grinding and his hands were wrestling with the flesh of her buttocks and she was shouting oh oh oh and he licked harder and sucked and ate and she shouted again oh oh oh and then... ooooohhh!

For a full minute she stood, head bowed, her hands on Fleming's head, her hips moving ever so slightly as the last ripples of coming slipped away, and then she released her hold. Fleming's hand fell from the roundness of her buttocks as he toppled, totally played out, sideways onto the carpet where he was instantly asleep.

'I think that's enough for one night,' pronounced Annabel. 'Come on. We need some kip too. We'll just lift him into bed and then we'll be off. Duty again tomorrow. Early call. 6pm, don't forget. Cocktails and canapés for the thousandth time, all in our uniforms, all with our hair combed straight and our smiles fixed. There we are. Oops a daisy. Night night, sleep tight. Mind the bugs don't bite.'

It was 4am by this time. The night porter was in his

cubicle having a brew and a smoke, which was a pity for him because he wouldn't often see three of the blondest, most lovely, tall, perfectly-built off-duty PR girls walking through the lobby making final adjustments to their recently re-donned clothing.

Had he seen them, he might have been glued to the telly next day hoping they'd be on, but they weren't scheduled to appear on camera until the winner's presentation, and by then he would have had a lot of difficulty telling which were his three from the twelve immaculate dolls who stood, smiling and clapping their hands, as the chairman of the tobacco company gave a cheque for some unimaginable sum to a guy who could knock ivory balls into a hole with a long thin stick.

Meanwhile, things were moving on the sponsorship front. A phone call from Annabel to Elspeth had assured her that the job was well done and that Elspeth's money had been a sound investment. Elspeth could therefore meet Fleming that night at the snooker knowing that he had been through the sexual mangle.

They watched a couple of frames but couldn't really enjoy it, being under the constant gaze of smart-arse businessmen who, unlike Elspeth, were only after Fleming's money. Elspeth was, after all, wanting his money for the admirable purpose of furthering her daughter's career, not simply to line her own handbag or to promote an insurance policy or a brand of aperitif. There was a difference.

Another difference was that Elspeth was prepared to do more for the money than those smart-arses were and, after the blonde bombshells, the second stage of her four-point plan was to get Fleming in the mood for the third stage.

She expected to do this by taking him to an intimate Indian restaurant which she had found out about, being fairly certain that all men connected with computer software like curry. She was right. She could not have chosen better.

The restaurant was dimly-lit, like all such places, but Elspeth smiled sweetly and got them to bring some extra candles so they could see what they were eating, which was chicken tikka, seekh kebab and prawn pathia to start, with nan and puri, followed by murghi mahal and lobster biryani with three of four vegetable side dishes.

The food was excellent, a fact which was important to Elspeth, but not so much as her ability to convince Fleming that no true curry fan drank lager with his food.

'My dear Richard,' she told him, 'I once went to an Indian restaurant in the east end of London, somewhere in Aldgate it was, with an Indian of the Brahmin caste. Apart from the surprise at seeing us treated as if we were king and queen of the heavens, I was also astonished to find that a bottle of whisky had been brought to the table. What's this, said I? My companion, who was a gentleman of the oldest school, just smiled and said that it was the only drink to have with such food. Tea did not go, not really. No wine could cope. Water was for the holy cow. So what else could there be? And so, dear Richard, put away your pint of lager and join me instead in a large Grouse or two.'

Richard Fleming found that his very good friend Elspeth was quite right. Whisky did seem to go well with this subtle but strong mixture of flavours. And after a few more whiskies he felt benign as well as pleasantly full, and there seemed no harm in another one or two, and so he began to feel nostalgic about last night, warm and cuddly towards Elspeth, and generally as randy as hell in his new-found confidence with the opposite sex.

Elspeth noted all the signs and saw that it was time to pay the bill and get a taxi back to the hotel penthouse as soon as possible. This achieved, and with a bottle of Glenfarclas sent up by room service just in case he hadn't had enough, Elspeth felt ready to deploy her third phase tactics.

These were simple enough. She showed him swiftly round the penthouse, ending with the loaded phrase 'and this is the bedroom'. Even Fleming, pissed as he was, could get the hint. He took Elspeth in his arms and kissed her, placing one hand clumsily on her large and willing left tit.

'I trust your intentions are totally dishonourable,' she said, looking up into his eyes with mock challenge.

'Absolutely,' replied Fleming. 'Totally disthingy.'

'In that case, let me pop to the loo, you get into bed, and we'll be totally dishonourable together.'

She left with a little glance back over her shoulder, in time to catch poor Richard trying to untie his shoelace. She had better give him an extra minute or two.

Elspeth collected the whisky from the sitting room, took all her clothes off in the bathroom and put on a flimsy peignoir in black lace. She poured a whisky, drank it, then poured two more. Armed with these, and with her peignoir open at the front, she breezed into the bedroom. There, lying on top of the covers she was surprised to note, was poor Richard, not so poor now he remembered what a stud he had been the night before. No. If he could shag three cigarette dollies several times each (Was it that many? He couldn't be entirely sure), then one lady of a certain age should be no problem. He waved his half-erect cock at her in jolly and boozy greeting.

'All the girls say I've got a big one,' he said, grinning.

Elspeth, with the knowledge gained from a long telephone conversation with Annabel, smiled. She hoped he appreciated what she was doing for him.

'I'm sure they're right,' said Elspeth. 'And I' – she took off her diaphanous robe and stood with her hands on top of her head – 'have got two big ones.'

Fleming stopped waving his cock about and gestured her towards him. She knelt at the foot of the bed and crawled up beside him, her massive tits swinging like rowing boats at anchor. This was new to Fleming. All the cigarette girls had had decent-sized tits but not really big, and none of his previous women had been so well-endowed. Blimey O'Reilly, these were gigantic. Like you used to see on Page Three.

She swung them over his face, glancing down at his

cock to gauge the reaction. She was pleased with what she saw, both in terms of the increased stiffness wrought by her tits, and the anticipation of what might well turn out to be a fun evening. That was no mean weapon to be speared on, she thought.

Fleming reached up and grappled with her wonderfully warm and cosy bosom. What a sensation it was to be among all that flesh. How he loved licking those nipples and watching them rise up at his touch. How he enjoyed the feeling of her sweet little fingers gripping his cock and moving the skin up and down, and what a momentous event it was when she got athwart him and plunged his cock in her hot pussy up to the hilt, and collapsed herself onto his body so that he was entirely smothered in tit.

He couldn't see a thing. He could only feel tit all around him, and he could feel an energetic quim leaping up and down his shaft. Elspeth, also not perfectly sober and suddenly eager, was going for a quick kill, and was shagging him as hard and as fast as she could. She gripped the body beneath her with her elbows, shut her eyes, and fucked to her utmost.

At high speed she pushed, pulled, rotated, banged and rattled, and soon she could feel the big cock stimulating her towards her destination. She sat back, with her hands clasped on the man's waist. Her head tilted rearwards, her hair flying, she rode him faster and faster. He looked up and saw these great tits wobbling from side to side and wondered at her incredible skill and energy.

And then he felt it coming himself, and as she went into her last throes he could push up, and just as she cried out in pleasure and pain he pumped his spurts into her. Seven, eight, nine! Elspeth still had enough control to count. Well. I wonder if he can do that much again. If he can, I'll make sure it's in my mouth next time.

By the time Elspeth dismounted and snuggled up to her latest conquest, he was fast asleep. Elspeth drifted off too, to dream of herself receiving an Oscar for Best Supporting Actress in a film which also won Best Director – Carole the cameraman – and Best Actress – Katrina Mulloy. Yes, she said at the press conference, she knew this was the first time Oscars had been won by mother and daughter. No, it was not true that they had both slept with the producer and the producer's brother in order to get the parts; no, it was not true that there was only one woman in the world who had fucked more men than Katrina Mulloy, and that was Elspeth Mulloy . . .

She awoke in a sweat. The lights were on, there was a sleeping man beside her, and a whisky on the beside table. She drained it and looked down at the man. He was slim to the point of thinness, with that slightly translucent paleness of the nocturnal animal or the person who spends the whole of his time indoors. His big floppy sausage of a cock looked out of proportion to his thin hips and waist. Pity about the ponytail, she thought, otherwise he was quite nice. Pleasant face without being chunkily handsome, obviously intelligent, no hint of malice or cruelty in his facial lines.

Well, OK, she had to admit, if it wasn't for his money and his cock, she wouldn't be bothered. Either on its own would be enough to awaken her interest, however. Where was that whisky bottle? Ah. On the floor beside the bed. Good. Just another little tot, and then we'll give him a suck.

He was three-quarters on his back already, so she could roll him over without disturbing him. She put one hand beneath his balls and held them securely but with tenderness, and then placed her lips over the end of his soft banana.

Gently she tongued him and kissed him and licked him. His cock began to stir, and so did he.

'Hello,' he said. 'What a very nice alarm clock you make.'

Elspeth looked up from her work.

'I'm going to show you something,' she said, and she grasped his now almost completely erect prick in her right hand while bending down to lick it. She licked only the very central point on the glans ridge where skin joins meat, where there is a sharp upcurve of line and where sensation is concentrated.

She licked that point only with the very tip of her tongue, patiently and for what seemed a very long time. She stopped only when Fleming, teased beyond endurance, tried to force her head down and his cock between her teeth.

'I told you I was going to show you something,' she

said. 'And that something is how to make you come with nothing but the tip of my tongue.' She bent to work again.

Soon the man was squirming on the bed, his sighs of frustration and groping hands showing Elspeth that she was near her goal. Still she resisted the temptation to plunge the whole thing in her mouth, or to grab the shaft and wank it, or even to lie on her back and invite him in. She just kept on licking, the tastebuds on the end of her tongue rasping the hot spot on his dick.

His sighs became cries, and his cries became one shout.

'I'm coming!'

Elspeth gave the cock one last lick, opened her mouth wide and placed the end of it carefully and not too far inside, ready to gather up the large quantity of sperm she was expecting. And here it came, spurt after spurt, nine, ten, eleven! She sucked and swallowed as fast as she could, bringing a cry of ecstasy from Fleming with each suck. What a comer! It was like swigging a warm mugful of chicken-and-sweetcorn soup from the Chinese takeaway.

Well! That was some pumping orgasm. She looked at the spent beast lying wet in her hand. Here was the key to Katrina's future. Had she turned it enough?

Chapter Nine

Let us now praise famous men . . .

. . . who have pricks of inches ten, thought Katrina as she stretched lazily in the deep armchair, king-size cigarette and queen-size gin and tonic in either hand, plus an emperor-size cock in full view before her.

It was being kissed, gently and teasingly, by a young woman whose face was little known but whose voice was familiar to all in the room as the presenter of one of the most respected news programmes on national radio.

The cock she was kissing belonged to the Duke of Kinross, Britain's second wealthiest man and one whose tastes included very private parties, parties which featured himself as the host, life and soul with a small but highly select group of famous women as the only guests. How did he do it? His philosophy was simple. Every man and every woman had their price. He could afford to go as high as most women wanted, particularly the women from the showbiz, arts and media worlds which was where he liked his party partners to have gained their fame.

You might find the occasional female politician who would be propositioned by the Duke at some function and, disbelievingly, ask a million – and thus put herself out of any reckoning – but actresses, newsreaders, journalists, fashion designers and, of course, weather forecasters would usually ask a perfectly reasonable price.

Katrina was on twenty thousand pounds for tonight. She, the radio news analyst and the other woman, a pop star of some years before and now a TV quiz show presenter, had all agreed to the same personal appearance fee. Had they known that the Duke of Kinross possessed the biggest cock in the aristocracy, and that it was virtually unassuageable, they might have asked for more, but never mind. That was the bargain, thought Katrina, and they had to stick to it.

Sticking to it just at that moment was the tongue of the radio journalist. The Duke knelt on the desk in front of her. She sat in a chair, fully clothed and wearing her reading glasses. Scripts which had been set tidily in front of her were now in some disarray, scattered by the Duke's knees, but the big radio microphone was still there and in fact was being used as a prop to the Duke's left hand as he pulled the woman's head towards him with his right.

The particular thing about the Duke's little parties was that not only had the three or four ladies present to be famous, and from the entertainment industries, they also had to perform their sexual acts in character, as it were. They did it for the Duke while playing the roles for which they had become well-known.

Thus was the voice of authority in British radio news now sitting in a small theatre set made to be exactly like a radio studio, and she was dressed and positioned as she would be for her regular broadcast at 7pm.

Katrina smiled. Those headphones were really bobbing now as the Duke thrust his gigantic rod where usually flowed only golden words. The poor woman was spluttering and coughing as she tried to cope with the huge volume of hard meat being rammed into her mouth.

Thankfully the Duke didn't want to pump his load down there too. As he reached his climax he pulled out, turned ninety degrees to face his audience, and with a triumphant laugh spurted his come onto the carpet.

As he dismounted from the desk and went over to the drinks cabinet, great cock hanging half-slack and swinging, he gave his recent benefactor an airy wave and told her to carry on.

The red-faced woman adjusted her headphones, straightened her glasses, and picked up the sheets of paper which had fallen on the floor. While announcing to the mike that it was indeed seven o'clock and this was *News Magazine*, she found the sheet she wanted.

'The news headlines,' she began, reading from the paper. 'The Duke of Kinross, Britain's second wealthiest man and most eligible bachelor, has just been sticking his fucking great dick in my gob.'

The woman looked up, appealingly, but no help came. The Duke just shouted 'Carry on!' again, and the other two women giggled, enjoying the other's discomfort in the full knowledge that it was their turn next. What could the newsreader do? She cleared her throat and soldiered on. She had taken the Duke's shilling, being at that time desperate for some extra cash to buy the perfect country cottage just now on the market, and so she must do her duty as contracted.

'It was without doubt one of the biggest cocks it has ever been my privilege to suck, and I recommend it heartily to all of you, whether you like knobbing with your cuntal labia or that other set of tackle with which you slurp your soup. And now it's time for the weather, with Katrina Mulloy.

'And for fuck's sake get me a drink, somebody,' she added as she took off her cans and left her little set.

Katrina looked questioningly at the Duke, who gestured her towards the second custom-made piece of scenery, which was basically nothing more than a well-lit screen with a map of Great Britain on it. She went and stood in her customary position but looked in vain for a script.

'Make it up, girl,' said the naked Duke, his dong now half-erect as he stood behind Katrina, and so she did as she was told. Smiling to the front she began to describe a normal day's weather. The only abnormality was that as she did so the Duke, cock gradually rearing its head, was taking her clothes off.

'Later this evening we can expect this low, currently over central France, to start moving towards us, causing some showers and gusty winds along the south coast. These showers could be heavy at times, so any young lovers intending to take a romantic walk in the woods tonight, don't forget to take some protection with you.'

Katrina had had to deliver the last couple of lines in muffled tones as the Duke, having taken off her necklace and earrings, lifted her sweater over her head. While he busied himself with her bra clasp, eventually freeing her mighty globes and giving each and both a thorough squeezing, she continued.

'Moving further up into East Anglia, the Midlands and central parts of Wales, we can expect a reasonably fine night although again there might be some breezes and showers along western coasts.'

As she stepped out of the skirt which the rampant Duke had wrestled to the floor, taking the opportunity to kick her shoes off too, she took a quick look at the other two women. She expected them to be chatting to each other, having a smoke, sipping a glass of vino, but no. They were staring, fascinated, at the Duke's now fully-erect penis which she could feel occasionally knocking into her back as he fiddled around with her remaining clothes – just a waist slip and a pair of skimpy briefs.

With them off, and she standing naked, still gamely and smilingly nattering about the likelihood of fog in the Highlands, the Duke pushed his arm between her legs and rubbed her crotch first with his fingers and then with his forearm. She, faltering in her forecast, looked down to see a big bony fist appearing and reappearing between her thighs as the noble lord sawed at her quim with his wrist bone.

Soon, Katrina thought, the ducal cock will be taking

the place of the arm. She looked desperately around for something to lean her hands on. If she was going to take the Duke from behind, she was going to need a little support.

Seeing her plight the newsreader got up and brought her a chair over. Katrina could hold onto the back of it – and not a moment too soon, because he was even now pushing his prick in and out between her legs, its great length enabling him to show as much in front of Katrina as if she had had a normal length cock of her own.

She grabbed hold of it and wanked it. What a whopper. Swallowing hard she spread her legs, bent over the chair, and presented the head of the great weapon at her pussy entrance. With a cry of hurrah the Duke gave a shove and pushed the first six inches in. Katrina, knowing that was by no means all, gripped the chair and tried to relax her knees, thighs and pelvis.

The Duke reached around and took a tit in each palm, rotated the nipples between finger and thumb, shouted something about God and Merrie England, and then whacked the rest of his scimitar into Katrina's willing sheath. She could not help but cry out, at the size and shock of it, but her cries of astonishment soon turned to moans of delight as the Duke began a long, patient, steady fucking, gripping her tits and slapping his thighs against her arse cheeks in slow march time.

Across the room the other two women were still entranced, both of them wondering if they would be able to take it as well as Katrina seemed to.

The Duke shifted his hands now, taking Katrina just below the waist and leaning back a little as he increased his strike rate. Slap, slap slap went his hairy, muscular thighs against her smooth, round, white-skinned flesh. Oh, oh, oh groaned Katrina in the back of her throat as she felt this enormous dick filling her to the utmost.

The Duke was galloping now, and Katrina could hardly stop herself from collapsing over the chair. She, like the newsreader with the dreadful script, looked up for help. It was the erstwhile pop star who came over to sit astride the chair and hold Katrina's hands on the chair back, and then to kick the chair aside and stand there herself, Katrina's hands on her shoulders while, bent and exhausted, she absorbed the last few blows of the Duke of Kinross.

'Ahaaa!' he shouted, as if he'd just hooked a monster salmon, and pummelled Katrina's bottom with his hairy torso as his final thrust went home and his tribute with it. For Katrina it had been a bit of an ordeal. If only she had been able to have this man in a bed instead of on the weather forecast! The Duke, however, had enjoyed it immensely and pulled his cock out to show everybody. It was red and wet and shiny, and he waved it around, the last fews drops of come spraying from the end.

'Just time for a drink before the telly,' he shouted. 'Whoo-hoo. What a weather forecast. Are you girls helping yourselves? Good. I'm really looking forward to this. I've always fancied myself on one of these shows. Do you know this one? It's called *Wankety-Wank*!' –

and he laughed uproariously at his own brilliant wit. 'Now, you girls get ready. You're all in this one, you know, what?'

Katrina took a few extra minutes to shower and then to dress in a ridiculously low-cut, short, black cocktail dress with nothing whatever underneath. The newsreader was also ordered to change into something more appropriate for the telly, in her case a red satin number with a V slashed to the waist. Our friend the faded pop star was already dressed for the occasion in a smart double-breasted suit with a short skirt and neat little jacket which had an amply open space between its lapels, wherein could be observed the curving upper surfaces of two creamy white spheres.

The Duke didn't bother dressing. He sat naked between his two fellow celebrities as Sandra Beech, the quiz queen, introduced that week's edition of *Wankety-Wank*.

After a bit of the usual drivel, Sandra began the serious business. On their cards would the celebrities please fill in the blank, or wank, following the first key word which was HAIRY.

Would the answer be: BALLS? MINGE? ARSE? Or ARMPIT? On the computer, which tonight was taking the place of the non-celebrity guest, when Sandra pressed the button, appeared the words LEGS. The newsreader showed her card. On it she'd drawn a massive hairy cock. Katrina showed hers. She'd written PUSSY. The Duke showed his. He'd written KRISHNA. The Duke was feeling very witty tonight.

So, the computer got no points on that one. Let's give it one more chance. Fill in the wank after this word: STIFF.

Would it be DRINK? SENTENCE? Or CLIMB? Sandra pressed the button and the computer screen showed COCK. Surely, in the circumstances, that was a good guess. But no. Katrina had ONE. The newsreader had, feelingly, put UPPER LIP. And the Duke had put NECK.

No points for the computer again, so it was out of the game, taking with it a *Wankety-Wank* packet of tissues and a video of last month's party at the Duke of Kinross' London flat, featuring a famous lady novelist, an ex-ballet dancer turned choreographer, and an Olympic medallist from the American women's four-by-one-hundred relay team.

Sandra looked questioningly at the Duke. In answer he gave a push with his feet and sent the desk, behind which he and the two girls had been sitting, rolling across the floor, revealing a sight for sore eyes. Both girls' skirts were round their waists, both bare bottoms were nestling in a noble palm, and both the ducal index digits were inserted into neat, sweet but definitely hairy CUNTS, as the Duke now shouted out.

He also shouted, 'Get 'em off, Sandra!' and so she removed her high heels, lifted her skirt to show a fine pair of thighs while she undid her suspenders, took off her jacket and then her bra, slipped the skirt, suspender belt and panties off, and stood there as naked as the Duke, the main difference being that she had two large and pointed tits sticking out in front of her while the

Duke had an absolutely huge and very, very stiff PRICK.

She walked over with a secret smirk on her face, making sure that her tits wobbled nicely. As she arrived in front of her chief spectator she saw that the two seated girls now each had a hand on his mighty dong, giving it unsynchronised stimulation as they wriggled their botties on the Duke's fingers.

Sandra turned her back and shuffled up until the Duke's knees were against the backs of her thighs. She bent her own knees, put her hands on them, pushed her bottom out, gave it a tremendous circular grind, then began to sit back.

Katrina and her newsreader colleague took aim. The Duke laughed uproariously and shoved four fingers up each of them. Sandra's bottom approached. Surely she wasn't suggesting putting this huge machine in the wrong place!

But no. At the first touch of his cock end on her rectum she swiftly reached behind her, hoisted her arse up and over, and pushed the end of his knob into her quim. She sat back with a sigh, luxuriating in the phenomenal sensation of that great cock surging up through her.

The Duke had no hands free – the other two girls would not let his fingers out of their hot pussies – and so Katrina and the newsreader took a Sandra tit each and massaged it as the quiz queen began heaving her buttocks up and down along the length of the Duke's cock. Soon she was making strange noises, ghostly cries like a lost soul in torment, long wails which seemed to come from some remote misty place and float through the night. Owoooooooooo! she cried, and Ayeeeeeeee!

The Duke was pushing too, and forgetting his fingers. The other two girls could only watch in envy as his ancestral weapon plunged with enormous force and vigour into Sandra, and Sandra rode it like she'd been bucking broncos all her life (which, actually, she pretty well had, ever since she seduced the boy next door at the age of thirteen).

'Tally Ho!' shouted the Duke. 'Tally Ho!' and then, as Sandra gave out her last wail, a fragile, falsetto call like a curlew making a kamikaze dive, he blew a hunting call with his lips and bellowed, 'Gone away!'

The fox had indeed left its cover as Sandra, in her semi-unconsciousness and blissful enthusiasm, heaved her arse too hard and let the big cock slip out just as it was spouting. The come shot into her arse crack and began dribbling down her buttocks. She, fulfilled and exhausted for the moment, fell forward onto the carpet. The Duke could only watch as his cock fountained, frustrated at the last.

Well, that was a jolly good edition of *Wankety-Wank* nevertheless. Now it was time for refreshment. The last party game, called *Perversity Challenge*, would take place in about half an hour.

Two hours later, three very tired and sore females were sitting in a flat in Mayfair, making inroads into their third bottle of Frascati and expressing their amazement at what they had just done.

'I never thought I could cope. In fact, I wish I hadn't.

If the bastard's battering ram had failed in its mission I wouldn't feel like the turkey feels on Christmas Eve.'

'That's certainly the most sausage meat I've ever had stuffed in me,' added Katrina. 'At least, there, anyway.'

'There', eventually and with much trepidation, had been their several back passages. All three of them, after annointing with oils and great pushings and shovings, had been buggered by the Duke. He had shafted all three of their bumholes, he'd come in all of them in the space of forty minutes and then, taking pity on them, had paid them in cash and had them driven to Sandra's flat in his Rolls. They were past caring that almost anyone seeing them in that car would instantly connect them with the dirty Duke. They only wanted some time without a cock thrusting its nose into their most tender parts.

On Sandra's walls were many photographs. Quite a lot were of Sandra, some were of other famous faces – singers, rock bands and so on – but one stood out a mile. It showed the face of a young man, a boy, even, looking over a wall. He had a big grin and a light in his eyes which seemed to say that he was very satisfied with his life, thank you very much.

Unlike all the other photographs, obviously taken by professionals, this was an amateur snap. So who was it, Katrina wanted to know?

'That, Katrina dear, was my first lover. He is shown after having me for the tenth or eleventh time, by which level of experience he was getting distinctly confident, although I can assure you he was quite the opposite when the thing started.'

'The thing?' the newsreader wanted to know.

'My brother, who was older than me, fancied the girl next door like mad. She, he was fairly sure, fancied him but was too shy even to acknowledge him in the street. Now, I was sixteen and still a virgin. I wore a C-cup and I knew all about "it". My brother had told me what was what, and I'd played with his dick and seen it all stiff and watched the white stuff come out of the end when I stroked it. Of course my brother and I didn't actually do "it", because we knew that was wrong. He never even felt my tits, and he just showed me his dicky enough times for me to get the courage up to hold it properly and move it up and down until the white stuff came.

'So, he was fancying this girl next door, who was really good-looking except she wore these awful National Health glasses, you know, the ones which are round with wire frames, but he couldn't get through to her. Then one day he noticed her brother, as if for the first time, and saw that here was an opportunity. Her brother, the boy in the photograph, was just sixteen and, clearly, had never been kissed. So my brother, Nigel, asked me to arrange it. I set it up fairly easily. I just hung around the lane waiting for him, and when he turned up I asked him to help me with my homework, and that was that.

'Kissing was one thing which I expected to lead to another, but it didn't. I told Nigel. This boy, Derek, was backward in coming forward. Nigel said I had to take the lead. I reported back that I'd got him as far as holding my left titty in his hand, outside my jumper.

This seemed good enough for Nigel. I had no idea what he was up to, but I soon found out.

'Next day me and Derek were snogging in the sitting room as usual after school. This room had French windows giving onto the garden and little did I know that as soon as Derek had arrived, Nigel had phoned next door and told what's-her-name with the wire glasses that he thought her brother was up to something at our house and could she pop round please? Anyway, we were snogging as I said, and I'd just managed to get his hand *inside* my jumper when there was a knock on the windows and there she was, blushing like mad. We let her in. She told Derek that he had to come home straight away and was not to do that sort of thing ever again.

'Off he went, like a lamb, but he was back in half an hour like a lion. He wasn't going to do what his sister told him. She had no right to order him about. Anyway, he knew she played with herself in the bath. He'd seen her. And heard her. She wasn't going to make him be good when she was obviously thinking about being bad. Well, Nigel, listening outside the door would be delighted with all that, I knew. And so we moved onto Phase Two.

'It was well over an hour before our parents were due back from work so I invited Derek up to my bedroom, and I can tell you I didn't mess about. "Sit there," I said, and put him on the bean bag while I did a Salome in front of him. Well, his eyes were popping. I did it ever so skilfully, I thought, although it can't have been terribly good really, but anyway I ended up stark naked and posed, rather self-consciously, in front of this flushed boy. "Aren't you going to do something?" I asked. "I don't know what to do," he said, so I pulled him to his feet and got snogging again.

'There must be a very big difference between snogging a bird with her clothes on, and snogging a bird with big tits with no clothes on, because when I put my hand down to feel his bulge I found that it was damp. Once again I wasn't going to get anywhere, I thought, but I reckoned without the recovery powers of the adolescent male. "I'll just go to the toilet," he said. "Don't go away."

'I was lying on the bed when he came back, like that piece in the painting, the one with the black velvet band around her neck . . .'

'The Odalisque?' said the newsreader.

'Is that her? Right, so was half-lying, half-sitting, all curled up and sexy, and in came my boy Derek. He took his clothes off, except his underpants, which were white Aertex Y-fronts, I ask you, and stood in front of me. His bulge was back, I noticed, so I beckoned him over and felt inside. There it was. Not as big as my brother's but big enough for a virgin sturgeon like what I was.

'I fished the beast out and stroked it like I'd been shown by my brother and then, what do you know? The door opened and in came my brother and Derek's sister! Well, Derek leaped like a startled haddock and began frantically putting his clothes back on. Miss Iceberg from next door gave me a very strange look – not angry, not outraged at all, but sort of jealous almost, and excited in a weird kind of way.

'Two days later I was lying on the grass of our lawn watching the fruiting of my brother's scheme. I still didn't understand how he'd done it, but the ice of Miss Iceberg was broken and no two ways about it. Knowing I was there he came to the window and looked out, casual-like. He was wearing nothing. His cock was standing out like a barber's pole. And, balanced on it as if it was a nose, with the wire arms held in position by Derek's sister standing behind him, were the famous National Health glasses.

'Nigel, sure that I'd seen, turned his back and walked into the room leaving me a clear sight of Miss Iceberg. Bollock-naked as well, she was, standing there with her glasses hanging from one hand. Well, I'd promised to stay at binocular distance but when they disappeared from the window I thought fuck that, or whatever a precocious teenage girl might say as its equivalent, and I crept up as near as I dared. I could see right into the room, and I could see Derek's sister lying on her back with her knees drawn up and wide apart.

'In between them laboured my brother. He had his hands on the carpet on either side of her and was keeping his arms straight while he banged his cock into her gully. Her arms were flung out flat, and her head flopped on one side, and every time he made a stroke, her head turned to the other side. Back and forth, back and forth, going from one side to the other on every thrust. I couldn't hear anything but I could see her mouth working. Whatever my brother's other drawbacks, he was obviously a good screwer.

'After a while he began to speed up, and he got too fast for her to keep time with her head. She was just shaking it now, like a frenzied dervish, and he was banging away like a good 'un, and then it was all over. He collapsed on top of her. She wrapped her arms and legs around him. And I thought, I'd like to try that, so I went next door and there he was, young Derek, doing his homework. "Derek," I said, "come with me. I want to show you something."

'We shushed and giggled our way back to our garden and crawled to the French window. The scene had changed somewhat. My brother Nigel was on his back now, and hovering above his stiff knob was the open mouth of Derek's sister. We watched in awe and fascination as she lowered her lips slowly, and her tongue flickered out and licked the end of his dick, and then she had the end of it in her mouth, and then she was working on it like a greedy child with a stick of rock.

'This, Derek knew, was his supreme moment. He walked up to the window and just stood there, not knocking or anything, but waiting until, as he knew must happen, the performing pair became aware that they were being watched. Her face was a picture, I can tell you, as she slowed down her sucks and then looked to one side as if just confirming what time it was. She saw Derek. Her eyes opened wide, her jaw sagged, her hands went to cover her tits, and then she realised, as she saw me walking up behind Derek, that she might as well not bother.

'And soon after that I lost my virginity, supervised and encouraged by Derek's sister, and boy did we have some times. We went camping together. Boys in one tent, girls in the other – for ten seconds flat. And as soon as we'd got our boots off it was me and Derek shagging away and Nigel and the sister doing the same.'

Sandra took a deep draught of wine, sighed at memories of years ago, and smiled at the others. Oh, for the wildness and energy of youth. But still, there were compensations to being older. Like a sore arse and twenty grand in cash, she thought.

'My brother was younger than me,' said the newsreader, taking up the confessional mood, 'and I had an older sister. She was a right bitch. Very conscious of being older and therefore superior, and very careful not to let us young ones spoil her relationship with her latest boyfriend. I mean, we didn't have to do anything. Just us being there, and being younger, seemed embarrassment enough to her.

'The routine with every boyfriend, and she got through them like they were dolly mixtures and she hadn't eaten for days, was to ask them round for tea with the family and then retire, the two of them, into the sitting room, which was never used otherwise except for Christmas and funerals. My brother and me were anxious to know what went on in this sitting room, and we got more anxious as we became more aware of matters sexual after we discovered a book in our sister's bedroom all about how to have it away.

'We read this book together, looking at the pictures and then comparing them with our own private parts. We didn't do anything, except I did touch my brother's dick with the end of one finger, and he did explore my fanny with his fingers and his eyes. Our main concern was not what we might do, but what our sister actually was doing. Our parents seemed unconcerned. They trusted sister, obviously.

'Anyway, autumn came and the clocks went back and now it was dark after tea. Our idea was to close the sitting room curtains in advance of them going in there, but leave a gap we could look through and hope sister didn't notice. And what do you know? It worked first time.

'Tea was over. I asked if I could go round to my friend's house, and brother said the same, but we didn't go anywhere. We just hung around in the garden, waiting for the light to go on in the sitting room. There it was! And the crack in the curtains was untouched!

'We crept up to the window – funny how much sex education is acquired from the other side of a sheet of glass – and watched. They were on the couch, kissing, and the latest boyfriend, in there for the first time, hesitantly put his hand on sister's tit-filled cardigan. He needn't have worried. She wasn't going to push him off. Soon he had the cardigan unbuttoned and was feeling her tits through her blouse. She seemed to like this, so he stopped kissing her and, looking her in the eye, slowly undid the blouse with both hands. She smiled her encouragement. Hussy, we thought. He bent his head and kissed the bare tops of her tits. She put her arms around his neck and eased herself off the back of the couch, so he could get his hands behind her to undo her bra catch.

'He was a fast worker. He had the cardigan, blouse and bra off in no time, and there she was, naked to the waist. I have to say she was a fine-looking girl. Her tits were big but perfectly formed. They held their shape well, even without the bra, and this boyfriend certainly agreed. He looked at them for a long time, not believing his luck. I mean, in those days there were not so many girls with the class of my sister who would let boys make free with their persons.

'If this boy thought he was lucky so far, he could hardly believe it five minutes later when he put his hand up her skirt and she opened her legs wider. There he was, kissing her tits and fondling them with his left hand, and his right hand was on her knee, and then it moved a few inches onto her thigh, and a few more inches, and her legs sprung apart as if they were on a trigger!

'My brother, watching with me, let out a little groan. I bashed him in the ribs and he shut up. Boyfriend meanwhile was up to sister's knickers and pushing his finger around the gusset. Sister whispered in his ear and lifted her bottom. He pulled her knickers right down and off, and she lifted her skirt and spread her legs. He pushed his fingers in and then, when she said something, took them out. She put her hands on the back of his head and pulled him onto her.

'This was a novel concept to my brother and me. What was he doing? Obligingly sister shifted on the couch and we could see his tongue was out and licking her in her pussy. This went on for a few more minutes and then something truly amazing happened. Sister told him to stop and stood up. She took her skirt off, and her socks and shoes, and told him to lie on the couch. She unzipped his trousers and dug around inside and then fetched his cock out. She played with it for a bit, then undid his trousers properly and took his shoes and socks off, pulled the trousers off, and his underpants, and pushed his shirt up. She stroked his tummy, and his thighs, and massaged his balls, and – our eyes were on stalks now – she licked the end of his prick!

'This wasn't in the book we'd been reading. She must have got another one, more advanced! So, she licked it, and breathed on it, and moved it up and down with her hand, and before long there was come spouting out of it and landing on his stomach. She went over to the cupboard and got a couple of tissues and wiped the come off and put the tissue on the fire.

'I looked at my brother beside me. He was panting. I thought, well, why not, and so off we went, up to his bedroom. I knew he wanked, because he told me, and I'd told him I'd played with myself, but we'd never done it together. Well, we did now.

'I did what my sister did and stripped all my clothes off. He took all his off except he left his shirt on like the boyfriend had, and lay on his bed. I sat beside him and gingerly reached for his dick. I tell you, no sooner had I got my fingers around it than he spurted, all over my hand and my tummy. I couldn't believe it. There had to be more to sex than this. So I put my clothes back on and went to my own room and waited. I heard the sitting room door go. On the landing I met the boyfriend going to the bathroom.

'Looking back I was incredibly forward but I was also very excited by what I'd seen. So I said, straight out, that I knew what he and my sister had been doing, and I was going to tell my mum. Unless. Unless what, he said. Unless he would do it with me, I said. He seemed to find that idea perfectly acceptable, and we arranged for me to go round to his house when his parents were out.

'I couldn't wait. The two days crawled by. And then there I was, on his doorstep, and he was inviting me in and asking me upstairs. No. I wanted to do it in the sitting room on the couch, like my sister. OK, there was a gas fire, and there was a table lamp so it wouldn't be too bright, and he put me on the couch and kissed me. I didn't know much about kissing. I didn't know about tongues and mouths, but I soon learned, and then he put his hand on my breast. It was a gentle hand, and I liked it, and I wanted him to touch my skin, so I sat up and pulled my sweater over my head and let him kiss me on the neck, and lower down, and he unhooked my bra, and I wriggled it off, and he was stroking my nipples and kissing my tits and it was wonderful.

'Then he moved to my knee and up my skirt. This was new to me, apart from the rather clinical examination I'd had from my brother, and I wasn't sure what to expect, but I liked the feel of his hand on the soft cool skin of the inside of my thigh, and I was helpful to him in getting my knickers off and pushing his fingers in my quim, and he knew all about it and found my clit straight away. My legs leaped apart of their own accord, and then he bent down and put his tongue in!

'Well, I was transported. Totally gone. I loved it. I had no idea such a sensation could be had. He licked the stalk of my clit, and sucked it, and sucked my quim lips, and wow was I enjoying it, so much, in fact, that I never noticed him taking his trousers off and getting his dick ready, and then suddenly his lovely tongue was gone and there was this much bigger thing trying to get into me.

'I sat up with a little scream. I looked at his cock. He said he wouldn't put it all in, just the end bit, and so I lay back, and he got hold of his cock in his hand and rubbed the entrance of my quim with the head of it, and then began rubbing my clit with his finger at the same time. I relaxed. I was away again. I felt the cock start to move into me but I didn't care. I wanted it inside me. And soon it was. I hardly felt any signs of breaking. I just enjoyed the entering. And then he pumped away at me and came in about twenty seconds.

'Of course I hadn't reached any kind of orgasm but that didn't matter. I decided there and then that I liked sex and I liked it a lot, and I couldn't wait to try it again. He said that next time he would make it last longer, and told me that I was marvellous, and what a pity my sister wasn't as co-operative. I was surprised, but no, she wouldn't go all the way. She just did heavy petting. Nor would she put his cock in her mouth. She would just kiss it and lick it.

'Anything my sister wouldn't do, I would, so I told him there and then to go and wash his dick and I'd show him who was the real woman in the family. So he did, and he sat on the couch, and I knelt on the floor in front of him, bare to the waist, and took his floppy cock in my hand. I kissed the end of it. I felt it move. I licked it all over. It moved again, rather more this time.

'I closed my eyes, took a deep breath, and closed my mouth over it. I didn't know what else to do and so I just stayed still. Move your tongue on it, he said, and suck it a bit. So I did, and I felt it grow in my mouth until I had to take it out, it was so big. Go on, he said. Put it in again. But I can't, I said, it's too big. Course you can, he said, and he was right, and so I sucked my first cock.

'Before long he was breathing heavily. I'm coming, he said, so I pulled back and held his cock to my chest, and watched the come ooze out between my tits and slide down my cleavage. Now, sister, I thought. That's the way to do it.

'Over the next few months I began working backwards through the sequence of my sister's recent boyfriends. It wasn't difficult to arrange. They were mostly from wealthy backgrounds, so they had cars, or big houses, so we could always find somewhere to go to do it. And then the inevitable happened. My sister heard about it. Boy, was she mad. She called me every name under the sun. I just smiled, and said that doing it was much better than reading about it in sex manuals, and she ought to try it sometime. But she wouldn't. She gave me a lecture on non-penetrative sex and feminism and how men should be used for our pleasure, and we've hardly spoken to each other since.

'And talking of penetration, I think the noble duke's efforts have knackered me and I'm going home. Do you want to share a cab, Katrina? We can hear your story another time.'

Chapter Ten

A picture is worth a thousand words . . .

. . . or in this case, thought Katrina, a thousand fifty-pound notes.

It was Sunday morning, a day off work, and the day after the party at the Duke of Kinross' pad. Katrina had been luxuriating in a lie-in, dozing, waking, slipping in and out of that delicious halfway stage between sleep and alert consciousness. She loved the feel of the silk sheets on her skin – she always slept naked – and the marvellous sensation you got when moving a long, elegant leg from the warm part of the bed to the cool. So much better than the flannelette nighties and nylon fitted sheets of her younger days. This was the life. Life at the top, or near it, was everything she had imagined it to be. And then there came a low, quiet thud from the front door. The Sunday paper had arrived. With a white towelling robe wrapped around her, she trotted across the hall.

Katrina only took the one paper, and she rarely got through even that, and so was surprised at the size of the pile of papers on the doormat. The top one as they'd fallen was her usual, one of the qualities, but beneath it was a whole heap of copies of the most famous Sunday scandal sheet in the world. What was the paper boy playing at . . .? Just a minute. That was a familiar face on the front page.

'SOAP DISH!' read the headline. 'Warm wet fronts!' read the sub-head. See page six . . . and there was the picture in its entirety. Katrina stood full frontal, soap bubbles clinging to her in various convenient places, a slightly quizzical look on her face plus the complete relaxation of pose which only comes with total ignorance of any photography going on.

Katrina took one copy of the paper into the kitchen and left it on the work surface while she made some coffee and warmed a croissant in the microwave. With breakfast on a tray and the newspaper, she returned to her bed.

'Gale warnings in all sea areas!' ran the big type right across two pages. 'Katrina Mulloy, Weather Dish of your dreams, has decided to get out of the bath to answer the door to all our readers. Carpet layers, eat your hearts out. This is Katrina reporting from all her coastal stations. If you feel an area of high pressure while imagining what's under the bubbles, turn to page eight!'

Oh no, not more – and wow! Another picture, again obviously taken while the commercial was being shot, showed Katrina with almost all the soap bubbles gone. She wasn't full frontal, but half-turned and seemingly about to sit down in the water again. One hand was on the bath side, the other was frothing up the bubbles. You could see all her bottom, including the tuft of hair between her legs, and one large breast dangling.

Nothing was left to imagine in this picture. It was all there. How embarrassing... and then the telephone rang.

'Katrina Mulloy? Hold please, I have a call for you.'

'Hi, Katrina. Presswell Cody here. I'm calling from New York, where it is six a.m., and where one of my secretaries has just rushed into my private apartments with wired copies of the pictures of you in today's newspaper. Katrina? You still there?'

Am I still here? Katrina wasn't too sure. Presswell Cody was one of the world's biggest media tycoons. He owned newspapers and TV stations around the world. Didn't he own the paper with Katrina's pictures in?

'OK, that's great, Katrina. Listen, my only regret is that we didn't get to those pictures first. Meanwhile I'll tell you that we had already heard something about you over here, and I have to tell you that several of our TV stations have now gotten their own girl forecasters, but I've been making a few inquiries about you and that little ole Weather Dish broadcast you do, and I've got a proposition. I want to put you on American television. No imitations. The real thing. What do you say, Katrina?'

Katrina couldn't say a lot but her new friend, call me Presswell, honey, was insistent. He would be in London next week and sure as hell they had to meet up.

She lay back on her pillows, looked again at the

pictures and saw them in a new light. A thousand fifty pound notes? Make that a million dollars. But how had they got the pictures? And why publish them so long after they were taken? It must be six months since she was in the bath, lusting after Brian the carpet layer. Whatever happened to Brian? Must look him up sometime. Telephone again. Hello? It was her boss, the priapic owner of Satellite Morning Television!

'Katrina, hi. Don't say anything. I just want to thank you for pulling the biggest publicity stroke on behalf of SMT that's ever been known. You couldn't have done better if you'd gone three in a bed with our royal princes. It's great, and I'm going to see you are properly rewarded. Come up to my office first thing Monday and we'll discuss your new salary.'

And your cock, thought Katrina. So, that's weather forecast USA, or more of the same with extra pocket money. So far, quite good. Could do better? Perhaps. Main thing is not to jump too soon. Telephone.

'Katrina Mulloy? My name is Victor Handley, MD of Quickstep Productions – you know us? Yes, that's right, those are our main shows for Channel Four. Well, we're working on a new show right now, for ITV, which is a kind of upbeat version of *The Clothes Show* on the BBC. We're calling it *Catwalk*, and we want a really zippy and totally knock-out female to lead the presentation team. Until now I thought I'd have to go to America to find her, but maybe not. Can I meet you sometime? Soon?'

It was only now that Katrina remembered she was

ex-directory. SMT had her number, of course, but where were these other guys getting it from? Telephone again!

During the next half hour there were offers of centre-fold portfolios from the three biggest men's magazines in the world, a possibility of making a pop record, a chance to appear in a soap opera, and a request for her life story plus more pictures from a newspaper even more scurrilous than the one she was holding.

It was too much. She took the phone off the hook and stepped into the shower. As she stroked body oils into her skin she toyed with the idea of fingering herself to a private orgasm. Her hands somehow drifted across her breasts, down her stomach and onto her hairy mound. As the hot water cascaded down her perfect body she could rub the sides of her breasts with her arms and at the same time put an index finger from each hand between the welcoming lips of her centre of passion.

On Monday it would be her boss's giant prick which would be forcing its rampant way in. Later in the week, she had no doubt, Mr Presswell Cody would be looking for the same thing. Or maybe he would be one of those guys who only liked you to get on your knees and suck. Katrina didn't mind. She liked doing it. In fact, she loved doing it. And it was her greatest asset and greatest joy that the thing she liked doing most was the thing that men most wanted, and could help her most in advancing her career.

What about Victor Handley? He'd sounded a bit sort of, well, you know, as if he liked boys better. But she knew from experience that some camp-sounding men were the ones who never stopped rogering. There'd been that chap she'd met at a party, ever so super darling with tight little trousers and pink lambswool jumper, and she thought he was an A1 queen, and once he'd got her alone in one of the guest rooms he'd been unstoppable. What a cock. Like iron. She could feel it now as she stroked her clitty and the shower warmed her back and breasts. What a man. He'd just stood in the room, whipped his cock out, and waited. Never said a word. She could have turned around and walked out, or she could have done what she did, which was pull her skirt up, pull her knickers off and lie back on the bed.

Half an hour later, she'd come three times and he was still at it. He'd said it was ginseng tea which he drank four times a day. It made his cock hard and delayed his coming. Katrina had said he should cut it down to twice a day before he killed somebody.

What had happened to that chap, what was his name, Paul? Matthew? She couldn't remember . . . mmm, her fingers were working . . . ah, that was better, a little faster . . . yeeeeees. Ah. Nice.

It was while she was towelling herself dry that the thought crossed her mind. Mother! I bet it was Elspeth the Guardian Angel, that must be it. Otherwise surely she'd have been on the phone herself. Unless she hadn't seen the pictures. Or maybe she hadn't been able to get through, and now the phone was off the hook. Then she would have called round, surely. She only lives twenty minutes away. So. That's it! The scheming old bag. It's one of her brilliant promotions for her brilliant daughter. So, that's where we're going this fine Sunday morning.

Elspeth had a ground-floor flat in a detached, rather grand Victorian house in Chalk Farm. The doorbell didn't seem to be working, and nobody heard Katrina knocking, so she walked up the little path beside the house, which led through a tall wooden gate to the gardens behind.

The French windows were open, and there were sounds coming from the room. Katrina stopped and listened. She could make out a man grunting, and a woman kind of whimpering. Every so often a voice said something, as if it were an instruction or a critical comment.

Stealthily, Katrina made her way to the window and peeped around. She needn't have bothered so much with concealing her presence. The people in the room were totally preoccupied with what they were doing.

Lying on his back on the carpet was the biggest black man Katrina had ever seen. He had nothing on and his muscular body rippled and glistened in the sunlight which was streaming into the room. He was side-on to Katrina. Head-on to her, and with the head in question bowed down over the black man's central portion, was a slim, trim female. Katrina could see the lines of her body but not much else, apart from a small white hand which was grasping the black man's huge member.

Well, grasping wasn't quite the word. The fingers

nowhere near met around the adamant shaft but served only to hold it vertical so she could, with great stretchings and gulpings, get some of it into her mouth.

Above and to one side, also naked, was her mother. She was holding a camcorder and was filming the action.

'When he comes, make sure you pull off and get the come in your face,' ordered Elspeth. 'Don't let him come in your mouth like I did. The viewers want to see your face spattered with it. Are you coming yet, Cliff?'

Cliff indicated that he wasn't far away. The slim girl redoubled her efforts. Elspeth got closer with the camera, kneeling on the carpet so she was level with the slim girl's head.

'Now!' shouted Cliff. The girl pulled back and tried to keep her eyes open as come shot into her face. And the face, Katrina now saw, was a familiar one. It belonged to the camera operator on the commercial shoot. What was her name? Chloe? No, Carole, that was it. Carole the cameraman. And Katrina had thought she was a les. Far from a les, she was a front-of-camera cocksucker.

With the scene now relaxing, Katrina realised she'd soon be seen. Her thoughts weren't yet collected enough, so she slipped away and walked a few yards down the road to a café. Coffee and a bun would help her organise her mind.

She had of course realised that her mother was pushing her, and was very probably willing to do anything in the cause. Clearly, for example, Katrina could not be the only Mulloy who had been shafted by the sex-maniac boss of SMT. Such a man would not have been able to resist Elspeth any more than he could resist Katrina. All beautiful women, big-titted or no, would make his cock rear, and if he offered it to Elspeth, as he surely must have done, then she must have embraced it or Katrina would never have got to the interview.

But the pictures in the newspaper were different. There was nothing casual about them. They had been planned, and the co-operation of Carole had been bought – how, she wondered? With the black man's chopper? Possibly. And what was the idea of the blue home movies? Surely Elspeth was above that kind of thing.

Restored by the coffee and bun Katrina decided to confront her mother. Time it was all out in the open. As she rose from her table she looked out into the street and saw the black man and Carole walking past. What an amazing sight. The man-mountain walking beside the slender reed. Of course, not such an amazing sight as the one of half an hour ago . . .

Elspeth was smoothness and charm itself as she answered Katrina's knock.

'Come in, darling, do sit down, would you like a coffee? Ah.'

The 'ah' came when Katrina slapped a copy of the newspaper, open at page eight, onto the kitchen table.

It was the way she slapped it. It was a challenging, positive slap. It did not say, 'Have you seen this, Mother dear?' It did not say, 'What do you think of your daughter now she's got her bare arse in the paper?'

It said, 'What the fuck do you know about this?'

'Well, you see, darling, at the time, you see, I wasn't entirely sure that the, er, well, that the weather forecasting thing would, you know, be . . .'

'So you bribed Carole the cameraman to take piccies of my tits and tush, and no doubt received thousands from the *Sunday Screws* to splash my cunt hairs all over the nation's breakfast tables?'

'There's no need to be so coarse, dear. And how did you know it was Carole, might I ask?'

'Because, Mother dear, I had the privilege, not half an hour ago, of watching the said Carole with her mouth agape, collecting black man's come in her eyesockets. And guess who was photographing the whole thing for posterity? Elspeth the camcorder wizard, mistress of the backstreet porno movie. Fucking hell, Mother, you don't need to do this sort of thing.'

'What sort of thing, dear? Sell your pictures to the paper, or take pictures of that sweet little Carole and her friend the American footballer? I was only doing favours in both cases. One was a favour to you, because I thought it would advance your career. And one was a favour to Cliff, who has been asked to audition for a series of skin flicks in Hollywood and needed to demonstrate and confirm his abilities in a sort of show reel, you might say. So Carole obliged.'

'And you did, too. I heard you say he'd come in your mouth.'

'Oh dear, are we getting all accusing? Have we forgotten how we got the job at SMT? And how we so enjoyed ourselves at a party given by a certain Scottish laird?'

'How did you know about that?' Katrina was astounded. The Duke's parties were supposed to be the most secret thing in London.

'There is nothing I don't know, daughter of mine, so don't get all hoity-toity with me. I know you come across for whoever might advantage you, and sometimes just for the fun of it, and I don't blame you. I'd have done the same. Now, here's some coffee, here's some sherry, and here's an ashtray. Let's hear what has happened since the pictures came out.'

'You must know half of it already, seeing as you gave all those people my phone number.'

'Very good guess, darling, but I don't know what they said, do I?'

Elspeth smiled sweetly and listened while Katrina told her all about the offers.

'Well, forget the centrefolds,' said Elspeth. 'As you have already pointed out, your botty is already as familiar to the nation as it was to me when you were a baby and I was wiping it. I think your current boss is being a mean bastard, over-confident, and counting on you being forever grateful to the miserable, stiff-cocked old sod. I should say the American weather offer will pay the most and the *Catwalk* the least. Probably even less than you're getting now. So, it has to be ... *Catwalk*.'

'What? Less money? I think I'd rather go to America. I might get a really big chance there. Films. Hollywood.'

'You will get that anyway, my dear, and when you do you will be more than just a jumped up reader of weather scripts. You need some good solid experience, and fronting a show like *Catwalk* will give you it. You can become a famous face in every home, whether they have satellite or not, and maybe I can twist a few arms and get an American network interested in buying the show. More important, I think I might be able to persuade someone with lots of sponduliks to sponsor the job. *Catwalk*, Europe's top TV fashion programme, brought to you by . . . never mind for the minute.

'Anyway, that's your road, my girl. Go down it. But first, let's pop out for some lunch. I think we can afford to celebrate. Do you fancy the Étoile? Or Langan's Brasserie?'

Katrina had an extra-capacious, deeply-padded, floral-print-covered rocking chair in her flat, and after a lunch with plenty of wine she sank gratefully into the chair and was zizzing inside a minute. As her mind meandered through a mist of tiredness and alcohol, and her breathing became regular, and her magnificent chest rose and fell in gentle rhythm, her eyes began moving under their closed lids.

In her mind she saw a black figure, gigantic even at a distance, a man of Herculean proportions, dressed in a special costume of some kind, as if he were taking part in an old Hollywood film. The clothes reminded her of jailers and executioners in medieval stories, when they had leather jerkins, cloaks and – yes – he had a leather hood over his head.

This man was important to her. He was going to judge her, and he was not open to any kind of bribery, especially not the sort Katrina specialised in. Oh, hell, what should she wear for the trial? Something innocent-looking, it had to be. But her wardrobe was full of femme fatale outfits, little black dresses, tight trousers, strapless backless ballgowns, skimpy sweaters, low cut blouses. What could she do?

Someone came in with the latest designs from Claudio Lastigni, who was to be featured on next week's *Catwalk*. They were perfect! The famous Italian designer had gone back to the age of innocence with his latest collection. Here was a white cotton dress, reminiscent of A-line with its long flat bodice and shortish skirt, and it came with a pale blue blouse with sleeves, shiny pale blue tights and white shoes, and a wide-brimmed straw hat with white and blue ribbons. Brilliant! She could appear before her accuser without fear, looking like a girl out of *Salad Days*.

The black man was waiting now for her, impatient and angry. How would she plead to the charges, which were that she had no talent and that she was not as sexually attractive as her mother?

Katrina would plead not guilty to both charges, in which case she would have to prove to the black man that she was innocent. But she thought she was innocent until proved guilty? Not so in such a case. Innocence in this court meant guilt also. She would have to prove to the black man that she had talent and that she could seduce him while he preserved in his mind thoughts of her mother, naked, with her legs wide apart, waiting for the black pacifier.

She smiled. The challenge pleased her. She would

Jennifer Cross

lead the way up the stairs, making sure that her skirt swung just perfectly, giving him a glimpse of thigh but not too much, and her bottom wiggled as they mounted the staircase, but not too obviously. This seduction would need to be slow and patient. Any crudeness in her approach and she would lose the case.

The room at the top of the stairs was like a restaurant, an old-fashioned sort of a place with waiters dressed in black tail-coats. They showed no surprise as a beautiful young woman, dressed as if for a summer picnic in 1948, came in with the most enormous black man, dressed as if he was the active constituent in the execution of Anne Boleyn in a film made about the same time.

They sat opposite each other at the table in the centre of the room. There were no other diners, and the twelve waiters, all good men and true, stood around the walls. Katrina took off her hat and placed it on the chair next to her, shaking her head a little to allow her glorious long blonde hair to fall in a golden cascade around her shoulders. She smiled again. The man was unmoved. She held up her glass to him, but he would not chink his with hers.

She asked him about himself. She rubbed her knee against his. She allowed her hand to brush his. She moved her fingers up and down the stem of her wine glass, and placed a slim bread stick between her lips and moved it slowly in and out.

She asked him if he would like her to give him a massage. He said he was obliged to co-operate with her in her attempts to prove her innocence, and so the

194

waiters pushed two tables together and stood and watched as the black man took off his cloak and the rest of his clothes, all except the leather hood and, unashamedly naked, with his massive penis swinging soft, he climbed onto the tables and lay on his stomach. Katrina had a few aromatic oils in her bag – sandalwood, juniper, elderflower, all reasonably masculine – and with a few drops of these, one at a time, she began work on the backs of the man's legs. Slowly she moved up to his thighs, and then his buttocks, great masses of muscle, and she rubbed and pushed and worked in circles, her small white hands dwarfed by the task.

She looked around the room. Every one of the twelve waiters had an erection. She could see the bulges in their trousers. Perhaps the black man would have one too. She half rolled him over to see. Nothing. The black mamba just flopped there, its length a threat but not a promise. She rolled him back and decided on a more positive approach.

With his eyes following her every move she walked up to a waiter and gave him a white shoe. She gave the second to the next one. Her dress, unzipped and removed in an instant, she gave to the third waiter, and the fourth held her light blue tights, the fifth her blouse, the sixth her bra and the seventh her panties. Naked she walked around the other five, giving each of them a light-fingered touch along their hardened ridges, before returning to the black man.

She found a new bottle of oil with a pungent, gingery tang to it and poured the whole lot into the small of the black man's back. Climbing on top of him she began to rub the oil in first with her knees, then her breasts, and finally she sat astride him and massaged him with her mound of Venus. Her hands had been working all the while too, and her soft kisses had brushed his neck, and now a hand strayed between his buttocks and searched there. She dismounted and rolled the man on his back. His cock still lay inert. This is not possible, she thought. Not a man in the world could resist what I have just done, and for confirmation she looked at the twelve waiters. Three of them had damp patches, four had their cocks out and were wanking, and the rest looked as if they were about to lose their inner battles with their self-discipline.

The black man stood up, towering over her. She stepped back, fearful, her naked white body suddenly seeming a weak and vulnerable thing when a few moments before it had been the proud instrument of arousal.

The black man spoke. She had failed. She would have to be punished.

Katrina's hands went to her neck and she screamed. As the black man took a pace towards her she collapsed and fell against him. He picked her up as if she were no heavier than a lily wrapped in a silk scarf and carried her across his arms, a white, frail female resting in the shining black bone and muscle of the judging male.

She was in the dungeon when she came to, chained by her wrists and ankles to the wall. The only light was from a fire in a brazier, and its flicker was just sufficient for her to make out the two figures in the place with

196

her. One was the black tormentor, still naked except for his hood. Next to him was her mother, also naked, except she had a black leather collar around her neck and a pair of black riding boots on her feet.

They walked towards Katrina. Mother took a short riding crop from the wall and placed it under the black man's cock, which instantly reared up into the most magnificent erection. Mother smiled in triumph and went to the wall where hung two iron rings on chains. She stood on a stool to reach these, her back to the wall, then kicked the stool away and hung there. Slowly she parted her legs. The black man, massive erection preceding him, walked to her and thrust his cock home. She pulled herself up on the rings and wrapped her legs around him as he banged his mighty rod into her delicate body.

They fucked as if in a ritual, he keeping a steady rhythm and she calling out words which Katrina had never heard. At last he increased his speed with ten rapid pushes, then they both called out as he withdrew and turned to Katrina, his cock standing in an iron curve and shining wet with Mother's juices and his own come.

He stood there until the meat softened and the cock hung loose. Then he turned to Mother, still hanging from the rings. He lifted her down and they both took up short whips.

As they walked menacingly towards Katrina she knew this was going to be her last moment. This was her punishment. She was going to suffer now for all the innocent men she had seduced against their wills, and for all the sinful flaunting of her body, and for all the gratification she had had of cocks and tongues and hands, and all the writhing orgasms and shouts of delight and all the shaggings she had until her sensibilities were exhausted. For all this she was now going to suffer. Pain was her due reward. She deserved pain.

The black man pushed the handle of his whip between her thighs and searched her private parts with the knob on the end of it. He seemed satisfied with what he found, and stepped back. Mother placed her whip under his genitals and again, instantly, his cock reared up.

Mother strode over to the wall and began winding on a handle. There was a rattle and Katrina felt the tension increase on her chains. Her arms were being pulled, and Mother kept on winding until Katrina's arms were vertical above her head, and still she kept winding as Katrina felt herself lifted off the floor. She rose until she was about two feet off the ground and then Mother locked the handle. There was another one beside it, and she wound on that, and Katrina felt her legs being pulled apart.

Now she hung there, arms up, legs spread, and watched as the black man came towards her, vast cock rearing and pointing. He stopped in front of her, the very tip of his prick resting on her stomach.

Mother stepped forward, gripped the cock and placed it at her daughter's entrance. The man pushed. It was in. He pushed more. Another few inches slid inside her. And more. And once more, and the entire length was within her. She could not have taken another tenth of an inch. She was full of cock. And now it began moving inside her, and Mother watched and said these words again, and the ritual fucking relentlessly continued until Katrina's eyes were starting out of her head with the tremendous waves of sensation which completely overwhelmed her. The pain in her wrists and arms was irrelevant. The rasping of the stone wall against her naked back and buttocks was of no account. She cared about nothing except the reciprocation of mankind's most impressive piston as again and again it engendered feelings which she knew so well and yet she had never felt with such intensity before.

Mother reached over and touched the man's bottom with her whip. He moved faster. She touched him again. He moved faster still. Katrina was virtually out of this world, in a trance of fulfilment, as the huge weapon speared her for ever and ever.

Still he went faster, responding to a rather more urgent tap on the arse cheek from Mother's whip, and soon she was tapping with every thrust, and the taps became more insistent, and the man was shouting, and Katrina was wailing, and Mother gave his arse one last full-blooded cut as he pushed his cock into her daughter as far as it would go and spent his spurts. Aaaaagh! he shouted. Ooooooh! Katrina wailed in a plaintive cry that asked for the gods to take pity on a girl who could take no more, and yet would surely hope that this was not the last time she would make such a prayer to them, transfixed to the utmost on the end of a giant prick.

Oh no, not the last time. She wanted more than this. It made her feel that she knew at last the meaning of the word ecstasy. It made her body zing with pleasure, her heart sing with joy, and her ears ring with bells . . . bells? What kind of bells?

Katrina's eyes opened with relief on the familiar sights of her living room, with the log-effect electric fire flickering in the late afternoon gloom and the door bell ringing loudly. Who the fuck wants to call on me on a Sunday afternoon? Without switching the light on she went to the window and looked outside. There was a man standing on the doorstep. He was dressed in some sort of awful anorak thing, and he had a beard. Must be a newspaper reporter. Sod him. And now the phone was ringing.

'Hello, darling,' said her mother. 'I'm expecting a very important person to call on you shortly. He's called Richard Fleming, he's a bit scruffy and insists on looking like a second-rate polytechnic teacher but he's very very wealthy, made his money out of computers, and he's going to sponsor the *Catwalk* show. So when he calls, be nice to him, won't you, darling? By the way, I've also called the production company and accepted their offer on your behalf, with triple the salary you're getting at the moment. So I repeat. Be nice to Mr Fleming. Bye, darling.'

Katrina ran to the door and opened it just as the anorak-coated figure was disappearing round the corner. She hurtled after him and grabbed him by the arm. Of course, he knew who she was. He'd seen her on telly. And she was even better-looking than the pixels allowed.

'You knocked?' said Katrina, panting.

'Ah, yes, well, you see, I've apparently, I mean, this show, the *Catwalk* programme, I'm going to . . .'

'Yes, I know. Isn't it wonderful? It will be such fun. As the sponsor, you'll be able to meet all the models, and the designers of course. And me.'

'Actually, it was meeting you which, well, you know, I do so like your weather forecast, you know, sort of, the way you . . .'

'Come back to the flat and I'll get you a drink. What do you like? G & T? Scotch?' Katrina burbled harmlessly on until she had him sitting on the settee, coat hung up, and in hand cut-glass tumbler containing large measure of Talisker.

'Have you had anything to eat? Can I get you a sandwich or something?'

'Well, actually, I . . .'

Katrina went into the kitchen and continued their conversation through the hatch. While she spread butter and placed thin slices of German garlic sausage, tomato and pickled gherkin on a foundation of lettuce, she told him about her lunch with her mother. Yes, Richard knew her mother, quite well, actually. And then, Katrina said, she was just about to take a bath when there was this man at the door.

There was the sandwich, and would he excuse her? Perhaps when he'd finished the sandwich he'd like to come through and scrub her back for her?

It was not that long ago that such an invitation would have been completely lost on Richard Fleming. He would have declined, politely. Said oh no, that was all right, I mean. Recent experience, however, had sharpened his perceptions and he knew what the invitation meant.

Sexual advancement had not improved his conversation, and he could only nod and take a mouthful of sandwich as Katrina swung on her heel and walked enticingly from the room.

He took his time, not wanting to appear too eager. He even helped himself to a little more whisky. Finally he forced himself towards the bathroom and gave a timid knock on the door which swung open at his touch. Opposite him, in a rounded triangle of a sunken bath with foam up to her chin, lay Katrina.

'Come in,' she said, putting many, many layers of meaning into two such simple words. He did as bidden and looked uncomfortably around for somewhere to position himself. Katrina sat up, giving him just a tiny glimpse of the top curving surfaces of two fine breasts, and offered him the loofah.

'Come on. Give us a scrub,' she said, turning half away from him. With loofah in hand he could gaze down at her marvellous back, its shape a model for any sculpture of the Three Graces. He could also see, as she bent forward, a superb cleavage and the upper halves of two tremendous tits.

With hesitant touch he made a few half-hearted attempts to scrub her back. He was told to put some beef into it. He did, and dropped the loofah.

'Here, try this,' she said, passing him a flask of Chanel body lotion.

His hand became firmer now as he stroked the lotion into her skin, and his attitude became bolder. She felt his fingers straying over her shoulders, giving gentle massage to her neck and then to her collar bone. But they would stray no further.

She leaned back, bringing her breasts more into view. His hands began their exploration, marvelling as they went at the bounty of her bosom. What beauties they were, and how soft and yielding to the touch, and yet how firm in their shape.

Fleming felt his rod begin to stiffen. Katrina sighed, shifted into the water a little, and pushed her left tit upwards as if to say, stroke this little bud for me, please?

Fleming tickled the bud and watched it flower. It stood up and brought another sigh from its owner. Fleming reached for the other one and felt it do the same.

'You know, Richard,' said Katrina dreamily. 'I don't know which would be best. For you to get in the bath with me, or for me to get out of it to be with you. What do you think?'

Richard's answer was by way of demonstration, and inside a minute he was stepping into the bath with her, his prick, not a bad size at all, Katrina noticed, standing out but not yet fully stiffened.

He sat opposite her. She reached for his groin with her foot and felt his cock swaying in the water. He made his foot available and she pushed his big toe into her crevice. Such titillation could not last long and soon he was kneeling beside her, his cock asking to be soaped. She squeezed some cool gel into her palm and softly coated the surface of his prick with it. Then she moved her hand up and down it to bring up the foam, then she rinsed it with handfuls of water from the bath.

As he looked down on her work, she looked up, smiled, and then plunged his cock in her mouth. She thought perhaps he wouldn't last long so she sucked hard and fast. She was wrong. He put his hand on her crutch and pushed three fingers inside. She was wriggling now, a fish hooked on his cock and being grabbed from beneath by a bigger fish.

In her thrashings she pulled the plug with her foot and the water drained out, leaving her stranded and flapping. Richard, in charge, pushed her knees up to her chin and got between them. She gratefully guided him home and closed her eyes. This, she said to herself, might be the stuff that dreams are made of, but it's a hell of a lot better in real life.

Chapter Eleven

It's my party . . .

. . . and I'll fly if I want to, thought Katrina as she slipped the fun-fur coat over her underwear, which tonight was nothing but a short, pure silk camisole in pale peach. The coat had come from the boss, given to her at the leaving party she was just leaving, as a thank-you for her successful but all too brief stay at Satellite Morning Television.

Her colleagues on the programme had had a whip-round for a present too. They'd produced a Santa's sack of goodies, all to do with self indulgence – wines, Harrod's hamper-style foods, several luxury vibrators, an electric dildo with individually adjustable speeds, and a mind-boggling range of exotic lace garments with peepholes. There were also framed originals of the pictures which had appeared in the Sunday paper.

The leaving party went well enough although it never built up that careless energy which everybody had expected – perhaps because they expected too much – and most of the guests just got quietly drunk.

The boss made his usual demands, of course, and several of the regular girls had had to slip out with him at one time or another. Katrina, feeling strangely spaced out, became slightly jealous and possessive about this, and no sooner had he returned to the party from one priapic lusting than she took him by the hand, smiled her most killing smile, and led him out again.

The party was being held in a suite of rooms in a West End hotel. Katrina led her erstwhile boss to one of the three bedrooms, which, the hotel management had found, were a major selling point in the hiring of this suite. They were fully equipped with mirrors, king-size beds, satin sheets and in one of them was a video camera linked to the TV screens in the other rooms.

This particular facility had not been mentioned to Katrina or her boss, but somebody must have known about it because no sooner had the couple arrived in their bedroom than the TV set in the main reception room was switched on. All the party guests who could still stand, and see clearly enough, were gathered around it.

Of course the camera was focussed on the bed and so at first they only saw a few items of clothing being thrown on it. Katrina was determined to have her boss naked and on a bed, instead of up against a wall or back against a desk with his cock sticking out of his trousers.

The boss, off-camera, stood co-operatively while Katrina stripped him, and then lay back on the bed with a large whisky in his hand to see what happened next.

The TV audience at the party saw their head man lying with no clothes on, his famous dong in the resting position, obviously watching something very interesting which, unfortunately, they couldn't catch themselves.

Katrina was becoming quite an expert at the striptease, and even though she had not a great deal on to start with, managed to spin out the exquisite agony for long enough. It must have taken her three minutes to take the single orchid from her hair, sitting at the dressing table, brushing her golden cascade, leaning forward so the boss could see her cleavage reflected in the mirror.

Her shoes had an ankle strap with a small button. With foot up on the dressing table stool, she could make a delicious meal of removing these, and the stockings came off – and at last the party guests saw a bit more than just the boss with his silly grin and twitching recumbent cock.

Katrina came into view and tied one of her stockings in a bow around the big cheese's still-slack member, lifted it up to her lips and gave it a kiss. She wandered out of shot again and the boss looked on with approval as she unzipped her dress, yet another example of her range of little black cocktail frocks with a short skirt and low-cut neckline, and now she was dressed only in a silk camisole and a pearl necklace. The loose bodice of the undergarment draped itself revealingly over her large bra-less breasts, and as she shrugged her shoulders the thin straps fell sideways.

She came into shot again and the guests saw her from

behind as she slipped the silk from her luscious form and remained still for a moment, a picture of feminine perfection, then turned to walk unknowingly towards the camera, her breasts gently bouncing, as she raised her arms to remove the last article of dress, her necklace.

Now she returned to the man in the gift wrapping. Slowly, ever so slowly, she undid the silken bow, and massaged his testicles with the stocking. The renowned serpent began to stir, and so she took it in her hands and rubbed it lightly between her palms as if she were a Girl Guide trying to start a fire with two sticks. She certainly started something, because the monster began to rear up.

Those females watching the screen in the other room who had never seen the monster, and there were quite a few who had only heard about it, gasped their amazement. The larger number of males who had never seen it either, and what's more had never seen the lovely Katrina with no clothes on, gulped and swallowed in their deep, deep envy – first of the boss's situation, being ministered to by heaven's most agreeable angel, and second of the size of his prick.

For Katrina, the sight of the boss's cock was nothing new, but it was nice to have him lying down for a change. With him on his back, Katrina could sit on his stuffing machine and feel it fill her to the maximum . . . but first, she would make sure it grew until it could grow no more.

To more gulps and groans from her unseen audience, Katrina bent her beautiful head over the rampant beast.

Her lips parted and the tip of her tongue flicked out, and with the greatest care she ran it over every square millimetre of hard meat, holding it in both hands the while. She felt fairly sure it was as stiff and as big as it was going to get, but to make certain she opened her mouth wide and lowered her head over the great purple knob.

She sucked it and slurped it, then sat back, absent-mindedly wanking the curved column, to admire her achievement.

The moment had arrived. Katrina shuffled herself across the boss's chest, rubbed her minge on his chest hairs, reached behind her, raised her impossibly desirable bottom in the air, and to wails of envy from audience males and females alike sank, an inch at a time, onto the unparalleled penis.

Every eye watching the screen was open wide. The boss's eyes were closed in gratification as he felt Katrina's hot pussy sliding up and down his prick. Widest open of the lot were Katrina's eyes, as she marvelled at her own capacity in taking within her the entirety of this cock. What a length! What a girth!

The TV audience could see the great prick very well, and watched in total fascination as it disappeared and reappeared. It would stay in sight for a few seconds as Katrina hovered, gathering herself for the next plunge and then it would be sheathed to the hilt again.

As she drove up and down and did her own private little bumps and grinds, the man's hands reached up and cradled her tits. Gradually he became more active in his participation and pulled her body to him. His hands were on her buttocks now, grappling and grabbing at the miraculous globes, and he was thrusting up into her as she went down hard on him. Now he turned her over and raised her legs right over his shoulders. The audience could see only the man's arse and his balls swinging below as he whacked his incredible cock into Katrina faster and faster.

Her feet, waving in the air around his neck, told the story, and as the pace built up they became frantic signallers. No more! they said, no more! But there had to be more, and the boss was reaching his climax, and Katrina went shooting past the most overwhelming orgasm into temporary unconsciousness as the boss pushed home with his last thrusts and flooded her insides with his tribute to her beauty and sensuality.

As he collapsed on top of her somebody in the other room turned the set off, and it was a subdued and thoughtful group of party guests who went in search of their next drink and a couple of canapés.

They had, they felt sure, witnessed the fuck of the century. Some of the women wanted to try it themselves with the big man. Others were afraid.

All of the men, without exception, wanted to try it with Katrina, but all except one managed to maintain proper decorum when, ten minutes later, she returned to the party. The big boss, knackered at last, was left asleep in the bedroom. Katrina, for some reason feeling that the night was still young, looked like she had just stepped out of the beauty parlour.

Somebody got her a drink. Somebody got her a smoked salmon sandwich. She smiled and looked around the room. Nice people. In some ways it was a pity she was leaving. She'd enjoyed being the Weather Dish. Doubts began creeping into her mind about the wisdom of this new leap into the bigger time. It was one hell of a job, presenting *Catwalk*. Was it too different from the weather? Could she cope with all that extra pressure and exposure?

Lost in her thoughts, she didn't notice the approach of SMT's notorious drunk. This was one of the floor managers, a reasonable enough bloke when sober but unable, when alcohol was about, to stop himself becoming a stinking, swaying slob.

'Howzzshabout a quick – pardon – fuckerooni? Fucker – oops – ooniooni? Hm?' he slurred, dropping ash from his cigarette and spilling wine out of his glass.

'No thanks, Sid, I've just had one,' said Katrina, looking around for rescue.

'Know that,' said Sid. 'Sawt on telly. Cmon. Quick fuck, Jshta ssing. Jsh wotta doctrorder. Jshta quick one. Frold timessake. To member you by.'

Katrina wondered briefly what he meant by seeing it on the telly, but dismissed it as the drink talking. Still she couldn't catch anyone's eye, and when Sid stubbed his fag on the floor, placed his glass with extreme care on a table and made a grab at Katrina, she thought she had better do something.

'For goodness' sake!' she hissed. 'Not in here. Come on. Follow me.'

She took him outside and down in the lift to the hotel's admin floor where she found some sort of general office, a medium-sized open plan room with desks and Swiss cheese plants and computer screens and, of course, no people. All the accounts clerks and administration workers were long gone home.

It was fairly easy to convince Sid that she liked bondage, although she had to strip to her camisole before he would agree to have his wrists tied with telephone cords, and he would only have her little black dress draped over his head after she had taken his trousers and pants off and tried for a few minutes to get his cock to stand.

This was why she was now leaving her party, in fur coat and practically nothing else, and why it was that the first office junior to get to work at the hotel next morning found the senior SMT floor manager, sound asleep on the carpet without his trousers.

After last seeing Sid, wrists tied, head hooded, groaning incomprehensibly in his drunk confusion, Katrina found a taxi. Forgetting her state of déshabille she ordered him to the Cassandra Club, a discreet little casino with a dance floor and bar, where a slow and sleepy band provided just the atmosphere Katrina sought.

She had been there a few times with the girls from SMT and, once, with the boss. She wasn't a member but guessed correctly that it wouldn't matter. There were no intentions of gambling anyway. Katrina just wanted the soothing sounds of the wheel and the cards, the quiet discipline of the croupiers, the facility to wander next door and listen to the piano, bass, drums and plaintive clarinet of the band.

In a place like this, being famous was not such a disadvantage as it could be elsewhere. Here the patrons were well-mannered enough to leave her alone if that was what she wanted. Here, nobody would be asking for her autograph, or making jokes about bathtime with the carpet layer, and nobody would be trying to stick their hands up her skirt.

Luckily there was no one else at the hat-check counter and so nobody saw the dreamy Katrina half take off her fur coat before remembering she had no dress on. She asked if she could keep her coat, but there was a rule against it, something about aces up sleeves, and so a search had to be made of the hat-check girl's wardrobe of lost and forgotten gowns. There was a surprisingly large number of these. Apparently the clientèle of the Cassandra Club was not always so restrained and polite. Sometimes, if a few Hooray Henries were in, and one of them ran out of money, his girlfriend would be placed as a bet, and if she had to lose her clothes and her jewellery, so be it.

There were also a few women who would tell their husbands they were going to see mother, then would come to the Cassandra Club where they kept some spare clothes, change into something a bit more knock-out than mother-visiting sweater and jeans, and spend a glamorous evening with whichever lantern-jawed specimen happened to be the lucky boy of the moment.

Katrina chose a dark crimson, ankle-length gown in

the Empire style, tied beneath the bust with a black ribbon and cut in a wide scoop to show her soft expanse of breast and cleavage. She looked imperially feminine and, in her vacant mood, regally elegant.

There was even a black choker with costume diamonds. Without any real intention to do so, she looked absolutely stunning. She couldn't help it.

Every head turned in the room when she walked in, but only one pair of eyes could hold her gaze. He was a dark-haired man aged about twenty-eight, sitting at the roulette table, a modest pile of chips in front of him, and to Katrina he looked kind and sympathetic as well as one hell of a hunk.

She found herself standing behind him. He looked up, questioning whether these chips should go on red or black. She nodded red. She also picked odd correctly, and soon they were being bold enough to place bets on single numbers. Two of them failed but the third won. Satisfied, the man rose. Would the most beautiful woman in the room care to dance? She would, and two hours later she was still dancing, her head on his shoulder, her eyes closed, their bodies swaying almost imperceptibly.

The man asked if she would like to go home. She said no. She wanted to stay with him and so, about half an hour later, the man took the shoes, the choker and the crimson gown from her sleeping form, laid her in his bed, and went off to sleep on the couch.

Next morning he didn't hear the shower going, nor the hair drier, nor did he hear the rattles and clinks of coffee being made, and the spitting sizzle of bacon being fried, and the first thing he saw when he opened his eyes was a mug of coffee in a small, feminine hand. His eyes travelled from the neat little hand up an arm covered in the white towelling of his own dressing gown, and up to the long blonde hair, and the smiling lips which told him that breakfast would be served in ten minutes. He took his coffee into the bathroom while she did toast and eggs.

They never spoke a word during breakfast. They just stared at each other. Katrina had never seen such a good-looking man, and the man had never had a Weather Dish in his flat before. He might indeed be good-looking and be used to handsome women, but he didn't have the money to mix with the social scene and get himself into close contact with TV personalities. Last night at the casino had been a blue-moon occasion, a case of trying to turn a sudden little windfall from Auntie's will into enough of a wad to buy himself into a business of some kind. Well, thanks to Katrina's luck, he'd done that. Now, with some luck of his own, he might find himself being able to give Katrina pleasure in return.

As the last finger of toast disappeared Katrina arose, still without a word, and headed towards the bedroom. At the door she turned, slipped off the robe, flung it over her shoulder, and walked away from the man with the robe hanging down her back from one finger.

The man, dressed in a tracksuit, went after her as fast as manners permitted. She was standing by the bedroom window, looking down into the street, the dressing gown still hanging over the smooth, light golden skin of her back.

He put his hand on her bare shoulder. She turned, and they kissed, a long passionate embrace. Katrina felt a highly satisfactory bulge in the tracksuit trousers, pressing up against her, and sighed with contentment as his hands, warm and gentle, stroked her breasts and nipples. This was a caring lover, she was sure. This was a man who would seek her own satisfaction as much as his own.

Her hands found the spot where tracksuit top met bottom and ran first up his back, and then down. She squeezed his buttocks, and then wriggled her hands around to the front where she found a strong, hard curve of desire which she lovingly caressed with her fingers.

The man led her over to the bed and laid her, naked this time, on the covers. He swiftly removed his own clothes and lay beside her, his hand moving over her body like a blind man's, softly touching, searching, stroking, memorising through their sensitive fingers the contours and textures of the loveliest female form he had ever been close to.

Katrina closed her eyes and let him play at will. She was going to enjoy this. She sighed, and smiled, and breathed, and made little noises of encouragement as he worked her. Sometimes he would massage, sometimes he would make no more contact than a floating feather might, and then he began to use his lips and tongue. The game was moved beyond the stage where

Katrina could be a passive player. Now, with his lips around her nipple and his fingers in her quim, and now with his tongue rasping her clit while his hands palpated her breasts, she could not help but reach for him.

His cock was stiff and hot. It wanted action. She pulled him towards her and raised her knees, guiding him home and giving a low 'mmmm' as the rod slipped in. He didn't move for a while. He just lay above her, keeping his weight off her, and kissing her breasts. He liked to see the nipples stand, and he used his lips and teeth skilfully to maintain them both at full erection.

She also felt his fingertip slide a short way into her alongside his cock, and she knew it would find her little joystick and stroke it, and she wondered how long she could keep still. The tension was almost unbearable, and then it became completely unbearable as he rubbed her clitty suddenly and hard and sucked her nipple and grabbed handfuls of arse-cheek. With a choking cry Katrina began pushing her pelvis up, desperately seeking the deepest penetration. Still he held off, stimulating her everywhere and every way except in the place and by the method she most wanted.

Soon she would have given anything for a fucking, and the man judged it perfectly. Just as she reached the point of panic he began thrusting, slow and deep, and Katrina began gurgling and groaning.

The man put his hands under her buttocks and raised her to meet him. She grabbed hold of any part of him she could get and willed him into her, deeper, faster, harder, longer.

Katrina was shouting words which might have been

'yes' or 'more' or 'now' but the man couldn't really tell what they were. He was going for it, flat out, full throttle, and as he felt his own coming approach he also felt the mad spasm of Katrina's contractions in her orgasm, as the chemical messages in her passage of bliss moved her mind into another world and her body into its ancient task of trying to take the sperm from the man's cock and force it ever upwards.

His last dozen strokes were fantastically quick, and his very last thrust was as deep as could be, and he sighed as his cock spurted and Katrina shuddered again in a second coming of her own.

Katrina's life changed from that moment. This was the supreme episode of her sexual existence so far. Nobody had ever done it nearly so well, never mind better. The man, called Calvin Bryant, became her only lover and her minder, and nothing was agreed or decided unless Calvin agreed or decided it.

Elspeth, watching from a distance, was distraught. Calvin, without a career or means of his own, was living off Katrina and living very well. Some of his influence was beneficial, Elspeth had to admit. With no other sexual distractions, Katrina concentrated on her work wonderfully well and made *Catwalk* a raging success. Fathers and their teenage sons who had never had time for the fripperies of fashion were suddenly to be found by their firesides on a Saturday evening when *Catwalk* went out – along with almost every other sexually aware segment of the viewing public.

Elspeth was kept very busy with the show's sponsor Richard Fleming, who couldn't quite understand why Katrina had gone off him. Elspeth's own soothing ways, plus the occasional excitement of being shagged to delirium by a pair of long skinny models, more or less made up for lack of Katrina.

Other senior TV and media men obviously thought they too had some sort of call on the girl at the front of *Catwalk*, and lookalike mother had a lot of serious poking to do to keep them all at bay. So, while Calvin minded Katrina's person, her money and her business career, Elspeth protected her from too many sexual attentions by satisfying the applicants' needs herself.

Katrina went blissfully on her way, largely unaware of the help she was getting. She knew she was making a brilliant job of *Catwalk*, she knew she was getting fantastic sex whenever she wanted it from Calvin, and provided she had lunch with her mother once a month, during which Calvin was never mentioned, she thought she was doing OK.

But there was a devil in Katrina, a devil which had always made her willing to try whatever was going, and if nothing was going, had made her want to seek it out. And so, after one full season of *Catwalk*, and the summer break, and halfway through the next season, the devil began to bite.

The party after the school play became a recurring dream. She saw herself as leading, as the one who would take the others, willing and unwilling, into uncharted waters. She would wake from these dreams and find

Calvin asleep beside her, and at first this was reassuring, but then it became boring – he was always there, so dependable, so bloody dull – and then it became irritating to awake always beside a man so reliable. He was so considerate, so kind, so thoughtful. He protected her from everything. There was no risk in life any more – nothing to be scared of, and therefore nothing to be willing to try.

And on the morning she realised that, Katrina, without a word to anyone, disappeared.

Chapter Twelve

If you can't beat 'em ...

... you can't possibly do the job, thought Katrina, as she whacked the boy's bottom for the sixth time with a whippy and artistic, if cumbersome, rattan cane object which at one time had beaten the dust out of carpets rather than the fuck out of teenage boys. This boy, a well-made lad of nineteen, lay prone on his stomach on a wooden table with no padding.

Katrina was now in her third month at Holy Sepulchre College and in a badly paid but otherwise perfect job. It was perfect because it was undiscoverable – nobody would think of looking for the sexy hostess of *Catwalk* in an obscure Irish academy for prospective priests of a renegade and disregarded religion. The job was also perfect because it allowed Katrina to indulge in the three things she liked best – leading people into temptation, having wild and often repeated sex, and walking a tightrope of excitement.

Her mother knew she was safe and well, but that was all. Every track had been covered and the papers had given up trying to find her. Other girls with long blonde hair, big tits and willing smiles had succeeded Katrina in the tabloids' hall of fame, and she didn't mind one little bit.

There were six more strokes to administer before she turned the boy over, and between the two sets of six there had to be a five minute rest for whipper and whipped. She admired the red marks across his naked buttocks and, as she often seemed to do these days, paused for thought and began a meandering reminiscence of life gone by.

Always she had been guided. This was the thing. First her mother and then Calvin had pointed her always in the direction they thought she should go. It had worked well, she had to admit, but freedom was preferable. Such freedom as she had now was hard-won – there had been the emotional wrench of giving everything up which she, mother and Calvin had worked for. There had been the period on the run from the press, in France mainly. Then she had gone to ground in the Netherlands, working as a waitress in a bar in Leyden. She cut her hair short and dyed it black, just in case any of the customers had ever watched the weather forecast on Satellite Morning Television and then, anxious for a more exciting time of it, looked for employment in some rather different kinds of establishment in Amsterdam.

She admitted to little professional experience – they didn't seem to be interested in her fully-flowered amateur career – and so they started her off in a peep show. They asked about costumes. She hadn't got any. They told her where to go to buy what she needed, which was fancy underwear and a theme costume of some sort – waitress, schoolgirl, policewoman, teacher, doctor – gave her a starting time, and that was it.

The other girls working at the place didn't want to give her any help. They were all on performance bonuses, so tricks of the trade meant guilders in the handbag and were not to be disclosed. So, in she went, deciding to make it up as she went along.

She felt as if she was inside a barrel, a very large barrel with bright lights and low music. She stood, not knowing what to do, and then she heard the sound of coins being dropped into slots and a number of little hatchways sliding back. Behind the hatchways were small windows. Katrina could see nothing through them, but assumed there was a man watching intently at every one.

This was it. Let's go. She was wearing a nurse's uniform with a short skirt. She bent over, right over, and circled on the spot as she took her knickers down, making certain all the blank-faced windows got a good opportunity to see her naked arse. She glanced up at the clock, which had started when the coins were dropped. She had five minutes, and had already used one and a half. Dire warnings had been issued: she must be bollock naked well before the five minutes were up or the customers would want their money back.

Better leave the hat on for the moment, she thought, and got busy with the apron and uniform dress. Underneath it she had a black and red basque with a high

223

platform bra. Her breasts, previously covered by the starchy apron, were pushing upwards in their attempt to escape. She put her hands underneath and pushed them further. The cleavage was astonishing and the contrast likewise when she undid the hooks and eyes at the back of the garment and released her snowy globes from their torture. How soft and appealing they looked now, as in fact did all of her as she swiftly released the whole of the basque and stood dressed only in elastic topped stockings and a nurse's hat. She spun slowly again, leaning back, the fingers of one hand going to the black-dyed hair of her crutch while the other hand's dainty digits played lightly with her nipples, teasing them erect.

She parted her legs and pushed her pubis forward so that the windows got the chance to see her labia parted and stroked. She wondered briefly about using her breast-fondling hand to stick a finger up her bum but never had time to make the decision. Five minutes was up and the hatches snapped shut.

Katrina gathered up her clothes and walked from the room, to be met by the fearsome-looking old harridan who was the management as far as the girls were concerned.

One of the windows had, apparently, enjoyed her performance especially and had requested a private viewing. Katrina knew little of the business yet but she did know that this was what the girls were always after. This was where they got the real money in extra fees and tips. Not that Katrina wanted the money especially.

She had more than enough for a quiet life, but of course she couldn't help needing to do well and was flattered that she'd scored a hit on her first ever peep.

The room for her second show was smaller, and it had a couple of props – a chair, a footstool, a low coffee table, a bowl of fruit, a telephone (for emergencies, Katrina assumed, until she saw it wasn't wired up).

Now she walked into the job already nude. The harridan had taken her costume, given her a less than motherly smack on the bottom, and told her to use her imagination.

As she took stock the window opened, a much bigger window, and she could see the man, vaguely, behind it. She smiled at him, and began a slow, leisurely kind of dance which involved balletic movements of her legs over the back of the chair. She got more expressive still as she knelt on the footstool and placed her forehead on the floor, and then went into some warm-up exercises, feet apart, fingertips to the floor, then arms swinging.

The man must have seen everything she had by now, Katrina thought, and turned to sit in the chair, leaning back, legs spread wide, as if exhausted. She looked up and was shocked initially to see the man standing at the window, his cock in his hand. He was staring at her and slowly wanking.

Of course. That was what they did. Nothing to be surprised at, really. Katrina took an apple from the bowl and rolled it up and down the inside of her thighs. Replacing that she took a banana and rubbed it between her breasts, leaving her mouth slightly open. She made as if to insert it in her vagina, and then decided to peel it instead. Would she put it in peeled? No, she would eat it instead, which she did with enormously suggestive relish. Then she took the telephone handset and stroked herself with it, and pushed it to the entrance of her pussy, and began to excite herself with it, and opened her legs more to get more of the instrument inside her.

She glanced up again and saw the man wanking at high speed, and she saw the come spurt onto the window, and then the harridan was there, shoving the hatch across with a bang. The show was over.

Katrina didn't last very long at the peep show. After a couple of weeks she found it deeply unsatisfying, putting all this effort into provocation and then getting no self-reward from it. She wanted a cock inside her quim, or at least in her hand or her mouth. She didn't want to watch come spattering windows, or the old harridan cleaning it off while telling her in broken English which was the best window cleaning product for removing come. So, she looked for another job.

There was a club down by one of the canals which advertised REALFUCKING, one word. Katrina, firmly resolved to be willing to try anything at least once, asked to see the manager. He wasn't so keen at first. She didn't have a partner. Most of the acts, he explained, were performed by couples who lived and worked together. If she came into the show it would upset the balance. If she could find a good partner, which was one with a very large cock who could produce erections at any time and who could fuck for long periods without coming – then she could have a job. Meanwhile, why didn't she try one of the other jobs he had?

It would appear that the nurse's uniform would come in handy again, but the difference this time was that she was performing her strip in a private room, like a sitting room in a house, and her audience were in the room with her. It would be a small group of men, usually three or four, and usually they were on holiday together or knew each other from work.

They would relax in the armchairs, smoking and drinking, and Katrina would come in and take her clothes off. They would applaud politely and then one would stand up. Katrina would take him by the hand and lead him into the bedroom next door, where he would fuck her.

Sometimes these sessions were good fun. Sometimes they were not. The worst was when all four wanted a fuck and they just walked into the bedroom one after the other, stuck their cocks in Katrina, grunted and pumped for a few seconds, came, and went.

The best was when just one wanted sex, and he wanted good sex not just perfunctory poking, and the best time of all was when one particular group came in, four lads from Manchester or Leeds or somewhere, and one of the group had never had it before. They were very polite and appreciative during the strip, and then one of them explained the situation to Katrina. She led the blushing boy into the bedroom, and half an hour later they emerged.

The lad was still blushing, but he had come three times in the interlude, once in Katrina's mouth and twice in her manhole. It had taken her back to schooldays, that one. Such a nice lad, too, and so very thankful and so very, very generous. The four of them must have pooled their money for this one great moment in their virgin friend's life. Boys! There certainly was something about them . . .

But she had had enough of that way of living after another month and took herself off to the south of Ireland. Now she wanted to try living rough, sleeping under the stars, all that kind of thing. It was all right, she thought, but the romance of it tended to dissolve in the rain, and she was glad when she went in a bar and met Declan.

Declan told her about his religion. This religion was unique, in that it didn't expect you to believe in any particular god. The main point was that it was trying to revive the ways of the original churches. Declan's idea was that a church shouldn't actually have churches or temples. It shouldn't have this great string of massive buildings all over the place, and it shouldn't sit there waiting for people to come into these churches as if they were going to the theatre or a football match. It should have priests who roved the land, with no money and no property to speak of, just like the Nazarene and the twelve apostles did in Galilee.

Declan's priests would take the message of peace and goodwill to the people, not spend their lives counting the collection and waiting their turn to be a bishop.

Katrina thought it sounded marvellous, and she thought Declan was marvellous, particularly when he took her to the rambling old house which he'd called Holy Sepulchre College, and gave her the first square meal she'd had in days, and the first bath she'd had for two weeks, and never tried once to feel her tits, pinch her bottom, touch her thigh, anything.

Declan explained that celibacy was vital for all the priests in his order, and he was having a lot of trouble with that side of it. In these days of unemployment and disillusionment with authority and Western civilisation in general, he had no problem finding volunteers to train, and they were all willing to say they would be celibate. Then, the first time some girl gave them a wink, their vows were forgotten and their cocks were plunging home.

What the college needed was some sort of testing process, so that the weaklings could be weeded out before they got too far. The last thing he wanted for his budding church was for his priests, sworn to the pure life, to be found out in bed with some newspaper-worthy woman who was giving them shelter for the night.

Katrina said she could devise such a test. How about if she stayed at the college and became tutor in celibacy? She could, she assured Declan, tempt Nelson off his Column. Any student who could resist her would certainly be made of the right stuff and could be relied on for a century of celibacy if necessary.

And this was why she was now laying into Brother Anthony with the cane carpet-beater. Brother Anthony was a nineteen-year-old student drop-out from Shannon. Brother Anthony had been caught trying to look into Katrina's bedroom, which was on the ground floor – on purpose – and which always had its curtains slightly ajar.

Katrina shook herself free of her reverie, gave him the second batch of six strokes, and after the twelfth stroke of the carpet beater gave the command: turn over, Brother. He did so, and Katrina was hardly surprised to see his cock standing in a curve which travelled fully eight inches from its bushy roots to its tip's resting place on the boy's stomach.

Katrina ran her finger along the vein which made a darkish ridge along its outward-facing surface.

'Would you like me to relieve you of this tension, Brother?' she asked, in a deeply sensual voice which would have melted butter in any mouth. In fact, it would have melted a cold store full of frozen butter.

'No, thank you, Miss Mulloy, I would not.'

'You know, Brother Anthony, beating your neat little bottom was hot work. Do you mind if I take my woolly off?'

Without waiting for an answer she pulled the jumper over her head, revealing to the boy's goggle-eyed gaze a magnificent pair of breasts encased, just, in an uplift bra which made the very most of their structural potential.

'Are you sure you wouldn't like me to help you return to normal?' whispered Katrina in her huskiest tones. 'You know you are free to go now that your punishment is concluded. If you don't want me to help you, why are you still here, Brother Anthony? If you don't want my hand to touch you, why don't you get off the punishment table?'

'Yes, I know I am free. I am going. I'm going now, Miss Mulloy. It's just . . .'

'. . . that really you want me to put my hand on your big, hot, hard prick like this' – and she grasped it firmly in her hand – 'and show you my tits like this' – and she undid the front fastener of her bra with the other hand – 'and slide my hand up and down along the whole length of your cock while I show you what joys could be yours if only you were allowed to touch me.

'Other boys of your age, Brother Anthony, have felt my tits, and put their fingers in my quim, and their cocks. Do you know what it's like to put your cock in a girl's hot pussy? Oh, it's a nice feeling. They all say so. All the boys who have put their cocks in my pussy have told me how nice it is. Wouldn't you like to do that? I could open wide for you, Brother Anthony, 'cos you've got such a lovely big one. Ah. No need.'

Her hand moved faster and the boy, unable to contain himself, shot his load a foot into the air.

'Well Brother Anthony, you have a choice. You can give up your course at Holy Sepulchre College now. Or, you can do a week's penance in the cave, and then return to see if your penance has made you better able to resist temptation.'

The thought of a week on his own in the cold, damp cave halfway up the west-facing cliff, open to every gale and rainstorm that the Atlantic could produce, was enough to make him waver. And there was also the question of the twelve strokes of the cane he would get as soon as he transgressed again. Then, the renewed thought of another wank administered by Miss Mulloy made him decide. He'd give the brotherhood one more try.

Of course, Brother Anthony was one of the most recent novitiates and it had become apparent almost immediately that he would never make it, not if he studied for a thousand years. His cock sprung to attention as soon as he saw Katrina, whether from the front, the back or the side.

Some other Brothers whom Katrina was about to examine were a different kettle of fish. These were advanced students, already well-versed in the art of disciplining their minds to push thoughts of sex into the furthest and deepest recesses. Declan had asked Katrina to give them the test of tests before he sent them out into the world, and Katrina was never one to refuse a challenge, so while Brother Anthony submitted himself to the Brother in charge of the punishment cave, she got herself ready.

The theme costume trick she'd learned in Amsterdam had also worked well for her at Holy Sepulchre. It was the contrast, she thought, between the familiarity – and yet it was a distant, unobtainable kind of familiarity – and the sudden availability of what was underneath. Men could have sexual fantasies about women who played everyday roles in their lives – at school, in hospital, in the street where they might have a naval or police uniform – but who were untouchable in a sexual way.

The obvious theme costume for the Brothers today was a nun's. What could be more untouchable? But she had rejected that idea exactly because it was obvious. If she was to take this job seriously, she had to try her utmost to get one or more of them to weaken. If she was to get one to weaken, she had to employ all the subterfuge she could. They would be expecting a nun. They might even have done mental exercises preparing themselves to resist a nun. And so she would not do the obvious.

The test was to take place in the seminar room, which was set out like a miniature lecture theatre. The seats were raised in curved rows – just four rows of eight, with an aisle splitting the rows into four and four. They were cinema-type seats with the front row starting about two feet, or four steps, above floor level, where there was a lectern, a desk, a chair and, on test days, a bed.

The Brothers sat and waited with the house lights out and the bed and surrounding area spotlit. It was an intimate atmosphere. They said nothing to each other.

As Katrina entered she noticed that the five Brothers to be tested had arranged themselves on the front row four and one. The one on his own might be the weak link. She might be expected to concentrate on him and let the others off lightly. On the other hand, he could be the strongest, put there to take the strain off the others. That was it. They were bluffing, trying to get her to waste her energies on an immovable object. Clever sods, she thought. I'll show them.

The Brothers were dressed, as Katrina had insisted for the advanced test, in nothing but a pair of thin briefs. They sat, cross-legged, holding the arms of their seats with the nervous confidence of patients in a dentist's waiting room.

Katrina's own costume was far more normal for day-time wear. It was ordinary in the extreme. Indeed, you could hardly call it a costume. You might even call it off-putting – and that was Katrina's plan. She was going to appear to be a push-over for their mental discipline, easy to resist, easy to dismiss from their urge processes. They would relax, thinking the test was going to be no problem. And then . . .

Katrina was wearing a headscarf, a fawn overcoat and flat canvas shoes. She carried a shopping basket which she placed on the desk before seeming to hear the door bell. At the door she spoke to the invisible caller before inviting him in and then she chatted away as she mimed getting him a cup of coffee. The invisible caller was not only a him. He was a Brother.

How predictable! All she was going to do was take the examinees through a mock-up of a house call. She would be a bored wife, husband at work, and she would fancy the young Brother and try to get him into her bed. Dear oh dear. Can't she do better than that?

'So, tell me about this church of yours,' said Katrina, sitting opposite the imaginary Brother, cupping an imaginary mug of coffee in her hands. 'Do you do a lot of wanking? No? I'm surprised. I thought all men who never got a woman did wanking. Do they not, so? So what do they do to keep their cocks satisfied? Nothing? Really? I'll tell you, my husband doesn't wank. He couldn't get it up hard enough. I mean, we have our weekly fornication on a Saturday night, and he can only just manage that. Crikey. What a man. It takes me half an hour to get his prick to stand, and it takes one minute for him to get it slack again. So it's not him that does the wanking. It's me. Look.'

Inside her shopping basket was more than the usual tea, sugar, butter, bacon and flour. Beneath these items, which she removed one by one, was a vibrator, a tremendous long thing with a ribbed shaft and a big knob on the end partly covered with short rubber bristles. Katrina turned it on and it shook and buzzed. She turned it off and placed it on the table next to the butter.

'You see, my friend, this is what I use to poke myself with. And I'm just feeling like one now, so if you don't mind, I'll just carry on while you finish your coffee. Of course, if you want to get your dick out and replace my machine with the real thing, you're very welcome. If not, I quite understand.'

Katrina stood to take her coat off. Beneath it was a utilitarian cotton print frock and white apron. At a measured pace she took all her clothes off, folding them neatly as she went and placing them over the lectern, something which required her to walk across the front of the sitting Brothers. She did this with every garment, taking it off, walking, folding and placing, then walking back to take off the next thing.

Somehow, the dullness of the costume made her stunningly attractive body all the more mind-blowing as it was gradually revealed, and it would be hard to conceive of anything more sexy than her naked body, headscarf still on, walking along the front row of the seminar room in order to place a single woollen stocking on the lectern.

All the time she kept up a stream of talk. She showed the invisible Brother how her bra fastened and the difference it made to the shape of her breasts. She offered him her panties to sniff if he wanted – no? She told him about the variety in sizes and shapes of cocks she had had in her past – how the milkman had a long thin one, and the postman a short fat one. What shape was the Brother's? She bet it was huge, with a great big curve to it. What it would be like to have that slip inside her. Was the Brother quite sure he wouldn't like to come over here to the bed and give her a length?

Oh well. It'll have to be the plastic. My flexible friend. Just rub a bit of best butter on the end, that's it, makes it slip in easier, there, that's just right. Now, I'll lie on the bed and put the first three inches in, and turn it on. There. Mmmmm. Nice, makes me want to wriggle my bottom. A few more inches. Ahhhhh. That's so good.

'Can you boys see properly?' She spoke for the first time directly to the Brothers sitting watching her. 'You on the end. Can you see?'

The Brothers nodded. Some were showing more signs of strain than others. The one who sat second from the left was sweating.

'Now, as I lie back here' – she had her elbows behind her, half sitting up, with her legs wide apart and the vibrator at work on its own, sticking obscenely out of her blonde-fringed pussy (she had long ago stopped dying it).

'Now, as I lie back here, I want you to know that I am thinking of each of you in turn. I am imagining what it would be like to have your cocks in my cunt rather than this electric substitute. You on the end with the curly hair – I'm thinking of you first. I'm closing my eyes and thinking about you and making your cock stiff, with my hand, and then letting you climb on top of me and push it right in. That's nice. Now I'm thinking of the one next to you, with the reddish face and the ginger hair.

'I bet there's a big ginger bush all around his cock, which will be white as white, and I'm betting that when I bend over to kiss it, it will leap up at me, and I'll be able to get astride it and ride it home. Isn't that right, Brother Ginger?'

Brother Ginger, whom Katrina had already decided was her chief target, could do nothing but look totally dumbfounded.

'And the next one along, the thin-faced boy. I bet he's got a cock and a half. I've always found with thin-faced boys that they have cocks like rattlesnakes. I'd be able to get both hands on it at once. Mmm, I'd stroke it and lick it and make it stand up stiff, and then I'd put it in my mouth and suck it. And when it came I'd swallow some of the come, but I'd let some out so it could dribble onto my tits. Oh, yes, that would be nice, wouldn't it? Your cock in my mouth, all hot and wet? I'm very good with my mouth. I'm the best cocksucker in all Ireland.

'And the big blond guy, what kind of a dick will he have? A stiff one, anyway. I think I might turn over for him, and he could take me from behind, then I could feel his balls on the backs of my thighs as he stuffs me solid. And the poor little one on his own, the one with the long hair. Small men are supposed to have small cocks, but it doesn't always follow. I've known little guys with enormous cocks, and I've made them as enormous as they can get, believe me.

'That's my speciality, you see, cocks. I know all about them. And the more I know, the more I like. I just love cocks. I love kissing them, and sucking them, and stroking them. And most of all I like fucking them.

'Now! Stand up!'

Katrina's voice changed suddenly from sultry and seductive to parade-ground official. The boys stood. One had a bulge. It was Ginger.

He was quite a tall lad, this Ginger, and when Katrina took out the vibrator and got off the bed and walked towards the row of Brothers, she could see that Ginger's bulge, the only one, was about level with her chest. She stood at floor level. Ginger stood four steps up. She reached for his bulge.

Ginger had to stay still while she stroked it and felt it judder. She reached for the top of his briefs and with both hands pulled them down, revealing a cock more than halfway to full erection.

She brushed her nipples with it. It leaped in her hand. She took the end of it in her mouth. It leaped again, and stiffened, and was now out of anyone's control but Katrina's. She sucked it, her cheeks distending, and then drew back. In four other pairs of briefs, nothing stirred. They were truly amazing, these guys. What discipline. Except, of course, for poor old Ginger. He wasn't going to make it after all, except onto Katrina's bed, where she now led him. She placed him on his back, gave his cock one more long suck, and then speared herself on the rebellious and disobedient member.

Ginger, realising that all was lost, thought he'd better make the best of it. No sooner was he in than he was grabbing at Katrina's tits, and fondling her bottom, and shouting with gladness. This was what he liked best after all.

He rolled the two of them over, pushed her knees up to her chin, and gave her a good rogering. 'Temptress!' he shouted. 'Jezebel! Take that, and that, and that!' His cock surged in and out of her and, where the vibrator had just been, Katrina felt the old sensations.

'Come on, Ginger,' she whispered. 'Fuck me!'

With renewed vigour the lad set to, pushing his dick in harder, faster and further, and shouting his joy at the top of his voice. Katrina wrapped her legs around his bouncing arse and pushed her tits up at him. He had no time for tits. His eyes were closed, his mouth was open, and as Katrina felt the first gushings of her own flood of feeling he went into rapid fire and came.

'It's not strictly allowed,' she said, 'but if you want to

do that again tonight, you can.'

It was Ginger who caused the leak which turned into a stream which became a flood which washed Katrina out of her ideal job. After leaving the Brotherhood he went back to farming, and got pissed one night in the barroom behind the Post Office in his home village in County Kerry, and there was a reporter there in the bar, a girl on holiday from England, who soon picked up from Ginger's drunken ramblings that there was a hot story here.

She was a neatly-made little piece, a bit intellectual-looking for some (including Ginger at first), which was hardly surprising when you knew that she was a graduate of Newnham, first class, and was expecting shortly to publish a new translation of Virgil's *Aeneid*. Miss Flora Bisham, however, was nothing if not ambitious. She wanted to be Editor of the *Sunday Times* at least, and there were very few situations she would dodge on the way to that goal.

The night after Ginger got drunk, Flora came in the same bar again. This time, instead of the horn-rimmed specs, she had her contacts in. Instead of the hair in a bun she wore it loose. The shaggy Norwegian jumper and hiking trousers were replaced by a tight T-shirt and even tighter jeans, and of course Ginger didn't recognise her. That was soon put right and the level of his reticence about his previous existence was just as easily established. No way would he be specific. He'd been some kind of monk, he'd seen the light, and that was it.

No, it wasn't a recognised order. Yes, it was a bit way out. No, it wasn't one of those cults you read about where they all commit suicide. Yes, he'd left it for good. No, he wouldn't tell her any more. What did she want to know for, anyway? Oh, she was writing a book, was she? Well now, that's very interesting, a pretty girl like you writing books. How about another drink?

Next morning, in a white-painted room in a stone cottage not far from Dingle Bay, a slim, dark-haired English journalist called Flora got what she wanted. She had had to take Ginger in her naked arms and give him everything he wanted, everything, short of having his cock up her arse which she wouldn't do on any account, not because she was against the act itself but because her arse was a sweet, pretty and very small thing while Ginger's cock was a bloody great ugly thing.

This she was thinking to herself as she licked it. She had been licking it for twenty minutes, a deliberate, slow, particular kind of licking, confined to the very tip of her tongue and covering only the rim of his cock head, apart from the occasional run up and down the curving vein.

Ginger was frantic. She wouldn't move her hand on his cock, she wouldn't put it inside her mouth, she wouldn't sit on it or let him push it in her. She would only lick it, with the result that after ten minutes he was hovering on the very brink of orgasm, but she kept him there, hovering, and would not let him make the leap.

He had made several attempts to grab his cock himself, to put himself out of his misery, but she had made it very plain that any such act would result in an immediate scream for help. No doubt the two farm workers outside in the yard, who'd just finished the milking without any help from Ginger, would be quick to respond. Wouldn't she be telling them a tale of rape and pillage, to be sure, begorrah?

'Flora!' Ginger implored. 'Please! You can't keep me like this. Do something!'

'A name, and a place. That's all,' she said, giving his cock another long lick from root to tip. She bent her head and took both his balls in her mouth, mumbled them gently, and then returned to her tongue-tip torment. This, she thought, is the fifth time of asking. If he doesn't give in now, he won't ever. And if he doesn't give in he's jolly well going to have to use his own hand to get where he wants.

Just as they had when watching Katrina and her vibrator, Ginger's powers of self-discipline failed him, as they would have failed virtually any male in the universe in the situation he was in.

'Declan. The name. Tobylights Farm, just outside Tralee. The place.'

The small but neatly-formed Flora raised up her spare but nicely-fleshed frame and smiled a glad smile. The smile became an anxious look as she swung her leg over her man and sank onto his cock – it was a very big one for her to manage – and then changed to a smile of bliss as, with two or three wriggles, she felt the warm come seeping into her.

That afternoon she was on Declan's doorstep. That

evening Katrina was in flight again, while Flora filed her first story about the mysterious, ascetic religion with the beautiful and strangely familiar woman who tested the young priests' willpower.

Chapter Thirteen

A horse, a horse . . .

. . . my quimdom for a donkey! Or a bicycle. Any fucking thing.

Katrina managed about thirty miles on the old Honda moped which was the only transport owned by the Brotherhood, and when it conked out there was no question of it starting again. Even to Katrina's unmechanical eye it was clear that this was a dead moped. No good pushing it, not any further than that bridge, anyway, because at that bridge she could give it its last push, into the river.

That done, and walking over the bridge in the gathering dusk, Katrina saw some lights. A village, maybe, with a pub, maybe, and a man with a bed, maybe. It turned out that the lights were off the road. There was an imposing gateway, with stone lions on the tops of the gateposts and a wide gravel drive leading to whatever was the source of the lights.

She walked up the drive, quietly, and found a large house, not quite a mansion but definitely in the eight bedroom class. There were lights outside the door and in some windows, but none she could see into. OK. So we're here. Let's knock on the door and ring on the bell.

The man who answered was short, slim, Mediterranean-looking, and wearing a short black kimono. His smile of greeting as he looked up at the lovely Katrina changed to one of slight puzzlement, as he noted the windswept hair and the scruffy clothes, but changed back to welcoming again when he had also made inventory of the expansive bosom and the many other attractive features of his visitor. He bowed, and ushered her in. He was so glad she had got there in the end. Better late than never, as the English say, is that not so?

It was Katrina's turn to be puzzled, but there was no problem in going along with the strange little man. The only problem might come later, she thought, as she caught a glimpse of his sexual organ, briefly revealed as his kimono lifted in the air while he turned.

Katrina had seen some big dicks. The boss at SMT. That black man she had watched being videoed by her mother. Others, since and before. That chap with the puppet at Boundary Television, his had been a big one. But this!

Katrina hoped she had got it wrong. No man the size of this pleasant and polite gentleman – Turkish, perhaps, or Greek – could have such a dong. It was a killer, if it was as big as it had looked in her tiny glimpse of it. The killer dong from 30,000 fathoms, she thought, as she followed him into a large and comfortable room furnished with antiques, carpeted with Chinese rugs, and populated by two girls of about the same age and build as Katrina.

'Your new colleague has arrived at last,' the man said. 'Better late than never, indeed, because she looks even better than she did in her photograph.'

The two girls tried to look as if all was going to plan, but failed, and Katrina just smiled. What on earth was this little man on about? She asked for the loo, and one of the other girls offered to take her.

'What's going on?' asked Katrina as soon as they were out of the room.

'I thought you looked better than in your photograph,' said the other. 'So much better, in fact, that I knew you were not the same girl. So you tell me what's going on.'

Katrina explained how she'd got there, more or less, and the other girl believed her, more or less, and so explained that the man, called Mr Soumian, employed her – Sharon – and the other girl – Ruby – as, er, housekeepers. He had recently decided that they needed some more assistance and had advertised. The applicants all sent photographs, and Mr Soumian offered one of them the job and explained what was involved, and she had agreed and was to arrive this afternoon at four. But she hadn't come, and Mr Soumian obviously thought . . .

Anyway, they had better get back. Mr Soumian liked things just so, and it was almost dinner time. Which might explain, Katrina thought, why the two other girls were dressed like waitresses. They had black dresses, stockings with seams, high heels, white pinnies, white lace caps, the lot. Straight out of Lyons Corner House 1948.

Reading her thoughts, Sharon explained that Mr Soumian's ideas about Britain, and especially England, were based on films of the Ealing Studios era. To him, England was forever a village in the Cotswolds where the vicar rode a bicycle and old ladies in wide-brimmed hats trimmed hedges and called out good morning. And when he found that England wasn't like that anymore, he came to Ireland, where the priests do still ride bicycles.

'And what do you and Ruby do for Mr Soumian?'

'Anything he wants,' said Sharon.

There was a short interval during which Mr Soumian disappeared to change into an evening suit. Sharon found Katrina something decent to wear – another of those little black dresses with the low necklines! – because, as it was her first night, Katrina was Mr Soumian's guest at dinner. This was to be served in a spacious dining room with glittering silver, candles, the glow of polished wood and the crackle of a log fire.

Over the soup – Brown Windsor, Katrina guessed, although it could have been oxtail, or anything really – Mr Soumian explained to her that he had made a certain amount of money when a very young man, supplying specialised goods and services to discerning clients back home in Communist Armenia. When he had made what he considered to be enough money, and the balance had begun to swing unfavourably between the risks he was taking and the likelihood of his apprehension by the authorities, he had decided to leave his home country. Now he could enjoy the kind of life he had dreamed of.

This chiefly consisted of living as he thought an English gentleman should live, except that he preferred female staff to male. He didn't want a butler and a valet. He preferred the company of ladies, if Katrina understood him. Katrina, remembering the size of his cock, understood him very well.

There was fish next, Sole Véronique (Mr Soumian's ideas of Englishness clearly included food from the School of County Town Three Star Hotels), served by Sharon and Ruby, and Mr Soumian continued talking and Katrina continued listening. He told her about the paintings he collected, and his own wish to be a painter, and about the antiques and some of the stories attached to them.

By the time they were through the roast beef, past the strawberries and cream and were on the cheese and port, Katrina was beginning to think that this was an even better job than the one at Holy Sepulchre.

Mr Soumian then talked about a completely different subject.

'English gentlemen are all sexual perverts,' he said. 'They prefer oral and anal sex because that is what they are brought up with, in their public schools, and so women find they are poor lovers. Of course, my own private member is too big for anal sex with any woman I have ever met, but I too do enjoy oral stimulation. I feel I can surpass those I am trying to imitate in my talents as a lover, as I hope you will shortly find out as we go into our after-dinner entertainment.'

As they walked from the dining room, through a passage and then a covered way across a yard, Mr Soumian confided that his other great interest in life was Imperial Rome, particularly in its more decadent years, and to indulge this taste for ancient fading glories he had built – this!

'This' was a small but perfectly-detailed Roman bath. Columns and mosaics, stone benches, plunge-size pools of water, one steaming, one looking quite icy – it all looked just right to Katrina. And coming into view as they stood there were two handmaidens carrying large jugs and wearing wraparound gowns in a flimsy, light material.

'Of course, in Rome, women would never have been allowed to bathe with the men. But here, we are more liberal.'

Mr Soumian disappeared through a door. Sharon and Ruby waited, formally, the light from the torches on the walls silhouetting their bodies through the gauzy cloth of their dresses. When the man returned he was wrapped in a large towel. Sharon held it for him as he walked into the hot pool and Ruby poured the contents of the two jugs, which seemed to be some sort of perfume in the form of a red liquid. Instantly the water turned a cloudy pink and the room was filled with the aroma of flowers. Katrina felt slightly dizzy with it.

'You too must get changed and join me in the bath,'

said Mr Soumian to Katrina, and she was led away by Ruby who still was acting formally, as a slave would have done, Katrina guessed. Ruby helped Katrina undress, her eyes being her only betrayer of indiscipline as they took in Katrina's marvellous bosom, her perfectly-proportioned waist and hips, her deliciously rounded bottom and her inviting thighs.

Draped in a towel like Mr Soumian had been, Katrina was walked to the steps of the pool where her towel was removed and, feeling oddly embarrassed by the whole procedure, she made her first movement towards the water.

Mr Soumian, his eyes glowing with delight at the endowments of his new member of staff, had been sitting in the water which came up to his neck. As Katrina made her entrance and then waited, the pink water reaching halfway up her thighs, Mr Soumian felt obliged to rise out of good manners.

Katrina should perhaps have looked him in the eye and smiled her acknowledgement of his presence, but she could not look anywhere else but at the Armenian's incredibly large cock. It was a monster and a double monster. Katrina could not help letting a little squeal pass her lips as she saw this thing lurking just under the water, half-erect, like a submarine ready to surface.

'Come along, my dear, and we shall have the slaves oil you.' He clapped his hands and the two girls walked down the steps, still in their diaphonous gowns, and joined the blonde and fair Katrina and the short, olive-skinned, moustachioed little man in the pool. There was still room to move around with all four of them in, but not that much.

Ruby and Sharon both had strangely-shaped bottles from which they poured some kind of oil into their palms. Sharon began massaging Mr Soumian's shoulders and chest, while Ruby did the same for Katrina. Katrina's chest, of course, was a different proposition altogether from the Armenian's, and Ruby found it impossible to keep up her slavish impartiality. As her hands rubbed the oil into the finest pair of tits she had ever seen, she could not help sighing with desire, and she could not help tweaking the nipples and looking mischievously at Katrina.

Katrina was aware of the other two watching also, and from the corner of her eye saw that Sharon's hand had gone down to the Armenian dong and was bringing it up to full stretch. The level of the water on the little man was just below his belly button. His erect penis, left to stand on its own, broke the surface by a good six inches. Katrina turned her head to watch as it came towards her, a moving column of meat with all the menace of a periscope taking aim at a cargo ship, or of a great white shark's fin making a run on an innocent swimmer.

Katrina felt Ruby pressing on her shoulders. She was meant to kneel in the water, in front of the little man with the big prick. She did so, and took the monster in her hands and marvelled at it, and watched transfixed as Sharon poured oil on the end of it. The green oil ran down the massive cock and dissipated in the pink water, making a dark cloud, and Katrina felt the coolness of the oil on her hands as she slowly slid them up and down the shaft.

There was room on this cock for another pair of hands, she thought. Never have I seen such a cock – or sucked one, she said to herself as she felt a hand on the back of her head. Opening her mouth as wide as could, she pushed the fantastic thing in between her teeth. There was not much scope for tongue work. All she could do was move her head back and forth slightly and try to give him stimulation with her cheeks. It tasted strange with the oil on it, a kind of bitter-sweet flavour.

While she did this she felt fingers probing her. A hand ran down her back below the water and a finger searched for the crease between her buttocks. Another hand was pumping her breasts but with her attention total and mouth completely full of cock she could not look to see who was doing what.

After a few minutes of this Mr Soumian clapped his hands. The groping stopped and her head was lifted from its task. She was led from the pool by the two handmaidens, their wet dresses clinging to their bodies, and placed on a stone bench on her back. Her legs were placed wide apart, knees well up, and a cushion was put under her bottom.

Now the great man approached, his cock swinging. He paused while Sharon and Ruby both anointed it with oil, their four hands rubbing in unison but still not managing to conceal all of the eager monster. Katrina eased her bottom on the cushions, opening her legs a little wider, and tried to relax.

The oil certainly helped. Mr Soumian climbed on top

of Katrina and presented his cock head at her opening, and Sharon made sure it was properly aimed while Ruby held Katrina's quim lips open, and then he pushed. In it went, halfway at the first movement, and Katrina had no problems with that except she felt she would burst. The feeling was redoubled as the man gave a grunt and a shove and the whole of it went in. Katrina cried out. She couldn't help it. It was the plaintive wail of someone who realises she is lost and at the mercy of a force far more powerful than she. Nevertheless she wrapped her legs gamely around the buttocks of the little dark-skinned man and held him there.

The sight of the long white legs on the olive, muscular back of the man must have excited Sharon because she felt compelled to join in. Her hand went to the man's balls and cradled them as he began to thrust in and out of the still-wailing Katrina. His head was buried in her breasts and he explored them with his lips and tongue as his massive rod pushed her rapidly to her conclusion.

After fifteen or twenty thrusts and fifteen or twenty eerie cries she was there, her wail becoming a shout and her body becoming a helpless jumping cracker. As he felt her come, Mr Soumian withdrew and nodded to Sharon, who bent over the bench, legs apart. He nodded to Ruby, who placed her mouth on Katrina's pussy and gently sucked and licked it. Katrina was being kept warm while Mr Soumian brought himself nearer to his own climax.

Sharon felt the man lift her wet dress up and prepared herself. In it went, and she gasped – as she always did, even though this must be the hundredth time and more – and gave herself up to the enjoyment of the largest cock ever.

The man managed about fifty thrusts in Sharon before she half-collapsed in a shuddering heap, and so he pulled out from her and walked up behind Ruby, who was still gently licking Katrina. Ruby also felt the familiar hands lifting up the damp gauze, and she settled herself for the onslaught, and here it came.

His hands grasping her firmly around the waist, and she bending still to her job of keeping Katrina lubricated and ready, the two of them performed, unseen by Sharon, who was now sitting on the floor with her back to a pillar, her eyes closed in tired bliss, or by Katrina who was dozing in a state of half arousal, half satisfaction.

Mr Soumian felt his own moment approaching before he had time to bring Ruby off, so he withdrew, leaving her disappointed but knowing that there was more to come. She moved out of the way and once more the man climbed on top of Katrina. If she had been almost asleep she had a very abrupt awakening as she felt something the size of her own forearm force its way into her.

She didn't know whether to shout help or hurrah, so she just made a noise which was a mixture of the two and began drumming her heels on the man's bottom. He went flat out, his cock pumping as fast as he could, and while Katrina for the second time that session shouted out in frenzied ecstasy, he spurted a full measure of his life essence into her spasmodically-contracting passage.

Mr Soumian was a vigorous man. He had made his money by sheer energy and hard work, daring anything and doing everything himself. That vigour was now put into enjoying himself, and while Katrina lay back as if her work was done, Ruby and Sharon knew better.

Mr Soumian returned to his bath and stood, his back to the edge and his arms resting along it, watching his two slaves. Sharon went first. She bent to the hem of her clinging garment and slowly straightened up, then lifted the whole thing over her head. She was a substantial girl, Sharon, with well-rounded thighs, a proper tummy on her, and big breasts. She was dark-haired – she wore her hair shoulder-length, and trimmed her very profuse pubes into a neat triangle – and dark-eyed, but her skin was fair. Mr Soumian liked fair-skinned women.

Mr Soumian also liked to watch women together, and so once Sharon was naked, and had given herself a rub-down with a towel – a sight to make any man stir with venial thoughts of being among all those plentiful mortal delights – she turned to Ruby.

Ruby stood, also dark-haired and fair-skinned, willing and silent, as Sharon lifted her dress over her head and began a slow, intimate drying of her body using only a couple of fingers wrapped in the towel. Ruby was not so statuesque as her colleague in the slave trade, but she was tall also – Mr Soumian liked tall women – and, of course, had large breasts. They were carried on a narrow rib cage, so that they looked even bigger than they actually were, and hung prominently above a narrow waist and slim hips. In fact, Ruby's figure was the type which can get girls into nude modelling for magazines, but it hadn't done that for Ruby because she had strict views on such matters.

Long ago, when she first began sprouting her disproportionately large tits, Ruby had decided that she would make her living with her body, but she saw a moral issue in having it photographed for public consumption. Naturally she would be paid, but that was by the newspaper or magazine. All those men who looked at her body and lusted after it – they were not paying her. A man might buy a magazine and then show her picture to his friends, or pin it on the wall in his factory. All those other people who saw it, men and women alike, were not contributing to Ruby's financial welfare and so were morally in the wrong.

So, Ruby would never agree to modelling, although she was pestered and pleaded with all her grown-up life. She chose instead to be a rich man's mistress, and had progressed from a bedsit in Dublin paid for by a restaurant owner, through a country cottage owned by one of the landed gentry, to this current position which was harder work than anything she'd done before but much, much more lucrative.

Sharon had had a quite different background. She had been around cafés and hotels, waitressing, cooking, cleaning – learning all the skills she needed in this job, in fact – and had been picked up by Mr Soumian while she was serving him a lobster salad in a wine bar in Cork.

Ruby was dry now, and Sharon dropped the towel on the floor. She pressed her ample frame against Ruby's and kissed her on the lips. Ruby's arms went around Sharon and they were immediately matched by Sharon's around her. The two girls writhed and squirmed their bodies together as their tongues worked inside each other's mouths, and then Sharon pulled away slightly so she could put her hand on Ruby's breasts. Ruby responded by slipping her own hand between Sharon's fleshy thighs and wriggling a finger inside her slit.

They kissed each other's breasts and nipples, and pushed more fingers into each other's holes, and kept going even harder when they heard the sound of a man emerging from water.

Mr Soumian, cock stiff and frighteningly huge, made for the stone bench on which Katrina still lay, idly watching the performance. She saw that she was about to take a starring role but wondered what it might be. The little man gestured to her to turn over. She did, and knelt, her elbows on the bench and her bottom sticking up in the air. She was facing the other two women, who broke off from their embraces and came over to Katrina to take a dangling tit in hand. While they massaged her melons and fingered their own pussies, Mr Soumian stood on a low stool, placed his cock at the divine entrance and gave a great heave.

She might have gone flying if the other two had not been there to stop her. It felt even bigger when it was coming from the rear. She saw what he meant about no woman's bumhole being big enough and hoped fervently he wouldn't take it into his head to try hers for size.

While Sharon and Ruby played with themselves and her, Katrina concentrated hard. She must try and hold herself back. If she came to orgasm too soon, she felt sure that the man would just keep going and that way oblivion lay. No, she wanted to stay conscious throughout, memorising the sensations, because she somehow knew that she would never see a cock as big as this again.

Katrina did her best to concentrate on what Sharon and Ruby were doing, and to put in the background the repeated surges of the battering ram now completely inside her private domain. It was impossible. No matter how sensational the two women looked, their bodies rubbing against each other, their pubic mounds pushed up against Katrina's face for a lick, their hands making intimate searches of organs and skin, there was nothing could blank out the even more sensational pillaging of the greatest cock ever to find its way between Katrina's shaking thighs.

He kept up his rhythm like some relentless machine, one, two, three, four, in, pause, out, in, and Katrina felt the tide of her own most dramatic senses building up. Soon the gates must open and let the river flow.

Now the man increased his speed. One-two-three-four, one-two-three-four, and Katrina, helpless, could not prevent the cries escaping from her lips, the shouts of pleasure mixed with abandonment of self-control. Possibly the sight of the women playing with each other had heightened Mr Soumian's own sensitivities, because as Katrina began crying out, he too let rip and pounded her backside at a faster and faster rate. Katrina stayed in position only because she was speared on such a huge gaff and couldn't get off it. Her limbs were like jelly, her self-possession had evaporated, and the massive dick kept on driving into her.

She was much too far gone to notice the triumphal shooting of spunk but was vaguely aware of him withdrawing, and of the three of them carrying her to another room where there was a bed, but she knew nothing more until the morning.

'Come on,' said Sharon, opening the curtains and letting in the day. 'You're not a guest any more. Don't expect breakfast in bed, at least, not the boiled egg and toast variety. Mr Soumian has rung down to the kitchen and he wants some tea taking up. Knowing him I should think you'll be having salami and mayonnaise for your breakfast, and hot salami at that, and woe betide you if you spill his tea while you're doing it.'

Over the next few weeks the newest member of staff got rather more than her fair share of the duties, and she sucked Soumian's massive dick until her jaws ached and she thought she could never face white sauce again. He still liked to watch Sharon and Ruby while Katrina sucked him, and he liked to watch Sharon and Ruby while Katrina fucked him, but it rarely happened the other way around.

Unbelievably, at least to Katrina, she was actually getting tired of sex. Her appetite was jaded. Nothing could excite her any more. She was going through the motions but, so good was she at the motions in question, that neither her boss nor her colleagues noticed.

It was time to go, however, but before she did slip away Katrina wanted a memento. She wanted something to prove to herself, later, when the memories began to haze over, exactly what she had been through.

One afternoon she persuaded Mr Soumian that she had a slight toothache and would not be able to give him his usual after-lunch sucking, but if Sharon and Ruby could do it, she had something else she would like to try.

For Katrina's objectives, the cock had to be at absolutely full stretch, and so she encouraged Sharon to lick the shaft while Ruby held his balls in her mouth. When it was obviously up as high as it would go, Katrina produced a warm pack of modelling clay and proceeded to slap it on the great cock. It was the modern, quick-setting sort and so Katrina had no bother at all in obtaining what she wanted – a plaster cast of the unforgettable dong.

By suppertime she had made a mould from the cast and from the mould a dozen candles, two of which she packed away. The other ten she placed around the dining room. Mr Soumian thought it a terrific joke to have his dinner candle-lit by his own cock, and was in even randier mood than usual afterwards.

Katrina gave her all for the last time. Later, when

everyone else was sleeping, she restarted her journey –
to where, she didn't know, or why, or quite how. The
first part she knew would be on foot, and it was dawn
before she reached anywhere big enough to offer the
probability of a bus service or a taxi. With a sigh she
found herself a quiet corner, sat, and waited for the
town to wake up.

Chapter Fourteen

'And now the end is here . . .

. . . so I draw my mother's curtains', sang Katrina quietly to herself, and looked out on a London autumn morning with sunshine and leaves of many colours along the tree-lined street. She shook her head in amazed resignation at the thought of what she had to do that day.

She was going to be matron of honour, or Best Woman as her mother kept calling it, at the wedding of that mother, the one who looked like an elder sister and was always behaving as if she were, to Calvin Bryant, Katrina's old boyfriend and manager.

How things had changed while Katrina had been away. Elspeth and Calvin had formed a theatrical and promotional management company, Bryant Mulloy, which had seen unparalleled success in supplying the best looking PR girls, the most active actresses and the most dishy TV presenters, all of them ready and willing to prove that they were multi-talented and could give the best sexual performances for influential persons at private engagements.

Business for Elspeth and Calvin became inextricably involved with personal pleasure. They decided to form a spiritual as well as a business partnership and so Mr and Mrs Bryant would be running a company by the name of Bryant and Bryant, and they'd made it quite clear that if Katrina was a very good girl and promised to do as she was told, she could, if she was very lucky, be a Bryant client.

Katrina, still looking out of her bedroom window, sighed. Calvin had reached thirty years of age while she had been on her travels. Katrina was nearly twenty-five, so Mother would be just about forty – but she only looked mid-thirties-ish and there was no doubt that there was more than enough life in the old bitch yet. Married! Katrina could not believe it. Married. Mother. To Calvin. Good heavens above.

Katrina had been back in town over a month. She'd spent a short spell in Scotland after her flight from Ireland, with the vague idea that she might look up old pals from Boundary TV, but what with one thing and another she hadn't really done very much. She met a rather nice, quietly-spoken chap in Kelso and spent a pleasant enough week with him, and there was another guy in Melrose, and that one she met on a trip to Glasgow . . .

Realising eventually that the search for something else was not going to yield her anything except more of the same, she bought a ticket to London and turned up on Mother's doorstep. She was welcomed warmly enough but her defection from The Great Career Plan had obviously taken the edge off their relationship. Mother's dream of her daughter's world stardom would not happen, at least, not in the way Mother had planned.

Things cheered up a bit when Katrina agreed to write the book which Mother quickly fixed up for her, with serialisation rights and a film option. It would bring in a few quid and keep the pot of fame boiling but Elspeth knew that her daughter no longer had the uncrushable urge to get to the top.

Some of Katrina's urges were as uncrushable as ever, and she was looking forward to meeting that French film actor at the wedding. Meeting him again, that was, for the two of them had already made close acquaintance after a dinner party of Mother's when they'd had to do it standing up in the kitchen while supposedly making a second lot of coffee.

This had not been the ideal opportunity for Katrina to check out the prowess of the Latin lover. As she turned, on Mother's wedding morning, from the window towards the bathroom, she pondered the great-lover legend as interpreted by a Frenchman whose main concern in the act of shagging had been not to rattle the milk bottles inside the fridge against which Katrina was leaning.

Latin lovers! As she ran the morning bath and poured in the scented lotions, she hoped that after the wedding, with Mother and Calvin gone on honeymoon, perhaps Katrina and her Frenchman could find more time and liberation than had been possible so far, with Mother always trying to sign him up for something. Katrina was sure it would be quite an experience if only she could get the circumstances right. He was certainly good-looking, and charming, and he had all the right equipment. Next time he wouldn't be in such a rush, trying to come before the kettle boiled. Yes, that was it. Next time, with more time, it would be wonderful.

Katrina stepped into her bath – she liked the water very hot so she could lie in it for a long time – and lay down, slowly. Her body, submerged in the perfumed heat, relaxed. Her eyes closed, and her mind travelled back to the last time she had had a truly remarkable encounter with anybody French.

In her last year at school there had been a young *assistante*, a French student teacher by the name of Mademoiselle Brussac who had electrified the entire eligible male population of the school. Every pubescent boy had wet dreams featuring the Mamselle, and every bachelor teacher (and some of the married ones) attempted to convince her that she needed them to show her the sights.

She was crackingly good-looking, no doubt, but it was that indefinable French something else which had everybody agog. The style she dressed in was that little bit more elegant, the clothes she wore were that little bit better cut, the way her hair was done, her make-up, even the way she held a coffee cup – it was all somehow extra classy. She had a poise and a confidence unobtainable by any English woman, and she was oozing with Latin femininity. The female members of staff, apart from the two who liked other females, were all frightfully polite but as jealous as hell.

The terrible thing about all this was that the Mamselle was only at the school for one term! How could everybody who desired her possibly get their rampant dicks into her in that time?

Katrina, studying French at A-level, and Mamselle got on well. Katrina could call her Elise, and could use the *tu* form in private conversation, and it was in such a chat that Katrina found out why nobody had so far succeeded in bedding the *assistante*. She had become very well aware of the effect she was having and, although she quite fancied some of the masters and even a couple of the senior boys, she had decided that she could not give in to one without giving in to more and thereby causing the most awful row. If she repelled all comers, she could not offend anyone.

Katrina thought that this was a logical and reasonable response. If you can't meet all the demand, don't just meet a little bit of it and therefore upset everybody. While Katrina said this she was also having a secret thought. Mamselle's stance was reasonable, that is, so long as she gave in to the pressure when it didn't matter any more, such as on her last night. And so a plot was hatched.

There was no problem at all setting it up. The only problem was keeping it quiet. Katrina selected the three senior sixth boys whom she knew were considered fanciable by Mamselle and swore them to utter secrecy. If there was the slightest hint of anything going on, there would be disaster. This was not a threat. Katrina did not promise them slow castration by Zippo cigarette lighter, nor inexact circumcision by electric carving knife. No, she just pointed out that if they didn't keep totally mum, they would never get to fuck the lovely Mademoiselle Brussac.

The plan was as follows. Katrina's mother was away and so Mamselle would be invited for a small, intimate little supper, just to say goodbye. When she turned up she would find the three boys there also. Katrina and the boys would then exploit the opportunities presented to them.

The doorbell rang at 7pm prompt. Mamselle was ushered into the sitting room and the three boys stood and chorused, 'Bonsoir, mademoiselle, comment vas-tu?' as rehearsed by Katrina. Mamselle smiled a secret and ravishing smile and said that they had better speak English this evening, since only one of the boys was a student of French, and she would hate anyone to feel left out on her last night. Also, would they please call her Elise?

Katrina and the boys breathed their collective sigh of relief. She had not turned to flee, and so supper could be eaten in high hopes. They had made a decent job of the supper. They served dry Martinis first, proper ones with gin and an olive in, and then a quiche with Roquefort, fillet of pork with a garlic and sage sauce, a big mixed salad, and pots de chocolat for dessert.

With the wine and the chat, everybody was feeling warm and friendly by the time the dishes were cleared away. The conversation was currently about the Miss

World contest which had been on the TV the previous week, and Mamselle was scathing on the subject of dumb broads who liked travel and wanted to work with children and whose only obvious assets were the ones hanging on their chests.

Katrina thought she was a little biased – Mamselle's was a slim figure – but agreed that it was wrong for men to goggle at women when there was no real equivalent chance for women to goggle at men. Admittedly you could go and see the bodybuilders, but they were grotesque. They were freaks. There was no chance to see a parade of normally-proportioned dishy men. There was no Master World contest where healthy girls with healthy appetites could drool over guys who were not covered in grease and pumped up like Michelin gorillas.

'In any case,' said Elise, 'I understand that the processes these man-mountains go through, and the drugs they take, make most of their persons much bigger but certain vital parts smaller. And so not only are they repulsive to look at, they are useless also when it comes to romance. Is that not so? In among all that contorted muscle you cannot find a little willy lurking?'

The three boys, already seeing what was coming, squirmed in their embarrassment. There was, they knew, no way out.

'I tell you what, Elise,' said Katrina. 'We'll have a Master World contest right here. The only problem is, I don't have three pairs of men's swimming trunks.'

The two girls giggled while the boys looked at each other in despair.

'This is no matter,' said Elise. 'If there are no swimming trunks, we shall be able to check for ourselves if they have been taking these drugs or not, which make their parts smaller.'

While the girls thought this a most amusing idea, the boys were not so sure. They wondered if perhaps Katrina had not set them up and there was to be no glorious mating with Mamselle but just one great joke played on them. Peter, the fair-haired one, spoke for all three.

'We'll do it, providing we can name the next game.'

'Fair enough,' said Katrina. 'This is a democracy. Your turn next. Anyway, we shall be so turned on by the sight of your wonderful bodies that we'll agree to anything. Won't we, Elise?'

'*Absolument.* I have been learning all the correct words. When the boys have come with their bollocks naked, we shall have the fucking, yes?'

The boys stayed in the dining room while Katrina and Elise went through into the lounge, glasses of port and Gitanes in hand. The two girls were relaxing on the couch when the first contestant entered the room – in his underpants.

Now that they were sure they were not being set up, and that a romp was certain to follow, the boys had their confidence back. Neil, a tall dark-haired lad with a sultry look, came in and did his own commentary as he paraded before them.

'Neil is from Thirlmere Street and works part-time as a paper boy and part-time as a quality control inspector for a chain of massage parlours. His ambitions include doing rude things with women, and having rude women do things to him. He measures 40–26–34, and about seven and a half.'

Neil stood, arms folded, while Peter came in.

'Peter comes all the way from Acton Walk where he fills his parents' garage with stuff for his equipment-hire business. Fave bits of gear include his travelling baby-oil jacuzzi and his compressor-driven multichannel vibrator. He wants to be a gigolo when he grows up, or a toy boy, and hopes eventually to be rich enough to be a sugar daddy. He measures 41–28–35, and about seven and a half.'

Kevin came in wearing the thinnest, flimsiest briefs. Every outline of what was in the pouch could be clearly seen, and it was impressive. Elise and Katrina exchanged glances.

'Kevin originates from the palm-fringed shores of the Union Canal where his mother threw him soon after he was born. After a line of hardship and deprivation, he is now ready for anything. His measurements are about the same as Peter's and Neil's, except he thinks they are boasting at seven and a half while of course he is not at eight and a quarter.'

The girls clapped delightedly but announced that each contestant would need a further interview before a decision could be made. Elise stood first and walked towards Kevin. She blew a tiny trail of smoke from her

Gitanes as she looked up at him, a glitter of fun in her eyes.

Her hand went to his full pouch and tickled it lightly, then plunged inside his pants.

'Katrina,' she said. 'I think you had better come and tell me if this is right. I only understand centimetres. I don't know what is these inches.'

Katrina didn't mess about. She just pulled the boy's pants down and he stepped out of them. While Elise watched with cool fascination, Katrina massaged the boy's cock until it stood up to full attention.

'About seven inches, I should say,' said Katrina, moving on to Peter whose bulge was already well up. Elise meanwhile stubbed out her cigarette in the ashtray and went to Neil. Both pairs of pants were removed and their contents stroked and examined.

'I should say all three of these boys are equal. There can be no winner. And so, *mes amis*, what shall we do?'

Katrina seemed sorrowful that no dick had proved conclusively bigger than another. Kevin's had seemed so when slack, but when all three were stiff it was too difficult to be definite.

'But also, there shall be no losers,' said Elise. 'I know we agreed the boys would choose the next game, but I am going to insist on something else first. I want to show you English what a French girl can do.'

Elise struck a pose in the centre of the room. She really was a hell of a girl, with a beautiful face, short dark hair which curved in at her chin, massive eyes which seemed to speak volumes, and the promise in her slim body of sensuality and athleticism.

'I think I shall keep on my stockings,' she said, as she undid the clasp on her necklace. She spoke no more as she undressed, and neither did anyone else. The boys – and Katrina – were transfixed as she took off the neat blue suit, the shoes, the blouse, the bra and the lacy knickers, and faced them wearing only a suspender belt and a pair of sheer silk stockings.

Her breasts were like two sweet pears. Her waist seemed incredibly narrow to Katrina, who was a generously-proportioned girl, and her hips also were slim and boyish. She beckoned to Peter who walked across in a trance. Elise took his cock in her hands and skinned it and measured its bulk. She did the same with Neil and Kevin.

'There is very little in it, but I think that the smallest of these very handsome dickies belongs to Peter, and so he will have the honour of entering me by the back way, Peter?'

She took his cock and smeared a generous fingerful of spittle around its rim. Peter could not believe it. The Mamselle of his dreams, the one whose thought-pictures had caused his cock to rear up every night in bed and forced him to fill every hanky in the house, was now bending over before him and kneeling on the carpet. He walked towards her and knelt behind her. She reached between her legs, held his shaft firmly, and ordered him forward. In he went, his eyes wide with incredulity.

'Now, Neil,' she said, straightening up and pulling Neil towards her. He'd been picked because he was the least tall and so the nearest in height to Elise. He knelt in front of her, she fiddled with his cock, and in it went.

Elise kept herself erect, a delicious sandwich filling between two well-risen bridge rolls, and beckoned Kevin. He was to stand beside her so that Elise could get his cock in her mouth.

'Before I give this dickie the French kiss, I want to ask you boys not to push too hard. Be gentle, especially Peter in my little place. Now, let us show Katrina what she must learn to do if she is to be a Continental lover.'

Katrina watched, half in fear, half in fascinated desire, as the boys moved slowly in and out of the slim French girl. Peter, from behind, could kiss the back of her neck and play light-fingeredly with her small pointed breasts. Neil had his hands on her waist and his eyes closed as he pushed his cock up and in.

Elise too had her eyes closed as she sucked and rubbed the cock she held in her hand. Katrina wondered who would come first.

To her surprise, it was Elise. Suddenly she let go of Kevin's cock and grabbed Neil by the shoulders. She pushed her hips in and out, let out a cry, and fell forwards on top of Neil. Peter was left on the point, his dick jerking and steaming in the open air, and two strokes of his right hand were enough to produce a fountain of come which mostly landed on Elise's prostrate buttocks.

Neil began thrusting upwards and then stopped, realising that Elise had fainted. He turned her over on her back and withdrew, then got up and walked towards

Katrina, cock in hand. Kevin came with him.

Katrina, wondering what a French woman tasted like, took Neil's cock in her mouth. Mm. Same as English. Some swift movements of her tongue and cheeks had Neil shouting for mercy and, thinking that there might be a lot more to swallow before the night was out, she pulled away as she felt the come surging up his shaft and collected it in her hand.

Bending over the waste basket and wiping the come off with a tissue, she was unsurprised to feel her skirt being lifted and a way being found around the gusset of her knickers for a rampant cock. Kevin pushed home without ceremony and banged her hard. Ten, fifteen thrusts were all he needed, and the only person left in the room who had not come was Katrina.

Looking towards the naked body of Elise, Katrina hoped to find inspiration and was relieved and excited to see the slender limbs on the move. Elise sat up, her pretty little tits hanging like ripe lemons on a tree, and smiled.

'Did I pass out? It has been known. The trouble is it creeps up on me and then bang! I'm gone. Anyway, it was lovely and I would like some more ... but Katrina, darling. You are surrounded by naked boys with floppy wet willies, you are confronted by another naked person who has just been closely connected with all three of those willies, and you still have your clothes on! Come here, my little cabbage. Let me release you from those buttons and bows.'

The boys, sitting around in armchairs, watched with

the closest attention, their cocks twitching and lifting, as Elise took the bigger girl's face in her hands and planted a huge kiss on her lips. The boys could see the mouths opening and the tongues meeting, and each one felt a thrill at the sight. An even greater thrill came when Elise's hand reached under Katrina's skirt, and Katrina's legs parted. The boys could see Elise working the English girl, fingering her pussy while continuing the mouth-watering kiss, and now her hand came out from there and felt instead the twin peaks of Katrina's bosom.

Katrina was also using her hands, running them up and down Elise's firm flesh and testing the delicate beauty of her small orbs.

Leaving the embrace, Elise got busy with buttons. She undid every button and every catch she could, but removed no clothes. Katrina stood with blouse undone and open, bra undone, skirt unfastened at the waist, stockings unhitched and beginning to slip. Elise put both hands beneath the loose bra and luxuriated in the great handfuls of breast. She ran her hands up Katrina's thighs, lifting the skirt and showing white, smooth skin in curves of desirability.

The boys all had erections now, Elise noticed, and so it was time to reveal Katrina to the full. Working as fast as she could, Elise soon had the astounding body of Katrina on naked view, and was kissing the nipples and putting three and four fingers in her pussy.

The pair of them collapsed to the floor and Katrina lay more or less still while Elise explored her every crevice. She covered every surface, concave and convex, with kisses, and intruded into every orifice with tongue and fingers. At one point the boys could see Elise forcing her tongue in Katrina's ear while the big girl's body writhed with a finger in its bumhole. Now she sat across Katrina's stomach, bending over to lick her quim while presenting an enchanting view of her own to Katrina and the boys.

Katrina began to moan. Elise got between her legs, knelt, and paid full attention with her mouth to Katrina's pussy. As her tongue shot in and out, so her bottom moved invitingly – too invitingly for Neil who was forced to come and kneel there himself and push his cock home in her arse while she continued to eat her young English friend.

Elise didn't pause, but simply allowed Neil's movements to give an additional frisson to her tongue work in Katrina's quivering love passage. As Katrina began to moan louder, and her lips thrust up from the floor, Neil speeded up too, and Elise had the double sensation of bringing Katrina off at the same time as she felt Neil come off inside her.

After a short while Neil withdrew and the puckered hole drew tight behind him. Elise swung herself round and placed her own quim above Katrina's mouth. Katrina responded eagerly with her arms up and around Elise's sparely-contoured buttocks, and Elise, with her knees either side of Katrina's head, lay herself as flat as she could across the big girl's chest, placed a finger from each hand in her quim, and opened it.

Kevin was quick to act in reply. He slid his legs under

Katrina's right thigh and lay across her, on top of her left. His cock pointed in all sorts of directions, but Elise could get hold of it and guide it in, and then she could rest on Katrina's tummy while watching the cock, not two inches from her face, moving in and out.

There didn't seem to be any room for Peter in this drama until Elise lifted her muff from Katrina's lips and offered it to him. By kneeling behind Katrina's head, and with Elise shuffling herself back a little, Peter could give Katrina the same kind of sight as Elise was enjoying, that of a red hot cock sliding in and out of a warm pussy right before her eyes.

The two boys signalled to each other with their eyebrows. Peter, shafting Elise above Katrina's face, and Kevin lying crossways and shafting Katrina before Elise's interested gaze, would try and come together.

Katrina reached up and held the lad's balls to one side so she could better see the hard column on its repeated journey in and out. Elise reached forward and got a finger to Katrina's clit . . . wow!

Today's Katrina, wedding-day Katrina, awoke from her reverie to find her fingers in her quim and her bath water cold. That had been some party. In a hotter bath she could have replayed more of the blue movie she had in her brain, including her own attempts to have all three boys' cocks inside her at once, but it was time to get ready.

The wedding went off well enough although Katrina imagined there could never have been so many doubtful characters at such a ceremony before – camera persons,

American footballers, TV executives, computer million-
aires, PR girls – what a gang! And the French film actor
was a disappointment; this time it was between the
prawn cocktail and the steak Diane, up against a trolley
full of desserts and gateaux in a corridor behind the
hotel kitchen.

Katrina waved goodbye to the honeymooners and
began wondering about the direction her life should
take. One thing was for sure. She'd never be willing to
do what her mother had just done: promise to fuck one
man only.

Headline Delta Erotic Survey

In order to provide the kind of books you like to read – and to qualify for a free erotic novel of the Editor's choice – we would appreciate it if you would complete the following survey and send your answers, together with any further comments, to:

Headline Book Publishing
FREEPOST (WD 4984)
London
NW1 0YR

1. Are you male or female?
2. Age? Under 20 / 20 to 30 / 30 to 40 / 40 to 50 / 50 to 60 / 60 to 70 / over
3. At what age did you leave full-time education?
4. Where do you live? (Main geographical area)
5. Are you a regular erotic book buyer / a regular book buyer in general / both?
6. How much approximately do you spend a year on erotic books / on books in general?
7. How did you come by this book?
7a. If you bought it, did you purchase from: a national bookchain / a high street store / a newsagent / a motorway station / an airport / a railway station / other . . .
8. Do you find erotic books easy / hard to come by?
8a. Do you find Headline Delta erotic books easy / hard to come by?
9. Which are the best / worst erotic books you have ever read?
9a. Which are the best / worst Headline Delta erotic books you have ever read?
10. Within the erotic genre there are many periods, subjects and literary styles. Which of the following do you prefer:
10a. (period) historical / Victorian / C20th / contemporary / future?
10b. (subject) nuns / whores & whorehouses / Continental frolics / s&m / vampires / modern realism / escapist fantasy / science fiction?

10c. (styles) hardboiled / humorous / hardcore / ironic / romantic / realistic?

10d. Are there any other ingredients that particularly appeal to you?

11. We try to create a cover appearance that is suitable for each title. Do you consider them to be successful?

12. Would you prefer them to be less explicit / more explicit?

13. We would be interested to hear of your other reading habits. What other types of books do you read?

14. Who are your favourite authors?

15. Which newspapers do you read?

16. Which magazines?

17 Do you have any other comments or suggestions to make?

If you would like to receive a free erotic novel of the Editor's choice (available only to UK residents), together with an up-to-date listing of Headline Delta titles, please supply your name and address. Please allow 28 days for delivery.

Name ....

Address ....

....

....